Anthony Gilbert and The Murder Room

››› This title is part of The Murder Room, our series dedicated to making available out-of-print or hard-to-find titles by classic crime writers.

Crime fiction has always held up a mirror to society. The Victorians were fascinated by sensational murder and the emerging science of detection; now we are obsessed with the forensic detail of violent death. And no other genre has so captivated and enthralled readers.

Vast troves of classic crime writing have for a long time been unavailable to all but the most dedicated frequenters of second-hand bookshops. The advent of digital publishing means that we are now able to bring you the backlists of a huge range of titles by classic and contemporary crime writers, some of which have been out of print for decades.

From the genteel amateur private eyes of the Golden Age and the femmes fatales of pulp fiction, to the morally ambiguous hard-boiled detectives of mid twentieth-century America and their descendants who walk our twenty-first century streets, The Murder Room has it all. **›››**

The Murder Room
Where Criminal Minds Meet

themurderroom.com

T0352384

Anthony Gilbert (1899–1973)

Anthony Gilbert was the pen name of Lucy Beatrice Malleson. Born in London, she spent all her life there, and her affection for the city is clear from the strong sense of character and place in evidence in her work. She published 69 crime novels, 51 of which featured her best known character, Arthur Crook, a vulgar London lawyer totally (and deliberately) unlike the aristocratic detectives, such as Lord Peter Wimsey, who dominated the mystery field at the time. She also wrote more than 25 radio plays, which were broadcast in Great Britain and overseas. Her thriller *The Woman in Red* (1941) was broadcast in the United States by CBS and made into a film in 1945 under the title *My Name is Julia Ross*. She was an early member of the British Detection Club, which, along with Dorothy L. Sayers, she prevented from disintegrating during World War II. Malleson published her autobiography, *Three-a-Penny*, in 1940, and wrote numerous short stories, which were published in several anthologies and in such periodicals as *Ellery Queen's Mystery Magazine* and *The Saint*. The short story 'You Can't Hang Twice' received a Queens award in 1946. She never married, and evidence of her feminism is elegantly expressed in much of her work.

By *Anthony Gilbert*

Scott Egerton series

Tragedy at Freyne (1927)

The Murder of Mrs
  Davenport (1928)

Death at Four Corners (1929)

The Mystery of the Open
  Window (1929)

The Night of the Fog (1930)

The Body on the Beam (1932)

The Long Shadow (1932)

The Musical Comedy
  Crime (1933)

An Old Lady Dies (1934)

The Man Who Was Too
  Clever (1935)

**Mr Crook Murder
  Mystery series**

Murder by Experts (1936)

The Man Who Wasn't
  There (1937)

Murder Has No Tongue (1937)

Treason in My Breast (1938)

The Bell of Death (1939)

Dear Dead Woman (1940)
  aka *Death Takes a Redhead*

The Vanishing Corpse (1941)
  aka *She Vanished in the Dawn*

The Woman in Red (1941)
  aka *The Mystery of the
  Woman in Red*

Death in the Blackout (1942)
  aka *The Case of the Tea-
  Cosy's Aunt*

Something Nasty in the
  Woodshed (1942)
  aka *Mystery in the Woodshed*

The Mouse Who Wouldn't
  Play Ball (1943)
  aka *30 Days to Live*

He Came by Night (1944)
  aka *Death at the Door*

The Scarlet Button (1944)
  aka *Murder Is Cheap*

A Spy for Mr Crook (1944)

The Black Stage (1945)
  aka *Murder Cheats the Bride*

Don't Open the Door (1945)
  aka *Death Lifts the Latch*

Lift Up the Lid (1945)
  aka *The Innocent Bottle*

The Spinster's Secret (1946)
  aka *By Hook or by Crook*

Death in the Wrong Room
  (1947)

Die in the Dark (1947)
  aka *The Missing Widow*

Death Knocks Three Times
  (1949)

Murder Comes Home (1950)

A Nice Cup of Tea (1950)
  aka *The Wrong Body*

Lady-Killer (1951)

Miss Pinnegar Disappears (1952)
aka *A Case for Mr Crook*

Footsteps Behind Me (1953)
aka *Black Death*

Snake in the Grass (1954)
aka *Death Won't Wait*

Is She Dead Too? (1955)
aka *A Question of Murder*

And Death Came Too (1956)

Riddle of a Lady (1956)

Give Death a Name (1957)

Death Against the Clock (1958)

Death Takes a Wife (1959)
aka *Death Casts a Long Shadow*

Third Crime Lucky (1959)
aka *Prelude to Murder*

Out for the Kill (1960)

She Shall Die (1961)
aka *After the Verdict*

Uncertain Death (1961)

No Dust in the Attic (1962)

Ring for a Noose (1963)

The Fingerprint (1964)

The Voice (1964)
aka *Knock, Knock! Who's There?*

Passenger to Nowhere (1965)

The Looking Glass Murder (1966)

The Visitor (1967)

Night Encounter (1968)
aka *Murder Anonymous*

Missing from Her Home (1969)

Death Wears a Mask (1970)
aka *Mr Crook Lifts the Mask*

Murder is a Waiting Game (1972)

Tenant for the Tomb (1971)

A Nice Little Killing (1974)

Standalone Novels

The Case Against Andrew Fane (1931)

Death in Fancy Dress (1933)

The Man in Button Boots (1934)

Courtier to Death (1936)
aka *The Dover Train Mystery*

The Clock in the Hatbox (1939)

The Man in Button Boots

Anthony Gilbert

To
M. E. Grainger Kerr
With love

CHAPTER I

1

WHEN men speak of the mystery of Julian Marks, as sometimes happens, since the affair only took place last autumn, they mean as a rule the extraordinary sequence of events leading up to and succeeding the night of the 31st October; but when experts, like Dupuy and Montstuart, use the same words they mean a record covering almost the whole of the man's life. For the mystery of his death was not much greater than the mystery of his earlier years.

The history of this remarkable creature starts abruptly at his forty-fifth year, when he flowered upon London with an establishment and a manner of living that compelled admiration even from the dilatory. Emerging from an anonymity that included both the sheep farms of Australia and the diamond fields of Johannesburg, he became at once the centre of attraction in London society. It is a little difficult to explain the power of his personality to those who have never met the man. This had nothing to do with his appearance, which, though trim and elegant enough, was scarcely distinguished; nor was his erudition, considerable though this proved to be, wholly responsible for such a state of affairs. The old convenient phrase, personal magnetism, intriguing and vague, serves him best. At all events, whatever the reason, his progress from one point to another was invariably in the nature of a triumphant advance, and the last journey of his life, from London to Monte Carlo, via Paris, where he was seen with a woman so beautiful that the

1

pair were the cynosure of envious eyes throughout a costly and elaborate meal at the Hotel Cosmopolitan, was no less of a public excitement than his previous excursions.

Harbinger of the *Gazette*, whose representatives had tried to interview the man time and again and never successfully, said it was the most magnificent case of a silent publicity flair, amounting to genius, he had encountered in a varied career; no reporter could interview Julian Marks, and the most subtle could not wring from him a definite opinion on any political, social or economic point; no one knew what he liked for breakfast; no one knew which brand of religion, if any, he favoured. His picture was never to be found in the expensive weekly papers, he had no wife obsessed by philanthropic activities, no lovely daughter to grace ballroom and hunting-field. Yet he remained one of the most discussed men in the metropolis.

Springing from a background too crude, one might have supposed, for any form of culture, this amazing man took a high place immediately in the world of intellect and of imagination. It was discovered that there were few subjects on which he was not competent to express an opinion; he could speak and read in several languages; books of philosophy, of poetry and of art were to be found in his library, whose contents were in his head. His house was soon as well known as a museum and far more jealously visited; he kept a large retinue of apparently perfect servants, he had unending resources at his disposal, and for him to hear of some treasure in art that he coveted meant its instant acquisition.

He had his detractors, of course, men who said he placed a cash value on everything he possessed, that he was incapable of disinterestedness, that he demanded from his guests a large percentage on the price of their supper. There were other rumours, more definite these, tales of excursions to the continent with no very reputable motive; of chance glimpses of the man in company that would never find its way past even the back door of his town mansion; of excesses whose details altered with the narrator. Most of these stories were pooh-poohed as being extravagant, unfounded, improbable; but even these added to the sense of rich and varied experience that the mere name of the man evoked in his audience. It was noteworthy that there was not a photograph in the whole of his house and no hint of his personal history. Lacey, the historian, who detested the man but loved his possessions, said once, "He's such an odd chap, like the fellow who couldn't throw a shadow. It's as if there was no substance to any life he lived before he came here, and yet even his erratic type of genius couldn't build this kind of present on shadows."

And one of the more audacious weeklies cartooned him with a label, a bit of a cynic, a bit of a bachelor and a bit of a wit.

Even when the slump came in the diamond trade, when other men were unostentatiously closing their grand establishments and disappearing from society, he abated not a jot of his splendid ritual; he was an intensely curious person, like a human jackdaw, with a finger in every conceivable financial pie; he had details of an hundred commercial concerns at his finger-tips; he was even powerful enough to ignore the rumours that presently began to circulate that he was not, after all, so untouched by the general distress as he appeared, that society might expect a colossal crash pretty soon; and indeed, when these whispers had been flying round for some months, Marks added body to them by disappearing one morning from his

palatial house, leaving no address more tangible than
that he had gone abroad. The date of his return was
unknown.

2

Up till this time, and indeed for several months to
come, he had been a person of concern chiefly to the
leisured and commercial classes, but at the beginning
of November, almost immediately after his return
from South Africa with the Marks diamond, whose
discovery sent the whole world of jewellers and their
satellites into a frenzy, he became, vulgarly speaking,
anybody's meat, and his past, his present, the motives
lying behind the latest dreadful development in a
sensational life, were discussed, not merely by hot-
headed criminal novelists like Bertha Hoult, who was
one of his fellow-guests at the time of the tragedy,
by solid scowling business men like Anthony and
Perrin and Frayle of Lombard Street, by astute dealers
in Hatton Garden and on the continent, but by anybody who cared enough to buy an evening paper or
lounge on a doorstep, with hair in curl-papers and
arms comfortably idle folded over shabby aprons, talking piously and with delight of the inscrutable ways
of providence and the apparently inevitable penalty of
wealth.

Probably this knowledge would have been the most
galling humiliation that trim and sophisticated figure
could undergo.

The affair took place with every circumstance of
pomp and splendour. The surroundings were as magnificent as even he could demand. He was to provide
copy for innumerable detective writers for a considerable time after his death; his name was a pleasurable
one on thousands of lips. Yet his ending was without
dignity, a dark and hurried affair that might have

happened to any sneak-thief skulking in an alley, a man who was of no value to the community and of no personal achievement. It took place, moreover, at a time when the Marks companies, whose shares had fallen during the period of uncertainty, were booming, when people were anticipating the reopening of the gilded doors of the resplendent house in Mayfair, when the great Christmas season was being prepared for in a thousand ways. Marks had read of these developments on board the boat that brought him home; heard that the market was besieged by buyers; that the Stock Exchange was wild with excitement. Telephones, he was informed, shrilled perpetually in every broker's office; one excitable man who, courting prudence, had sold out of his Marks holdings, unable to endure the crushing disappointment, flung himself under a tube train; and while the bell and telephone of the house in Mayfair never ceased ringing, Mr. Cameron, Marks' private secretary, spent several hours a day with outward patience and inward exasperation informing inquirers by letter and in person that his employer had not returned and that no date for his arrival had been received.

Ultimately, of course, the rumour went round that this apparent flight, this tale of impending ruin, was a put-up job to enhance the value of the Marks shares; there were people who couldn't speak well of the man and who said openly that he'd asked to be murdered and only got, in the shape of that narrow French knife, what he richly deserved.

3

When Marks returned to London at the end of October he stayed there no more than four-and-twenty hours. Then, unaccompanied, and with a quantity of luggage, plus the famous jewel that he insisted on carrying himself, he departed from Dover, whence he would go to Monte Carlo, breaking his journey at Paris. The reason for this delay was not given, but he was later seen at the Hotel Cosmopolitan in Paris with a woman of amazing beauty and charm, and his detractors had a further opportunity of looking at him down their aristocratic noses.

"Though," said Julian Marks briefly, "they're mostly pug."

He was always outspoken, and even this did not prevent his being an acquisition at dinner parties and luncheons. He curtly refused Cameron's offer to travel with him, or to take a servant. He didn't, he said, need anyone to button him into his coat or lace his boots; he'd got past that stage when he was four years old.

"These women," he mused, "can't do their own hair, can't lace up their own frocks. What's the matter with them? Premature senile decay, I call it."

So he went alone, had his evening of adventure with the nameless lady and next morning travelled in great comfort to Monte Carlo, where he would stay at the Hotel Fantastique, that hotel that is almost as amazing as Marks himself, that was opened by Giuseppe Potain three years ago, and was accounted to be the most luxurious and entertaining place of its kind in Europe.

And, with him, to Dover, to Paris and to Monte Carlo, would go, he insisted, despite all warnings, the great Marks diamond that made collectors' mouths water and drove certain women to a frenzy that Marks himself thought despicable and beyond understanding. Not even his own lawyer had been able to dissuade the man from carrying the jewel on his own person.

"If you want to commit suicide," said Horsley, "you couldn't choose a better way of doing it. Why not have the stone locked up at the Bank of England, or give it over to Lloyds, somewhere where it'll be safe? Its value is tremendous."

Marks, an elegant, imperturbable figure, slightly under medium height, remarked dryly that he was more likely to know its value than anyone, and that he had no intention of changing his plans.

"The third biggest diamond in the world," Horsley pleaded. But Marks would listen to no one. He had received innumerable offers for the stone and was now, he said, on his way to Monte Carlo, where he proposed to meet a Paris dealer.

"Why drag him down to Monte Carlo?" asked Horsley reasonably.

"I've met this fellow before," said Marks in an unemotional tone. "He gave me some trouble. This time he shall have a little. After all, it's only one day's journey." He smiled his flashing, bewildering smile that was never wholly free from malice.

"As for gossip, one's never free of that," he added carelessly. "I should know, considering how my name's been used during the past six months. And I'm taking all necessary precautions. The stone is attached to me by a steel chain particularly forged for the purpose. No burglar's tool is going to cut through that very easily."

"But why travel absolutely alone?" Horsley wanted to know. "Take Cameron—or one of your servants."

"Cameron's needed to do my work in London. As for servants, I've learned that money is a very powerful factor in life. Practically everybody wants it, and of course there are numberless ways of getting it. There are also a good many people who want that stone, and want it cheap. There are times, my dear

7

Horsley, when diamonds are indefinitely more costly than men. For instance, I think Driver or Penney, either of whom I might choose to accompany me, would command a comparatively trifling price compared with that stone."

"On my soul," exclaimed Horsley who, lawyer though he was, was repelled by the dispassionate argument, "I'm inclined to agree with the fellow who said that the world would be no poorer if every diamond in it were burning in hell."

Marks didn't smile. "I should be poorer," he pointed out.

"That's one of the penalties of being a rich man, I suppose," remarked Horsley viciously to his partner, as he watched Marks enter his glossy, long-bonneted car. "You daren't trust a soul. I dare say he meant that either Penney or Driver wouldn't be averse to earning a handsome sum for taking an afternoon off during the journey. Who was that millionaire who never let another man shave him, in case the fellow cut his throat?"

CHAPTER II

1

MARKS was accustomed to glance up from his paper during long train journeys and observe the numbers of well-dressed curious travellers drifting unostentatiously past his window, all wanting to have one glimpse of the millionaire. He knew that familiar look that feigns to be artless, the shrewd sideways slant of the eyes, the dropped lashes, the careful arranging of a fold of the wearer's frock, while the astute owner took in every detail of the small, neat figure, with its slightly pointed French boots, its down-bent head, its thin, hawk-like profile, and the long, well-kept hands grasping one of the many papers with which the carriage would be strewn. But on this occasion of the last journey he would ever take he was more than an object of interest; he was a sensation, mild as yet, since he was still alive and, indeed, no one had actively threatened his safety. But none knew better than he the wild excitement and the fearful joy that would fill the hearts of his fellow-travellers if, at his journey's end, he were found with his throat cut, since this is the accepted finale of such stories as his, and all part of a providential design to warn the unwary that there are quite a lot of things money can't buy, security being one of them. He had never been moved by this curiosity or inclined either to pander to or resent it. He had created, he knew, not merely an atmosphere and a fortune, a rich and glittering background in London, set off by a mysterious secret history whose details were his own property; he had created a whole world of his own which was not dependent on other personalities and their reflection on his life. At best, the world in general was no more than a setting for his own personal play, and he used every detail, moulded every circumstance to his own ends. That sense of playing always against an artificial background was so strong that it impressed other people. When, after an amateur dramatic entertainment in which he figured with conspicuous brilliance, someone said, " What an actor he would have made," others (of whom, later, Mr. Latymer, the Man in Button Boots, was one) instantly retorted, " But what an actor he is."

At his journey's end he alighted, safe and free from any hint of molestation, and, followed by a number of glances, was obsequiously bowed into the magnificent vehicle no one quite liked to call an hotel omnibus, and was driven to the Hotel Fantastique. Here, for a change, since it was early morning, there were few people to watch his arrival, but they made up for their negligence with interest at dinner that first night.

There were a number of English people staying in the hotel, and all of them glanced up as he entered the room, a short figure in conventional evening dress, with a head slightly too large for the wiry little body it dominated; he walked with a slightly forward motion, as if he must press on without delay, like the famous apostle, though the dissimilarity of their goals makes the comparison a little ridiculous. But he was impressive, no one could deny that. His presence was felt, not merely by muddle-headed sensationalists like Bertha Hoult (she called herself a criminal psychologist and was the author of *Murder Below Stairs*, the story of a rich society woman found horribly mutilated under Wapping Old Stairs, *Bloodstains in Paris*, and a host of other ghoulish tales), but by sober intellectuals like Gabriel Montstuart, the distinguished barrister, who had been hounded abroad by his doctors, who told him it was a choice between Monte Carlo and Bedlam. He had expected to be most horribly bored by six weeks of enforced idleness, and, indeed, some of his companions made him shiver. That frightful woman who trailed about after him in alarming gowns of violet and orange and jade and was forever asking him involved questions of law, " because this is such an opportunity, Mr. Montstuart," until he had silenced her brutally by recommending an excellent lawyer he had himself employed, who would deal with her points at six-and-eightpence a time; she'd even suggested he should read her books, but he had vetoed that, saying he had come abroad for a rest

10

cure and couldn't afford to have his brain teased. If the majority of authors were like this, he thought, not knowing much about them as a class, it was no wonder they had the name of being a bit peculiar and unmannerly. Still, the divine law of compensation had provided the odious Bertha with a niece whom Montstuart found wholly charming, one of those candid, gay-spirited, modern children whom he admired, forgiving them their crudities on account of their courage. Girls like that wouldn't submit tamely to parental embargoes as a girl he'd known had submitted thirty years ago. This girl, Sarah Blaise, would marry the moody, handsome, brilliant young man, Nicholas Marvell, whom Fellowes, the south-country politician, had brought over as his secretary and personal assistant. Montstuart, watching the impatient lines of that notable face, wondered sometimes how a temper, abrupt and masterful, stood the slavery so well. Fellowes, now, was another of those men he had no use for, a weak, tyrannical rat of a creature, a man of straw, who was perhaps as well off in Parliament as anywhere. Certainly he would be little enough use to a client at the Old Bailey, voting as he did with every majority, and pretty brutal, rumour said, to his plump, nervous, chattering wife, who talked endlessly because he'd reduced her to a state of sheer terror that couldn't face a mutual silence. Fellowes looked as if one of these days he'd wring her neck. " Chap's a fool," thought Montstuart unsympathetically. " Of course, it is annoying to live with a woman who's little more than a bunch of platitudes, but if every man with a talkative wife could get compensation in law, the income of most husbands would go in legal and maintenance fees."

Above all, there was that extraordinary man who

11

wore button boots and hung about on the edge of crowds, went for aimless little walks, smiled absently when spoken to, who didn't seem to have an idea in his head, but had brought a neatly rolled mackintosh and a bowler hat in his luggage, and hadn't thought of removing from his suitcase labels marked York, Eastbourne and St. Leonards. No one knew what he was doing here; he was absolutely out of the picture and didn't even seem to be enjoying himself. He never went swimming or surf-bathing, didn't gamble, played no games at all, except chess, of which he had a pocket set and put up a brilliant show. Montstuart had played with him several times, and found himself hopelessly outclassed. There were various theories about the man, that he was a peculiarly subtle hotel thief or alternately, that he was a private detective engaged by Potain to guard the valuables of his guests. Montstuart pooh-poohed both notions; a man in either capacity would seek anonymity, a task Latymer would find simple enough with his slightly under-sized presence, thin mouse-coloured hair, insignificant features and light melancholy voice.

" He's probably recently won a sweepstake and all his mates have told him he ought to do himself proud by way of celebration," thought the barrister, amused at the idea, for the poor devil seemed to be getting remarkably little out of his extravagant holiday.

He looked a typical minor civil servant.

Yet he was not altogether without wit. There had been the afternoon when that unspanked chit, Jane Lanchester, had impudently asked him what the I. in his name stood for.

" Because we can only think of the Jewish ones—Isaac, Issacher, Israel, Isaiah, and they don't fit; or Scotch names like Ian, and if it's one of those I don't see how you can be called really legitimate; or there's Ivan, of course, but then you're so definitely not Russian, aren't you?"

The honours that afternoon had lain with Latymer. He had looked the impertinent young woman in the face and said in his dreary, gentle voice, "Increase, Lady Jane."

That sophisticated young woman's poise trembled in the balance. "Increase! Are you sure? I mean, it's such an odd sort of name."

"I was one of a twin," Latymer excused his peculiarity. "Increase and Prosper."

At his apologetic tone Lady Jane recovered. "And did he?" she demanded airily.

"For some years now we have had no means of ascertaining," countered her companion.

"H'm, yes, there's more in Mr. Latymer than we've probed as yet," Montstuart decided, letting his gaze flicker across the room to the man himself, neatly eating his soup with no more enjoyment than if the exquisite dish had been turned out of a tin five minutes earlier in some suburban kitchen. Then Marks came in, and Montstuart's spirits soared again. Here was a personality with a vengeance. Montstuart had a sudden feeling as though he were at Mme. Tussauds, without any notion how soon anyone could go to that forest of celebrities and see an astoundingly life-like representation of the little man on payment of a shilling.

"I wonder how much truth there is in the yarn that he's actually got the diamond in his waistcoat pocket," brooded Montstuart. "Lord, I'd like to see it. It's a pity the world's so constituted that one can't ask a simple favour like that without arousing suspicion. What's his game, though? He wasn't born yesterday.

He knows what he's about. I don't expect we shall see much of him during his stay."

And there again he was right.

2

The reaction of the other members of the English group to the newcomer were as instantaneous as Montstuart's. Miss Hoult, who collected personalities as small boys collect moths, remarked excitedly to her companion, "Look, Sarah—no, don't turn round in that ostentatious manner, just drop your handkerchief or something. That little man at the corner table dining alone. That's Julian Marks."

Sarah Blaise, twenty, tall, golden-haired, with the outspokenness of her generation that to her aunt's contemporaries indicated a lack of manners, turned her head and coolly stared.

"That little squit. Who is Julian Marks, anyway?"

"Oh, Sarah," groaned Miss Hoult, "I told you not to stare so, not in that obvious way."

Sarah opened her eyes wide. "Well, I wanted to see him," she said, "and I haven't got eyes at the back of my head. What's so exciting about him, anyhow?"

Her aunt said something uncomplimentary about the back of a hairbrush, then went on in eager tones, "My dear, you must have heard of the man. Everybody's heard of him."

"Except me," said Sarah composedly. "Bertha, I know you adore French cooking, but at least in England they give you mint sauce with lamb."

Miss Hoult disregarded that. So like Sarah to turn her flibberty-gibbet attention to unimportant trifles. "He's a big diamond magnate," she said. "He runs companies and sits on boards. You must have seen his name in the financial papers."

" I don't read them. Why should I? I haven't any money. Besides, I belong to that affected generation that doesn't think money so frightfully important."

" That's only because you haven't got it. It's a case of sour grapes."

" It's wonderful what a lot you can get without it," retorted Sarah, with a grin so disarming that Miss Hoult had to smile back. " Besides, darling, you've got such heaps. Go on and tell me about the little creature, if you must. This reminds me of the time when I thought I wanted to marry Raymond, and he was always bringing me disgusting little beetles and things, in bits, and making me look at them through a glass."

" He's the man who found the great Marks diamond," said Miss Hoult.

Sarah threw back her head and began to laugh in the most disconcerting way. " I begin to see why you're so frightfully interested in him. A diamond million-aire in a Monte Carlo hotel. Trite, of course, but the public doesn't mind that. All the same ingredients. Who have you picked on for the murderer?"

" Sarah! " breathed Miss Hoult in agony. People at the next table were looking at the girl; the two young Frenchmen who had been padding assiduously after her ever since they had arrived, now looked over and laughed, showing very fine teeth; one lifted his glass a little and bowed. " I wish you wouldn't attract so much attention," the wretched woman went on. " And don't for a minute suppose those French creatures are serious. They haven't got a thought of marriage in their heads. And anyway, no Frenchman marries a girl without money."

" No. Aren't I lucky to be English?" agreed Sarah cordially. " Unless, of course, you were prepared to settle some of your colossal profits on me."

"No nice man will want to marry you," said Miss Hoult angrily, and added at once, "You really needn't have made a scene the very first time Mr. Marks is here."

"What's he to do with me? Anyway, it's probably pleasant for him to be looking on at a scene instead of being involved in it, for a change. These rich men seem to make havoc of their married lives."

"He isn't married," said her aunt coldly, and quoted what the Smart Set cartoonist had said of him.

Sarah laughed again. "And your idea is to make him less of a bachelor? Good hunting, my dear. I suppose you're sure he hasn't got a wife stowed away somewhere?"

"I think you're disgusting," breathed her aunt. "Women of my age don't think of such things. Now you . . ."

"Oh, I'm booked for Nicholas, so I should be out of the running anyway. And I couldn't marry a man four or five inches shorter than me. It wouldn't feel quite decent somehow. . . . Darling, don't look as if there were a bad smell under your nose. Probably the notorious Mr. Marks is watching you, and he'll think it's your reaction to him."

"You know my feelings about that young man," said Miss Hoult repressively. "I can't understand what you see in him. He's got no money, no position and as few manners as you have."

"I know you've never forgiven him for saying that your ancestors must have kept a tripe shop; but that's only our way of saying we don't care about the books you write. His father or that odious Mr. Fellowes would have said, Not quite my style, or something pompous like that. It all means the same thing, really."

16

" There's all the difference between the two methods of expression that there is between a piece of raw steak and a perfectly cooked tournedos."

Sarah shrugged her shoulders crossly. " Oh, if you're going to be epigrammatic! Of course, you'll like the Marks creature. He's meat and drink to you; he's more than that, he's bread and butter. I think if I were you I'd have him murdered by his mistress."

" Sarah! Be quiet! Talking about mistresses like that, where half the room can hear you. He's come alone."

" Well, of course he has. You didn't expect him to come trailing one with him, did you? There's plenty of opportunity for him in Monte Carlo. I dare say he'll inspire you to a fortune. And quite fair. I don't believe in these rich men suddenly arriving from nowhere. He's probably done the dirty on someone. He's a nasty looking bit of work, anyhow."

Which was quite unfair to Mr. Marks' elegant distinction. Miss Hoult said so. Sarah chuckled, showing an unexpected dimple, and said in her clear young voice, that rang through the dining-room, " I've got the exact word for him. Natty. Natty little pointed boots, natty little grey fringe, natty little manners. I expect he could go one better than St. Paul, and say he was a citizen of several cities, none of them mean. London, Paris, New York and Bohemia, and all the worst elements of each. If he is murdered while he's here, I shan't mind. A man as rich as that and as conceited as the devil—if he weren't he wouldn't be doing anything so foolhardy as cart that diamond about with him—deserves anything that's on the way. Why don't you try your hand, Bertha? You know all the ropes, and I'm sure outsize diamonds would be terribly becoming to you."

" My dear, if for no other reason, I shouldn't

attempt anything so ridiculous. There would only be one rope left for me, if I did. People who write crime stories have at least the merit of recognising their limitations."

" Perhaps someone else will," said Sarah hopefully. " There's a very odd collection here at present, what with the freak from No. 27, creeping about in button boots, like Whittington's cat with its skin off, and that perfectly foul Mr. Fellowes and his poor wife, who's like a sparrow in a gilded cage."

" My dear Sarah, surely you remember that Mr. Fellowes is Nicholas Marvell's employer."

" I know. I can't think how Nick stands it. I know P. F.'s a cabinet minister, but I believe he beats his wife. She's obviously terrified of him. And I dare say he floats bogus companies as well."

" Presumably you get your information from Mr. Marvell," observed Miss Hoult icily. " I must say I should have thought common loyalty towards his employer, quite apart from considerations of discretion, might have sealed Mr. Marvell's lips. And in any case, if you ever do get married, which is quite improbable, considering you've neither money nor manners, I shall think your husband perfectly justified in beating you whenever he feels like it. I only wish I could be in his shoes for a week."

3

" This really is a most interesting hotel," remarked Mrs. Fellowes warmly to her husband, as they lifted their soup spoons. " And such a change from the Hydro, though people were perhaps a little more friendly there. There's nobody quite like that nice Mrs. Prothero, or that Miss Lewis who gave me the new recipe for minced ham soufflé. Still, they're cosmopolitans and, of course, that makes a world of difference." That was the kind of statement that infuriated Fellowes. He couldn't think how any woman could be such a fool: was even inclined to believe that, in spite of the fifteen thousand pounds she had brought with her, that had been uncommonly useful at the time, she was one of his worst bargains. And sometimes he trembled with a bitter fury to remember the young, vivid girls in the world from whom she would separate him probably for another thirty or forty years. A woman who didn't even know the difference between Harvest Burgundy and Chateau Yquem.

She was babbling now about how pretty Miss Blaise was, and that seemed to him the crowning insult. Sarah was the type of girl he wanted to have for a wife, not this fat, senseless creature, who hung affectionately round his neck and openly tried to keep him in a good mood, because she was so frightened when he was annoyed. He knew the gamut of her conversational openings by heart.

". . . but I do so miss my nice china tea at four o'clock. . . ."

" All this gossip and sport. I do think the vicar's right when he says that of such is the kingdom of hell."

And at last, " And who do you say this new man is, dear? A millionaire? How strange! He doesn't look like one, does he? Oh, diamonds? Now, that's not a stone I ever admire much. Such a glassy effect, I always think."

In his exasperation Fellowes lighted a cigarette.

" Oh, Percy, dear, not with the fish. I believe you're wool-gathering. Oh, really, what an interesting lot of people there are here. A politician and a novelist and a lawyer, and now a millionaire. And, of course, there's Mr. Latymer. I know you laugh at me, Percy. . . ."

"And I know you think he's the Prince of Wales," broke in Fellowes desperately. "I keep on telling you he's no more like him than my boot is."

"That's just where the cleverness comes in," cried Mildred Fellowes in triumphant tones. "You know, he's supposed to be a model of tact."

4

The two young Frenchmen talked with greater emphasis and less discretion. One said, "Another publicity expert, heh?" and the other replied, "But not Hollywood, this time. London, by Australia and South Africa."

Degas shrugged his shoulders. "Of course, he is mad. And perhaps he will pay high for his folly."

"You think he may be stabbed?"

"It is possible."

His companion looked unconcerned. "If there is to be a murder by all means let him be his own victim. It is his diamond, is it not? This modern notion that you shall have your cake and leave your bill to be settled by your secretary is not good finance."

"I dare say there is a good deal that is crooked behind that gentleman. It might be better to have him at some other hotel."

"Potain would not agree with you," Degas laughed. "He has the handsomest suite in the whole hotel."

"Yes, and he pays less for it than we who have single rooms on the fourth floor. No, Potain has said nothing, but one knows the type. A man who knows so much about getting money out of a diamond mine supposed to be derelict is not easily fleeced."

"Perhaps that is why he will not part with the

stone. Did you know that that fellow," he indicated Fellowes with a jerk of his smooth black head, " declared that an honest man would have no fear?"

"And have you not observed that honest men seldom pay their neighbours the compliment of supposing them to be equally invulnerable?" Lecoq laughed grimly and beckoned to the wine waiter.

The only remaining English guest, Mr. Increase Latymer, looked in his drifting aimless way from table to table, as he sipped his bottle of cheap wine and wished these French hotels served the long crusty rolls you got in England. They might know a lot about luxury, he thought, but they had very little notion of comfort. He looked longest perhaps at Mr. Marks, but what he thought no one knew, and he never talked about his feelings. A baffling, unsatisfactory man, an exciting, mysterious man, a dull, insignificant little man, according to how you regarded him.

CHAPTER III

1

IT was Marks' second night at the Hotel Fantastique, and there was to be a gala evening to include a magnificent dinner at which guests would wear festive button-holes and carnival hats; gifts presented in the dining-hall, and afterwards what Potain fondly believed to be ineradicable English customs for the last evening of October, including biting the apple and slapping the candy. Afterwards, because there were a number of men and women of other nationalities at the hotel who might not care for this boisterousness, he would turn them adrift into the grounds to

21

play a game resembling hide-and-seek that, he calculated, should keep them engaged until it was time for supper, and the surprise item. Of course, there would be dancing for those who preferred it, but one danced every night and All Hallows only came once a year. Potain was delighted because Marks had agreed to join in the fun. Potain, like all his kind, stood in awe of a fellow-creature so successful and so powerful; moreover, had not the man demanded and obtained the hotel's most magnificent suite at a price that made Potain's ears red now when he remembered the language with which his wife had greeted the intelligence?

"You gave him the rooms for that?" she cried, incredulous, arms akimbo.

"He took them," said Potain humbly.

"Took them, did he? And what kind of man are you to let the first-comer take your rooms for a few sous?"

Potain knew himself to be something of a personality; at fifty-three he stood second to none in the hotel world; yet he cowered before the lash of his wife's tongue. But Marks was a man apart, a charlatan, perhaps, a rogue almost certainly, a man into whose past it might be wiser not to delve, but a man one certainly would not care to antagonise. And out of the component parts of his nature he had created something, some image, that Potain automatically worshipped.

Success! It was a lovely word. He was by way of being a successful man himself. This colossal hotel was the zenith of his ambition; he had bought up the estate in lamentable order, pulled down the existing buildings, erected this magnificent hotel, spent a small fortune levelling and laying out the grounds, planning tennis lawns and fives courts, a swimming-pool, a small wood, a quarry, where conifer firs marched steeply to the earth fifty feet below; he had even discovered an ancient well and had spread unfounded but most impressive rumours concerning it. In his practised hand it was soon an old monastery well, where innumerable miracles had been performed. He had even had some notion of selling the water in glass bottles, but examination had proved it to be thick, weed-grown and unwholesome, most probably poisonous, so he had been forced to abandon that part of the programme and leave the well shut down. Bindweed grew thickly over the wooden rim, and he had never been to the bother and expense of actually sealing it up. He and his hard-headed, sharp-eyed wife, Julie, grew most of their own vegetables, and addled guests, hungering for any occupation, no matter how trivial, would lean over the gate that separated the kitchen garden from the remainder of the grounds, near the vaunted holy well, and lay bets as to which would be the next lettuce to come up. But, as Montstuart had observed, Latymer didn't even join in this amiable futility.

2

On the morning of the 31st Julian Marks went to Potain in his private office and asked if arrangements could be made for a car to be at his disposal the following morning at 11.30. Potain, as curious as his companion, asked if the car would be required for a long journey, and Marks named a hotel, the Cordon Bleu, in the Rue Anatole France, where, he said, he had an appointment. And added that if a M. Salomon telephoned to him he would be out for the next two hours. Potain's ears sharpened as he heard the name, recognising it as that of a famous Parisian jewel dealer; he longed to ask questions, but discretion sealed his lips; he dared not even drop a hint. Already he knew something of the quality of this client's temper, and he only agreed in his demure voice that the car should await monsieur's pleasure at the desired time, and disappeared to pass the news on to his wife.

Julie Potain nodded her sharp-featured head. " So he is parting with the diamond to-morrow. That's as well, Giuseppe. We want no scandal here, and . . ." her shrug said that where the body is there will the vultures be gathered together.

The party that night was the most elaborate entertainment Potain had ever planned. The dinner was perfect, the wines of a quality that made connoisseurs sigh with envy and wonder where the fellow had got his cellar; the presents were, as outspoken Sarah observed, worth having, not bazaar junk like so much free stuff; and afterwards they came into the shadowy grounds where a minimum of artificial lights had been kindled.

" What's the idea of this damfoolery?" grumbled Fellowes, barking his shin against the lintel of the french window. " Why we can't be amused in a Christian manner . . ."

" It's Potain's idea of what will please the national tendency best, sir," Nicholas Marvell explained in smooth tones. " In fact, he's getting so distressingly rural I almost expect to find him spelling English— E-n-g-l-y-s-s-h-e. Still, you must admit, sir, that the sight of Marks in a thing like a bastard biretta made of pink cardboard, with a silk tassel falling over one eye, is refreshing," he suggested. " Your clown's cap," he turned to Sarah who came up at that moment, " is far less becoming."

" You needn't talk, you and your blue and yellow sunbonnet," returned Sarah with spirit. " I must say I think Buttons looks rather a lamb in that drummer's outfit. Don't you, Mr. Fellowes?"

"I think they all look intoxicated," returned the politician irritably. He knew his wife was going to make a fool of herself this evening; she always did when there was a party on, and later there would be tears and pleas for reassurance. "You don't think anybody noticed, do you, Percy . . . ?" He knew it all, had been wearied by it more years ago than he cared to remember.

Nicholas and the girl had moved off and now they were joined by Montstuart, who said humbly, "Enlighten my ignorance, won't you? What are we supposed to do?"

"Oh, it's like hide-and-seek," said Sarah. "Somebody hides and then we all hunt for him in the dark. And when you find him you don't hoot, like you do in hide-and-seek, you just stay put beside him and the last person home has a forfeit and is the next to hide."

"It's the game that's known as sardines, if it's played indoors," Nicholas amplified. "And I can't think why we don't play it indoors."

"The last time I played it," remarked Sarah pensively, "there was a very toothy, dictatorial female who insisted on joining in, and she thought she was being brilliant and hid in the bath, and the first person to find her was a plump old gentleman who nobly climbed in beside her, and the next was Reggie Fortescue, who turned on both taps. I dare say Potain's anxious to prevent that kind of thing happening here."

"He's more likely, don't you think, to be preparing the climax of the evening indoors," suggested Montstuart, "and he doesn't want any of us to guess what he's at."

"Most probably," Nicholas agreed. "Anyway, it's

a horrible game at any time. People invent such foul forfeits. I once had to ring the bell of a perfectly strange house and say 'I love you' three times to whoever opened the door. It was very embarrassing, and, as it turned out, rather compromising."

" For England's future premier?" Sarah teased him. " He will be, you know, one of these days," she added, as Nicholas turned in response to a summons from his chief. " Oh, here's Bertha and little Buttons. She's perfectly fascinated by that man. I can't make out whether it's S.A. or whether she still suspects him of being a notorious criminal hiding from the police. Anyway, she's getting all the hints she can from him. They've been discussing this man, Marks, practically without a break for the last forty-eight hours."

Behind them the voices of the oddly-assorted pair sounded clearly.

" I confess I should be immensely interested to know his personal history," Miss Hoult was saying. " Quite unscrupulous, I feel convinced."

" And yet not wholly inadmirable," suggested Mr. Latymer's pedantic murmur.

" Why, I believe you admire the creature." Bertha sounded scandalised.

" I must admit that, denied what perhaps I may be allowed to call an adventurous virtue, I prefer, with Mr. Auberon Quin, a rich badness to mere mediocrity. And I am certain that whatever Mr. Marks' private history may prove to be, it will not be mediocre."

" One of these days Bertha will find herself in the courts for libel," remarked Sarah heartlessly. " She hasn't got a thing against the poor little man except that he's got a diamond worth fifty thousand pounds and she hasn't, but she's like most people who have

26

to earn a living; she's quite sure that anyone who has more than herself hasn't come by it honestly."

And then Nicholas broke up the conversation by coming across and saying, " They've been drawing lots for who has to hide first, and you're for it, sir," so Montstuart had to go.

He wasn't a man who believed in wasting subtlety, so he simply walked out of the verandah and leaned against one of the posts in a patch of shadow. It was a long time before anyone found him and then he complained that he hadn't been able to smoke for fear of betraying his whereabouts. Miss Hoult was openly disappointed by what she called his lack of esprit de corps. " I do like a man to enter into the spirit of the game; but I suppose he thinks he's too important to take any trouble over us." She was angry at having incurred the first penalty, having laughingly warned the assembly that she expected her detective sense to discover the victims to her before anybody else. She hid in a cramped position under a window-sill and everyone found her at once. Degas was victim that round and in his turn was followed by Sarah, and then it was the turn of Julian Marks, who came ' home ' quite two or three minutes after everybody else.

Up to date the game could hardly be called successful. Miss Hoult was huffy, Mrs. Fellowes nervous, and after the third round Fellowes announced that he had lost his tie-pin, that he valued greatly, and the game was held up while he minced along the paths looking for it. Latymer, who had been standing at the back of the verandah unobtrusively manicuring his nails, went with him, peering through his tortoise-shell rimmed glasses at borders and the edges of lawns.

" That'll hold us up for a week," said Nicholas,

pulling out a cigarette case. "Smoke, Sarah? And if he doesn't find it, what a day we'll have to-morrow. I believe that if that man furnished from Woolworths he'd take out a policy at Lloyds in case one of the saucepans parted from its handle too soon."

But fortunately the pin was found, and Fellowes came striding back, with Latymer following him hurriedly, and whistling the Marseillaise, "to show how much at ease he is, poor brute," muttered Nicholas. "Well, thank God, he found the trumpery little thing. A fox-head, isn't it, to show you what a sport he is, and a whiplash for authority and a pearl horse shoe for luck?"

"Stoo-ard!" murmured Sarah sympathetically. "Now for our little millionaire."

"Now, I expect he'll be really subtle," remarked the novelist maliciously, realising that Montstuart was within earshot. "I saw him wandering about round the Holy Well a little time ago."

"Oh, dear," exclaimed Mrs. Fellowes, who was bending over a bowl of silver spotted fish that decorated the verandah, "I do hope he won't try to hide inside the well."

"He'll be hidden for good, if he does," grinned Sarah, but Montstuart, who was watching them closely —he could never conquer his love of youth—saw that the face of Nicholas Marvell was uneasy and almost irritable. He moved unobtrusively over towards them.

"I don't like this," Nicholas was saying, and as the barrister approached he turned, adding, "Not a bit. Do you, sir? I can't think what possessed Potain to suggest this insane form of amusement. It's too dangerous." And he stared apprehensively at the dark lawn, over which the elegant figure of Marks was walking away from the light into the darkness.

"Natty just describes him," murmured Sarah, refusing to be sympathetic. " Watch him settling his tie and smoothing his hair. I wonder if he's ever been untidy in his life. I should think that, like Moses in the song, he was born wearing his old school tie."

Nicholas repeated insistently, " Don't laugh. It's dangerous."

" Dangerous?" Sarah stared. " For whom?"

" Marks, of course."

" Ten minutes in an empty garden?"

" Ten minutes in a garden that ought to be empty. That's nine and a half minutes too long. The first half-minute's all right. It takes him that time to get out of our sight into the bushes beyond the lawn. After that—well, I don't like it at all."

" What a satisfactory M.P. you'll make," was Sarah's careless comment. " Such a magnificent imagination. You'll suppose that any measure you're proposing is already achieved. Like Ko-Ko, you remember. Don't worry yourself. Marks is no fool."

" Any man is a bit of a fool who becomes colossally rich and lets the world know it," Montstuart backed up the young man. " I'm inclined to agree with Marvell."

" Personally I shall be very thankful when this evening's over, without casualties, if it is," said Nicholas with more violence than the occasion seemed to warrant.

Soft steps sidled up behind them, and a high-pitched nervous voice said, " Have you any idea, Mr. Marvell, where Mr. Marks will hide? Miss Hoult thinks down by the well, but do you really think that's likely? You know, I'm so stupid I'm certain I shall be the last, and I shouldn't have any idea where to hide. Besides, there are forfeits, you know, and I believe they're terrible. I do wish I'd said I wouldn't play. I'm really not enjoying this game at all."

" Neither am I," returned Nicholas heartily. " Hallo, here's someone in a hurry."

To the amazement of them all Latymer was suddenly at their side, crossing the verandah faster than anyone had ever seen him move before. As the light fell on his face they saw he looked haggard and strange.

" Where's Marks?" he cried, and they all noticed the absence of the prefix. It struck them as odd.

Two or three voices said at the same time that he was in the garden. " He's gone?" cried Latymer. " What? Alone?"

" Yes," said Miss Hoult eagerly. " You see, he was the last home and according to the rules . . ."

Latymer flung out his hands in a despairing gesture. " And I was looking for that tinpot tie-pin," he muttered impolitely. " I hadn't realised it was his turn. . . ."

" But why?" Sarah began. Her two men were silent, watching Latymer intently. He swung round, speaking roughly in his agitation.

" Can't you see?" he exclaimed. " Of all the fools!" Though whether he meant Sarah or Marks no one was quite sure. " Has he no imagination? No memory? Quick." He caught Nicholas by the arm. " You come with me. I hope to God it isn't too late."

He stepped back quickly, his eye sweeping the verandah, Mrs. Fellowes fell back with him, and the great bowl of silver fish came crashing to the ground.

Latymer muttered something unchivalrous, hesitated, said to Nicholas, " Come on. There are plenty of people to pick up the pieces," and darted down the verandah steps.

Mrs. Fellowes cried out in alarm and dismay and promptly cut her finger on an edge of broken glass; Miss Hoult cried, " The poor darlings, look how terrified they are!" Sarah stooped and began to collect them as they flapped and wriggled on the floor of the verandah, saying coolly as she did so, "I don't suppose they are frightened, really. I think they're too cold-blooded to know fear. Fish . . ."

"Sarah likes to talk as if she knew everything," said her aunt crossly. "You ought to be a lecturer for the B.B.C., Sarah . . ."

Latymer turned from the foot of the verandah steps, beckoning to Nicholas. "There are plenty of people," they heard him say, but before Nicholas could move Fellowes said in his harsh voice, "Just lend a hand here, will you? The game can wait, I suppose. No, Mildred, do not touch that glass. You've cut yourself already. And don't," he added, in a lower, fiercer voice, "for God's sake, don't cry. Do you want me to look a fool in front of everyone?"

Nicholas hesitated. He had been apprehensive before and now was definitely alarmed, remembering a number of trifling details, such as the visit of that wild fellow yesterday asking for Marks and talking all that balderdash about rich men and their diamonds, but before he could stir Fellowes' voice said urgently, "Marvell! Good God, man, have you no decent feeling?"

Nicholas shook a despairing head at Latymer, who had already turned and was moving out of sight, and stooped to collect glass and fish indiscriminately. Out of the tail of his eye he saw that Montstuart was following Latymer, and, after a moment, goaded to fury by his employer's manner, and by the niggardliness of mind that could set a futile accident against a man's possible danger, he straightened himself, saying curtly, "The servants will clear this, sir," and without waiting for Fellowes' inevitable fretful protest went down the steps into the dark garden.

His fears filled his mind, though he could give them no precise shape. But Latymer's dismay had convinced him that something serious was in the wind. When so normally composed a man allowed himself to betray such strong feeling, then there was ground and to spare for alarm. Behind him was Fellowes, who had flung himself in exasperation out of the crowd on the verandah, after giving his handkerchief to his now panic-stricken wife. Fellowes was going in another direction. He himself cut across the lawn the way Marks had gone a few minutes before, not knowing quite what he expected to find when he rounded the bushes that separated the lawn from the shrubbery; and when he reached that point to find there was nobody in sight at all, living or dead, he drew a breath of spontaneous relief. Now he could admit to himself that he had been afraid of discovering a body, or, at best, a woefully injured man. He stood for a moment like a hound at scent; under his feet the grass was damp and close-cropped; his blood, that had chilled with fear, ran more warmly again. He forgot that the issue was still in doubt.

" I wonder what precisely Latymer did mean," he reflected, perplexed, looking this way and that without seeing a human being anywhere. " He's not the kind of fellow to get the wind up over nothing."

The garden round him had been dark and shadowy, but now the moon broke suddenly through a thick bank of cloud, shedding an ephemeral but brilliant light over the whole scene. The grounds of the hotel now presented an odd harlequinesque appearance, so much silver and black, where the shadows drowned even the light of the moon; and this effect was heightened in the most dramatic way by the sudden appearance of the man he was seeking, walking on a ridge at the farther side of the grounds. Nicholas knew the spot well; it was a good place for a man who wanted to be quiet and escape his companions; the ridge overlooked a kind of natural quarry, lined with trees of conifer fir; thick tall bushes bordered the place, but at one spot, where they were most exposed to the fury of the winds, they thinned and withered, so that a man standing at this height was clearly visible from practically any part of the grounds. It was here, then, that Marks was now moving, a fantastic black figure against the paler sky. Nicholas knew him at once by his fantastic headgear, whose absurd silken tassel was blown backward, stretched tight like wire, by the night wind. Like the central figure of a ghost story, reflected Nicholas, standing still, fascinated by the vision. In the dim light it looked as though some strange bird had settled on that sober greying head.

"What the devil's he doing?" speculated Nicholas, standing stockstill to examine the situation. For Marks was proceeding with a swift and stealthy movement, making such haste as he could, in the direction of the belt of trees to the right, that would in a moment screen him from curious eyes. He was peering eagerly at the dark ground as he went, though he could hardly hope to discern much in the evasive moonlight; the only other illumination was supplied by a sparse collection of paper lanterns in various colours, that did their best to fog the rays of the nightlights they contained; and by the spinney none of these had been hung.

"Perhaps," reflected Nicholas, forgetting his previous distress and watching the movements of his quarry with a fascination that made him oblivious to the rules of the game, "this is an example of the genius commonly allowed to extreme simplicity. By making for the trees across a stretch of absolutely open ground, he may think he'll put his pursuers off. No one would look for him in such an exposed spot."

"But he's infernally conspicuous," objected Nicholas a moment later, beginning to move slowly forward, and thrusting his hands into his pockets, in his favourite attitude. "Hullo, he's going back on his tracks. What's his game?" It was then that the absurd idea occurred to him that perhaps Marks had actually lost the famous diamond, and was hunting for it, before that loss must be advertised; and it was fully a minute before he realised that what the millionaire was really doing was deliberately keeping in some place where he was perpetually under observation. With so many people scattered on the grounds it would be practically impossible for him to be attacked secretly; clearly his walk across the dark lawn had been a blind. The instant he was behind the hedge he had doubled back and found this open position.

"So Latymer needn't have worried," Nicholas decided. "The fellow's no fool. He knows he's in danger, and he isn't taking any risks." His admiration of this simple subterfuge increased, as he realised that when the first of his pursuers reached him, Marks would still be so obvious to the others that no form of attack would be possible.

"We needn't have troubled our heads," Nicholas repeated. "If you come to think of it, a man in Marks' position must have been in plenty of tight corners before to-day. He knows how many beans make five. An interesting chap in his own way." Nicholas was as ambitious as Lucifer and could never wholly resist the man who had power in his hands, and had won it by his own efforts and enterprise. "There's something behind this stunt," Nicholas decided. "What's he carting this diamond about for in this conspicuous and highly advertised manner?

However, he seems to be able to look after himself. And he'll need to. Who's that chap who's been hanging about the hotel ever since Marks arrived? A scoundrel, if ever I saw one. I dare say Marks could give us his family history if he liked. It may be on his account that he's taking no chances. One thing, the fellow has guts. Old Latymer's right with his remarks about a rich badness." Then and only then did it occur to him that his proper course was to make for the ridge and prevent himself being last man home. He started, and as he did so the moon disappeared again and he was amazed to see the ridge was absolutely blotted out. For an instant he paused, irresolute. The figure of the pacing millionaire was now perfectly invisible. Nicholas thought, "I wonder if he allowed for that. Is he scared? Where's he got to? Good God, what's that?" He heard, or thought he heard, an odd cry, like a scream choked in its first utterance, and after that a crash. He was quite sure about the crash. He ran forward a few steps, stumbled, spread his hands instinctively to break his fall and found himself clutching at the shoulder of a man who had approached him in the darkness.

"All right," said a voice that he recognised at once as Montstuart's. "Did you hear that? The chap must have gone clean over. Damn! We're going to have a storm, I believe. The night's gone utterly black."

Nicholas, who had recovered himself already, said in a steadier voice, "Oh, I don't know, sir. As soon as the moon's through that bank of clouds we shall be able to see what we're doing? Did he fall or what?"

"I didn't see," said the lawyer. "He was on the ridge all right. Well, that was sensible of him . . ."

Nicholas nodded, glad to have his own impressions

confirmed. For a moment that horror that lurks just behind a man's consciousness, a fear that perhaps the things he sees are peculiar to himself, that his ears alone hear sounds that may terrify or elate, had almost overwhelmed him. Did I really see Marks on the ledge? he had wondered. Did anyone cry? Or fall? Montstuart's robust handling of the position calmed him at once.

"It's not a very even surface," the lawyer went on. "He may easily have slipped. The devil of it is that place is as steep as a precipice. I wouldn't care to come crashing down among the firs much, myself, though certainly Marks is a good deal lighter than I am."

"You know, it wasn't much of a crash," said Nicholas intently. "That might mean he didn't fall far, of course, or . . ."

"He didn't fall at all," Montstuart wound up. "He's a lucky fellow, if that was his game, though what he's up to I haven't the faintest notion. But this infernal darkness. Hullo, here's the moon again. Now we can see what we're doing."

By its light they made out other figures hastily climbing the ridge. One was Fellowes, with a tall slight man beside him, and someone else was mounting from the farther side. "That's one of the French lads, with Fellowes," said Nicholas. "Lord, what suppleness. That chap must be as agile as a monkey." The other figure, they decided, was Latymer, and when they reached the ridge they found him holding on to a stout branch and leaning precariously above the abyss. He had a powerful electric torch in his hands, and was casting the light downwards.

"You'd need to be a cat to get down there without injury," he observed, as the other two came up. "Look at that." They looked down, and saw that two of the trees just beneath the beam showed new white wounds where branches had been broken away. Below this it was impossible to see anything but the dark mass of foliage, that might conceal half a dozen bodies of broken men without revealing a trace of their whereabouts.

A soft voice spoke unexpectedly in Latymer's ear. " If monsieur would lend me his torch," he said, " I could investigate." It was the young Frenchman, Degas, whose athletic appearance had pleased Montstuart so much a few minutes ago.

" I'll go too," put in Nicholas, a little nettled that the first suggestion to make the perilous descent should come from a man of another race. " I've got a torch of my own;" he displayed it as he spoke.

A moment later, clinging to trees, finding what foothold they could, bumping, slipping, glissading, they were out of sight of the watchers on the ridge.

In the meanwhile Latymer had discovered a less precipitous if far less direct way down to the foot of the spinney, and this he and Fellowes took. Montstuart remained at the top, where he was presently joined by Miss Hoult and her niece. He had intended to stay there until he got some report from below, but the four men had scarcely disappeared before the most appalling shrieking broke out behind him, and involuntarily he turned.

" That's Mrs. Fellowes," said Miss Hoult almost at once. " What on earth's happened? She can't have been bitten by a snake." All of them went in the direction of the noise, so that for a few minutes the ridge was empty and unobserved.

CHAPTER IV

1

In another part of the grounds Mrs. Fellowes, one hand neatly bandaged, wandered alone, wondering where on earth everyone else had got to. And suddenly (so she herself phrased it later) she experienced one of those " premonitions " by which she explained two-thirds of the happenings of her married life; Fellowes had another name for them: he called them her damned nerve attacks. Probably to-night the feeling was started by the unexpected vision of that pink crown, dark against the dark sky, a thing so improbable and unnatural that the poor lady had some excuse for her collapse. For collapse she did. In an instant the garden had assumed a fantastic horror; by every black tree trunk, in the glancing treacherous shade flung by the wan lanterns, she discerned shapes of unnamable things, not human, not even animal, powers and forces that robbed her for the time being of her native reason. She felt as though she had been plucked out of her familiar world and set in the midst of a creation that menaced her at every turn. Waving branches became gibbering shapes; the soft rustle of the wind an obscene threatening. She stood (as she said *ad nauseam* later) rooted to the ground. And then she conceived the hideous notion that that cap was tracking her, that there were eyes, not merely in Mr. Marks' head but in the cap itself, and that those eyes were following her, that at any instant, like power released by an instantaneous pressure on a lever, the horror would be realised and come charging down upon her. That terror, quite inexplicable, and, as her husband pointed out later, so unreason-

able, held her for more than a minute; then, because
she was like a rabbit captivated by a snake and incapable of movement, she flung up her hands over
her eyes, and waited. When she opened her eyes
again the cap and the man beneath it had disappeared; there was now no one at all to be seen on the
ridge. At once she turned away, plunging in another
direction. But horror still pursued her. She
found herself in the neighbourhood of the Holy
Well. Probably alone of all the people on the premises she believed in the supernatural to an extent
that made the well at such an hour and in her present
mood a place from which she recoiled with the utmost horror. In spite of the fact that the death associated with it by common rumour—(admittedly a
death of peculiar ferocity and baseness)—had happened nearly 300 years ago, she still felt an aroma,
an atmosphere, that were appalling. And because this
feeling threatened to overwhelm her and she had begun to feel she was being hounded by something unnatural from any place where she sought sanctuary,
she hurriedly moved on again, and in another
moment found herself by the railed-off kitchen garden
where Potain grew such excellent vegetables. This
was separated from the grounds by a boarding fence,
and a gate, but the fencing was not so high that a
person of average height could not look over the top.
There were two men still at work in this garden, and
when Mrs. Fellowes saw them she stopped at once,
feeling the security of human companionship. Of
course, they were only gardeners, but even gardeners
are human beings, and Mrs. Fellowes actually felt a
stab of shame to think that she, a middle-aged
woman, a hostess whose husband had a certain reputation, whose name was well known, should be engaged on so childish a pursuit when men young and

vigorous, who could probably make much better use of an evening's leisure than she was ever likely to do again, had to go on working, sweeping leaves and wheeling them away, and probably not even paid double rates like they'd get in England for overtime, she reflected. Of course, Percy would approve of that; he thought British workmen hopelessly spoilt and pampered.

One of the men looked up and saw her there, and came politely across to her. "I do feel a fool," thought Mrs. Fellowes in a panic, and she blurted out, "I wonder if you've seen any of the others. I— somehow I've missed them, and its got so dark."

"I think they're over on the ridge, madame," said the voice—she really couldn't see the face at all clearly, but he pointed, probably knowing from experience that she would not understand his language. She realised that, and in a final flicker of pride she threw back her head and replied in a volley of French that made him smile, though whether with pleasure or derision she didn't know. Anyway, she thought, it wasn't worth while thinking what a French gardener had in mind. She turned and began to move towards the ridge; she was out of sight of it at present, and she made a good pace, alarmed at the prospect of being last man home. The penalties she had heard were fantastic, and she was an intensely self-conscious woman. But, as though fear would not this night leave her alone, a new thought darkened her mind. Suppose she came home first, found herself alone with this Mr. Marks of whom, really, they knew so little? In vain she reminded herself that he was suave, polished and courtly; her heart said he was sinister and mysterious. There were odd stories whispered —Percy had mentioned them to her—of pilgrimages he took abroad from time to time, of odd friends he made, of the quite peculiar places in which he was seen. He might be just mad, he might be actually degenerate. And suddenly all these fears combined to upset her nerves completely. She could not shake off the sense of being tracked by something sub-human; her blood was freezing, her hair lifted, and then, without in the least knowing its nature, she knew— afterwards, interviewed by M. Dupuy, the dapper smiling little inspector from the Sureté, who said so little and thought so much, she swore that at that instant she actually had known—that something frightful was going on not far off, but out of sight. Knew, too, her own powerlessness. She stated that she knew neither victim nor aggressor, could not warn the one or stay the hand of the other, could, in fact, do nothing but open her mouth and shriek as she now did, not a high crescendo of sound, but one pitched terrible scream following another. As she screamed she plunged wildly through the darkness in what was, she hoped, the direction of the hotel. For the most part she kept her eyes fixed on the ground, but once she looked up and immediately a round pale phosphorescent thing—not a face, it had not the texture of living skin, but was dry and crackling—touched her. She screamed again, plunging wildly backwards, and the little swaying Chinese lantern, slipping from its bough, seemed to be pursuing her, hopping across the tangled darkness.

Now, at length, she could hear footsteps coming towards her, but could not be sure whether these belonged to the dead, yet as it might prove, insufficiently dead, saints she appreciated so little, or the party of whom she was one. Then someone caught her arm in an unmistakable grip of flesh and blood, and a young kind voice said, "It's all right, Mrs. Fellowes. I expect you caught your foot, didn't you? They're perfect devils of weeds here." To her amazement that was Sarah Blaise; she hadn't supposed that a girl so modern and outspoken could show so much sympathy for a woman whom most likely she thought was a fool. But, before she had had time to derive much comfort from this unexpected friendliness and understanding, Miss Hoult came sweeping down on the scene, vivid in an orange frock that held every fragment of light, flinging it back into this place, long amber drops swinging in her ears, as picturesque, as inhuman and as hard as a polished stone. But for the green bonnet with its yellow strings that bustled about on the back of her head, she was a figure that could not fail to strike awe into a far more courageous heart.

"Dear me!" she exclaimed, "what's all the commotion?"

"Mrs. Fellowes slipped and hurt herself, I think," Sarah replied.

"Is that all? Dear me, I quite thought someone was being murdered. Not that I mean to suggest that one cannot hurt oneself quite severely when one falls." She looked round keenly. "I wonder what it was you fell over, Mrs. Fellowes?"

"A branch, I expect," said Sarah hastily.

Mrs. Fellowes took no notice of this last suggestion. She said in urgent shaky tones, "I wouldn't be surprised if there was a murder. Something horrible's happened, I know. It's time we gave up this ridiculous game—that is, if it isn't too late already."

Miss Hoult was going to say something else, but Sarah interposed hastily, "Let me help you back to the hotel, Mrs. Fellowes. I expect you're pretty well shaken."

Miss Hoult said, "Well, of course, if you really feel

bad . . . I think I'll go back and find out if they've discovered anything about poor Mr. Marks."

Mrs. Fellowes, who had gratefully taken Sarah's arm, turned back, wrenching herself free. "What's that about Mr. Marks? Why didn't you tell me? What's happened?"

"That's just what we want to know. We think he's fallen over the ridge."

"Fallen over?"

"They're finding out—Mr. Latymer and Mr. Montstuart. I've always thought that place a death-trap."

"A trap," repeated Mrs. Fellowes. "I wouldn't be surprised if it was. And Mr. Marks." She forgot all her sinister suspicions about the man. "Mr. Latymer said something frightful would happen, if he was allowed to go away alone. Oh, don't let's stand here doing nothing. Let's go and see what they've found."

Speechless, even the voluble Miss Hoult silenced by the sense of tragedy achieved in the enveloping darkness, they moved towards the ridge. Before they reached it they met the four men coming towards them.

"Did you find him?" called Miss Hoult jerkily.

Nicholas answered her question. "No, we didn't find Marks. In fact, we've no notion where he is. I don't think he can be in the spinney—we've searched pretty thoroughly, and a body isn't like a slate-pencil; you can't overlook it very well. But we know he was there, because I found this sticking to one of the long thorns on the bushes half-way down," and he opened his hand and showed them all the fantastic tasselled crown.

2

Two hours later the elusive millionaire was still not found, and the original admiration, changing presently to indignation, at the ingenuity of a man who could so successfully fool a whole party, had given place to a definite apprehension thickening to suspicious fear. Every corner of the grounds had been searched by guests and waiters, armed with lamps and torches. People had been plied with questions until exasperated nerves snapped under the strain, and the ugly word murder was heard on more than one lip. But at this stage no one definitely came forward with the suggestion that Marks had been done away with; a more general feeling was that, for some reason they couldn't plumb, he had disappeared.

It was Montstuart who said presently, in his downright way, " I don't know what the rest of you think, but if I were in charge here I'd send for the police. If it's a case of deliberate escape then there's something queer about the whole thing; and if it's anything else, then the sooner the police are on the job, the better."

They were gathered together on the verandah and, looking up as he spoke, Montstuart realised for the first time the absurdity of their appearance. Several of the guests still wore their extravagant carnival hats. Nicholas and Sarah, both absorbed in the mystery, were regardless of their appearance, but some of the older men were beginning to remember how foolish they must look. Fellowes had dropped his cap on the floor, Montstuart had removed his and was pleating it carefully, as he spoke. Across the table he saw that Latymer had folded his into little squares, and now he flipped it away from him, while Bertha Hoult's restless fingers were occupied in ripping hers into strips, that she scattered on the floor.

"Odd, how little control we have over the sub-conscious," thought Montstuart, rather contemptuous of so much childishness and recognising that probably not one of them knew what he was doing; and quickly he put his hands behind his back, as Fellowes looked up to say in a strained tone that if the police were called in every time anyone vanished for a couple of hours, you'd need to double the force. Then he took up the challenge robustly. "This isn't a case of a servant girl disappearing for an evening, who's probably having a rough-and-tumble in a sand-pit with her young man. It's a case of a fellow carry-ing an extremely rare and valuable diamond going off with no reason whatsoever that appeals to any of us —a very different kettle of fish. In any event, it seems to me that we lose nothing by appealing to authority, whereas by standing still Marks stands to lose not only his diamond but his life."

Potain, when the general feeling of the guests was put before him, showed himself extremely reluctant to fall in with their views. He even made one strenu-ous attempt to persuade them that there was nothing abnormal in a wealthy Englishman vanishing in the middle of a game, though he was at a loss when asked for any explanation that would hold water.

"But it is so bad for my hotel," he pleaded.

"Publicity," contradicted Montstuart hardily.

"But not the right kind of publicity. It is no good to an hotel to have had a rich gentleman disappear and the police called in."

"You'll have plenty of weak-minded fools come to look at his room and handle his gentlemen's under-wear if they get the chance," Montstuart pointed out.

"But it is the solid, rich, safe people whom I de-sire," cried Potain in an agony of anxiety and apprehension. "These, when they hear that I have the police here, will not pause to inquire, they will say, 'Oh, this is not a good hotel. They have the police here.' They will go elsewhere. Monsieur, I beseech you. Is not the missing monsieur human? May he not have a *petite amie*?"

"Dozens," agreed Montstuart amicably. "But I doubt if he'd draw attention to the lady so obviously. No, personally I favour the police. Though Potain's right," he added to Latymer, who stood placidly by, " it will put people off. They're so damned conceited it never occurs to them that ninety-nine times out of a hundred they aren't worth any murderer's money."

3

M. Potain, literally wringing his hands in a most passionate and dramatic manner, went to consult his wife about the latest development. Was he a philanthropist, his God? he demanded, enraged. Was he a humanist? His God, he was not. He was in trade for a living. Mme. Julie Potain, his sharp little gamecock of a wife, gave him even less sympathy than he had received from his clients. She told him fluently that if he did not summon the police at once, his hotel would automatically empty itself.

"Ma foi, do you wish it said that the Fantastique is the hotel where rich men disappear and no questions are asked? Would you ruin us? Besides, why should you fear? The English have a saying that a man who has nothing to hide does not fear the police."

"The English are crazy," flared Potain. "All the world knows that. Every man in his senses fears the police, as he fears anything with a strength he himself does not possess." Then he broke into a tirade against the missing man. "It is not fair, not right, not giving me a square deal," he cried. " If he wished to be murdered or spirited away, it should not be on my premises. He has enemies, no doubt. He is a rich man. As for us, we know nothing, Julie, nothing, nothing, nothing, except that he comes here with a big jewel. Perhaps he has been followed. How can we tell? Is it our fault? Of course not. Yet he takes the very bread from our mouths. Can you not see these other rich mesdames and messieurs who would have come to our hotel, saying ' No, no, we will not go to the Fantastique. That is the hotel where murderers get in through the fence. Let us go to nice pleasant safe Bournemouth or Tunbridge Wells?' I tell you, Julie, we are ruined."

"And I tell you you will be worse than ruined if you don't do what I say at once and send for the police," vociferated Madame. " Don't you understand that all the guests will be saying to one another, ' That old fox, Potain. While he fiddles, Rome burns. This is a pretty kettle of fish. A rich man vanishes, he may be dead for all we know, and Potain does nothing. He waits about, he makes excuses, he will not send for the police. And why?' What answer do you think, my poor Giuseppe, they give themselves to such a question? It is clear. ' He does not wish the criminal found, they say. He is saying in his heart, perhaps there will be rain and all traces will be washed away.' And moreover, what will M. le Prefet say when he hears you treat the disappearance of this man as no more than the straying of the stable cat?"

M. Potain, thoroughly upset now, muttered something about stable cats at least earning their living that was highly uncomplimentary to the missing man. But all the same he listened to his wife and with no very gracious air telephoned to the police.

CHAPTER V

1

AUTHORITY was represented by M. Dupuy, a dapper cool little man, slightly bow-legged, who received every item of information with a neat non-committal smile, only permitting himself an occasional faintly incredulous *C'est ça?* when the answer seemed beyond the bounds of probability.

M. Potain from the first dissociated himself from all responsibility and said as little as possible. The English gentlemen and ladies had been playing one of their outdoor games; he had been occupied in the hotel. Then they had come back asking for M. Marks; he had not seen M. Marks; he had interrogated his waiters and chambermaids; they had not seen M. Marks either. Everyone had explored the hotel; no M. Marks. They had borrowed lights and had gone out through the grounds; no M. Marks. One of the gentlemen thought he had fallen among the trees into the quarry, but though they had searched nothing had been found. It was very dark in the quarry, but so many gentlemen could not surely be mistaken. He spread his hands, a second Pilate disclaiming all responsibility.

M. Dupuy listened alertly and without comment to the stories of the guests. By common consent Montstuart had been chosen to represent them; he was a lawyer, he was accustomed to criminal procedure, he had been one of the party to see the missing man on the ridge; he might not know a great deal, but he knew as much as anybody else. He explained the position briefly. M. Dupuy nodded.

"Then you saw M. Marks on the ridge, and you

saw the ridge empty; you did not actually see him fall?"

Montstuart, with Fellowes like a Greek chorus, explained that the moon, their principal light, had been obscured for a moment; but the crash . . .

" Ah, yes." M. Dupuy stood nodding his head without further speech. Indeed, he might have been taken for one of those nodding idols that litter the junk shops of every big city in the world, so rigid was he but for that fantastically moving head. " The crash," he repeated presently in a careless voice, as though that were an affair of small moment. " But a crash is so easy. For instance . . ." He stooped and, picking up a pebble, tossed it at one of the small window-panes of the summer-house near which they were standing. " You see? I have broken a window, there has been a crash, but I remain where I was. I do not need to precipitate myself through a window to produce that effect."

" You mean, he needn't have fallen?" began Montstuart uncertainly.

" Precisely that, monsieur. Let me demonstrate." He called to the assistant he had brought with him, signing to him to remain where he was at the moment. The rest of the party lined up with him. Then Dupuy went forward to the edge of the ridge; in his hand he carried the cap Mr. Marks had been wearing; this was made of cardboard, with a tassel of silk. The assisting sergeant carried a very powerful torch, whose light he kept directed on the moving figure of M. Dupuy as he walked to the ridge and moved first in one direction, then another. There was a momentary shout from the ridge, and instantly the sergeant, whose name was Beret, shut off the stream of light. At the same moment Dupuy vanished; a second later the light played on an empty ridge.

M. Dupuy reappeared triumphantly. "You see."

"But there wasn't any crash," objected Fellowes stupidly.

"Certainly there was no crash. I have not yet examined the ridge, and we cannot afford to confuse clues. But I vanished—as M. Marks vanished. If you had heard a crash then I think you would have said, as you said before, 'He has fallen over the edge.' Well?"

"Possibly," agreed Fellowes reluctantly. "But there was a crash in the other case."

"You mean, he wanted to give the impression that he'd gone over, whereas really he'd simply concealed himself in the bushes? Well, it's true they're thick enough to hide him, especially in that light." That was Montstuart, eager and interested. "The idea, of course, was to get everyone searching the ridge, while he slipped off in some other direction. But why?"

"Monsieur," protested Dupuy in pained accents, "I have been on these premises perhaps half an hour, I have never met M. Marks, I know no more of him than one may read in the papers. How should I know the answer to your question? That is what we have to learn."

Nicholas Marvell looked up to say slowly, "Look here, monsieur. I don't know whether it has any bearing on the case, but ever since Marks arrived I've noticed a fellow hanging about the hotel. He was lounging at the corner when I went out before dinner last night, and I saw him again this morning. And just after déjeuner I heard two of the chambermaids saying something about some fellow asking impudent questions—they thought he was probably the vanguard of an hotel thief . . . I thought at the time he might be after the diamond."

"And you warned M. Marks?"

"Of course not. The man wasn't born yesterday. And, if he does not realise the risk he's running in carting a valuable stone like that about with him, he deserves to be either dead or in a lunatic asylum. Anyway, this modern craze for spoon-feeding the world, buttoning their shoes and holding their hands on every occasion sickens me. We've put off maturity, according to the psychologists, till thirty or later; presently I suppose adolesence will start at sixty. If Marks was such a fool, I've no sympathy with him."

"I think monsieur would have little sympathy with him in any case," suggested Dupuy.

Nicholas coloured, then laughed with a good grace. "These millionaires gall me," he admitted. "I never can believe they're honest men, and the world's tottering to ruin at the present moment, simply because we're run by grafters and men grinding their own axes to such an extent they can't hear anyone speak, much less spare time to lend them a hand."

Dupuy smiled once more, but it was clear that no red herring, however attractive, would deflect him from his purpose.

"About this man, monsieur. At all events, you warned M. Potain."

"I did not," said Nicholas. "And the same reasons apply."

M. Dupuy began to nod again. Fellowes said in an exasperated, audible aside, "What the devil does the fellow mean behaving like a mandarin? I've always maintained that the only country with an efficient police force is England and this seems to me to prove it."

M. Dupuy, however, did not seem disposed to explain himself. He turned and marched back to the crest of the ridge. The others found him stooping down, examining the ground with a powerful lens.

"Something has been moved from here," he said quietly. "I think a large stone." The sergeant came forward and took a photograph of a marked depression in the ground, of a roughly oval shape. "I think we may find the stone in the spinney where you have been looking for the body," Dupuy continued. "It is a pity there have been so many footprints; it will not be possible to obtain any clue from them. But— see here!" In accordance with his theory he pointed out a tree whose slender branch had been broken, and now hung dangling, not far from the top of the ridge. "Something was thrown down here with some force," he explained, "but it was not a body. A body would have crashed down more than that one bough. No, I think we shall find that M. Marks has the laugh on us this time. We shall see." With a surprising agility he made the difficult descent; his assistant was taking innumerable photographs. Montstuart, who had been involved in many criminal cases, but had never been actually on the scene at the time of the affair, was fascinated by all the detail. He cautioned the others to say nothing, lest Dupuy exercise his authority and dismiss them altogether. Meanwhile, they came quietly down the safer side slopes to find the French detective regarding with some satisfaction a large whitish boulder that, having broken several slender branches en route, now lay on the earth at his feet.

"I think this is the crash you heard," he said, smiling gently. "And I think, too, that M. Marks intended you to hear it. If the stone had slipped under his foot—but that, of course, it could not have done; clearly it had been prised out of its place in readiness —then it would not have travelled so far. It was flung down with some force. This M. Marks—he is a powerful man?"

"He's wiry," said Montstuart. "I daresay he has

a good deal of physical strength. None of us really know him, though."

"H'm." M. Dupuy caressed a blue-shaven jaw. "That is unfortunate. You have not, then, any idea why M. Marks should wish to concentrate the attention of the whole party on a place where he no longer was?"

"No. In fact, it's incomprehensible. One automatically links up anything that may happen to him with this precious diamond of his, but you wouldn't think he'd play any monkey tricks to-night of all nights."

"Monsieur?" Dupuy looked polite inquiry.

"I mean, he'd got some arrangement for disposing of it, so far as one could gather, in the morning. In the ordinary run of affairs, you'd expect him to be particularly careful."

"He spoke to you of this plan of his?"

"No. But he was telephoning from the public 'phone this afternoon to some fellow—I couldn't tell you his name, of course—arranging to meet him somewhere, some hotel, I think it was, to-morrow morning—that is, of course, to-day. It's struck midnight."

"You heard the name of the hotel?"

"I may have done, but I don't recall it."

"But he wouldn't arrange to display a diamond like this one at any casual hotel," expostulated Miss Hoult.

Montstuart turned to her. "You've heard of the great pearl robbery? When appointments were made then to dispose of part of the necklace the thieves met once at British Museum Station and once at a J.P. Restaurant. This notion that criminals frequent either the Ritz or underground cellars hasn't any foundation in fact. It's inartistic, but it's true.

I ought, of course, to recall the name of the place, but I only chanced to hear a bit of the conversation— he seemed to have no objection to our hearing all of it, if it comes to that—but I do remember thinking Potain would breathe more freely with the jewel out of the place."

"You spoke to M. Potain?"

"I didn't speak to anyone. It wasn't my affair."

"I see. Thank you, monsieur. Perhaps M. Potain will be able to add something. Or perhaps there may be a letter. That must wait. Now, monsieur," again he addressed Montstuart, "if you will be good enough to tell me exactly where you were standing when you saw M. Marks?"

The members of the party acted as alibis for one another. Nicholas and Montstuart had been together at some distance from the spinney. Fellowes and Degas had met on the ridge a moment or two after the crash; Miss Hoult and Lecoq went surety the one for the other; Mrs. Fellowes had seen him from her place near the vegetable garden; Sarah had seen nothing; she had been looking for the millionaire in the farther of the two summer-houses; Latymer had come racing up the slope from the opposite side at about the same time as Fellowes and his companion arrived from the other direction. Of course, one might suppose the whole party to be implicated in the affair, but short of such an explanation, that seemed monstrous to Dupuy, who knew how unwieldly a gang murder must be, committed within prescribed limits, one must seek the criminal elsewhere.

2

It was too dark for Dupuy to achieve much before dawn, and, in any case, the whole of the grounds had been so thoroughly trodden by everyone in the hotel that there seemed little likelihood of any clue remaining; and the guests, exhausted, alarmed or stimulated, according to their respective temperaments, allowed themselves to be shepherded inside the hotel, there to await examination at the hands of the police. Dupuy began his more detailed examination by cornering Potain in his private office and firing one patient question after another at his reluctant head.

"I know nothing, I tell you, monsieur," the unhappy maître d'hôtel protested. "Nothing at all. M. Marks comes here and engages a suite. The second day he is here he vanishes. That is all."

"You know nothing of his plans? Nothing whatsoever? How long, for instance, did he propose to stay?"

"He said for a week at least, and longer if it suited him."

"He travelled alone?"

"He arrived alone, monsieur."

"You know nothing of any friends or acquaintances he had in the neighbourhood?"

Potain spread his hands in angry despair. "How should I know, monsieur?"

"Or of his movements to-morrow—the day after?"

"Only this, that he asked me to arrange for a car to take him to an hotel in the morning."

"And the address of this hotel?"

"The Cordon Bleu in the Rue Anatole France."

"Do you know his business there?"

"He said to meet a gentleman. I do not know if that is true."

"And the gentleman's name?"

"He spoke of a M. Salomon who might telephone. I do not know if that is the same man."

Dupuy knew the name well enough. It was one

well known in Paris, but particularly at this moment did it interest the detective. For he believed he recalled certain rumours flying around concerning a reputation that had suffered, like others, in the recent diamond slump. Presumably, he and Marks were to have treated together regarding the great yellow diamond.

"I thought I had heard he was in rather low water," reflected Dupuy. "Now, before I go to see M. Salomon I think my good friend, Marnier, of Paris, might have some information for me. I will send him a message by telephone while I examine other possible sources of information."

He applied himself, therefore, to extracting any further information he could obtain from his companion, asking a good many questions about the exits and entrances to and from the hotel. Was there, for instance, a door near the foot of the quarry? Potain said there was not. What was the nearest exit then? There was a gate in the wall at the foot of the grounds, giving on to the high road, but this was an emergency affair, not generally used. There were only two keys to this gate, kept by his wife and himself. He was prepared to swear that neither of these had been used to open the door that night. The other doors were in the front and side of the hotel, so that any man entering or leaving the premises must come boldly to the central building and either walk through the hall or go round by the servants' entry.

"Entering or leaving," reflected Dupuy. "Well, a bold man might do it. There are a great many people here at present; a stranger could pass confidently through the hall without attracting attention. But could he enter the garden with no one observing him?

That is a horse of another colour. And again, how would he escape? And where is the body?"

He abandoned that argument for the moment, and asked to see the complete staff of the hotel. "I believe there has been a mysterious personage hanging about since M. Marks was expected," he said. "When was he expected, by the way?"

"Only just before he came, monsieur. I had no idea. It was, I thought, good luck that the royal suite, as we call it, was not occupied. He came on the 30th, and I heard only the night previous that I might expect him."

"And this mysterious man turned up—when?"

"Oh," exploded Potain irascibly, "I know nothing of these stories. They are told in the kitchen. There is always some foolish chatter in process there. And if there was such a man, doubtless he was following one of the servants . . ."

"I'd like to see the servants," said Dupuy, unmoved.

They came in varying stages of undress.

It was now almost three o'clock in the morning, and several of them had abandoned the search for the night and decided to go to bed. The detective questioned them all closely; he wanted news of a stranger, a pertinacious stranger who had been hanging about recently and visiting the hotel on some pretext, he did not know what. He wanted a description of the man and any details they could give him. Most of the servants were either sullen or alarmed, and were of little use, but one girl, a Mlle. Rose Gaudet, answered him with fire and energy. She knew, she thought, the man he meant. He was a rather short red-haired man wearing a red beard, with a gipsy face and an impudent manner. He walked with a slight limp, but added that she thought the limp assumed, for later when she had seen him in the street he appeared to be walking erect. He had come to the back door of the hotel a few hours before Marks' arrival, carrying a bundle of valueless knick-knacks, laces and soaps and ribbons, like the old-time pedlar, and had tried to persuade her first to buy something and later to accept a ribbon for love. She had refused, not caring for the look of the man. He had asked a number of questions, and immediately she had become suspicious.

"But you masked your suspicions, mademoiselle?" Dupuy suggested.

Gaudet tossed her head. "It was nothing to me whether he was pleased or no, monsieur. Any more than it was anything to him, or should not have been, who was staying at the hotel."

"He asked that, did he? Did he mention any names?"

"He was—coy, monsieur. He said this was a very rich hotel, that a great deal of money was passed here. He said that a girl who knew her business could do well in an hotel like this, and must make a lot of money. Then he said perhaps I would like to buy some ribbons, but I said No, I did not need such trash. When one is saving for one's *dot*, monsieur . . ."

"He mentioned no name in particular?"

Gaudet hesitated. Dupuy pressed her more urgently.

"I am trying to remember, monsieur," said Gaudet, who seemed an honest girl, anxious to give him any help she could. "I think it happened like this. He said that many rich people came here, millionaires and their friends. And then I think I said that we had only one millionaire, so far as I knew, and he had not arrived yet."

"Which was, I think, just what he wished to know."

"I believe you are right, monsieur, but at the time I only wished to be rid of him. Anyway, what harm could I do by telling him that?"

"It is the harm he proposed that is our concern," said the detective softly. "Did he ask you anything else?"

"He talked a little more, and then wished me to accept a ribbon. But I shut the door on him."

"He did not ask to see any of the other chambermaids?"

"No, monsieur."

"And that seemed to you strange?"

"I didn't think about it."

"A cleverer man would have asked," thought Dupuy. "But after all, he had learned what he needed to know . . ."

One of the man-servants further strengthened his conviction that the fellow had been hanging about in order either to intercept or to trail the missing millionaire. This man had gone down to one of the local cafés the previous night, at about half-past five, and a fellow had come in who seemed identical with the pedlar Gaudet had turned from the door some hours since. He was swarthy, rather short, with dark eyes and a clean-shaved bluish jaw. The man thought he might know him again. The fellow had come in and asked for a drink, had had two or three and had then acknowledged impudently that he had no money. When the proprietor became candid at his expense he had become abusive, and said that there was no one, either man or woman, who would help a lame dog over a stile. He added that he was as good as the next man, if that did happen to be a millionaire, with diamonds like rocs' eggs in all his pockets.

Pierre had not stayed to see the end of the affair, but he had heard later that the man had been evicted. One other scrap of information emerged from the mass of Dupuy's questionnaire; this came from another of the women servants, who said she had been doing an errand near the station at the time of Marks' arrival, and had seen a man hanging about, leaning against the wall with his hands in his pockets. When the train came in he hastily pulled out a paper and concealed himself behind it, but, as Marks entered the hotel omnibus, he had lifted his head and stared and nodded two or three times, as though some inward conviction was now confirmed. When she got back to the hotel she had observed to Gaudet, " I believe your friend was at the station. Fun if we have a murder here, won't it be?" She admitted she had only spoken the words in jest, and that the idea of a murder actually taking place had not been in her mind.

" But, mademoiselle, you thought something might happen—I think?" Dupuy insinuated, bright-eyed and urgent.

" Well, it would not surprise me if some attempt were made to steal the diamond," acknowledged the girl.

And that was all Dupuy learned from the staff.

Nevertheless, it was sufficient to perplex him. " This man," he thought, " is either very subtle, very foolish or else he has nothing whatsoever to do with the crime. If he is subtle, then he will argue that an old fox like myself will say immediately, ' This man has nothing to do with the crime.' For if he proposed to commit murder or theft with violence, which usually approximates to it, then he would not go out of his way to attract attention to himself. He would work in the dark. Then, my suspicions lulled, he can work as openly as he pleases. If he is very simple, then he is interested in Marks, and has gone in the most direct way for his information. Or else this is sheer coincidence."

He had been speaking aloud, under the impression that he was alone, but turning from his slow pacing of the carpet he found himself, to his surprise and a little to his chagrin, staring at that peculiar person, the man from No. 27, whose button boots made no sound as he moved.

"Unless perhaps it is expedient to be conspicuous," suggested the newcomer gently. "Oh, a very ancient trick, monsieur. The female peewit played it, probably centuries before man appeared on the earth."

CHAPTER VI

1

ALONE at last, and waiting for the light to make possible the work of investigation, Dupuy began to balance his theories the one against the other, brooding in particular on what was to him the centre of the mystery, why Marks had tried to give the impression that he was in one place when, actually, at the moment of search, he must have been somewhere else. What reason could there be for a man of his position and circumstances to sneak out of the hotel grounds like a stable tom, which was apparently what he had done? Dupuy determined to examine his problem in the light of this solution—i.e. that the true problem to solve was not who? but why? Suppose Marks had left the hotel of his own accord. How could he get out? There was no rear exit, and in any case the quarry was some distance from the road that bounded the limits of the hotel. He had already made a careful examination of the gate, and was satisfied that no one had tampered with the lock or attempted to scramble over the top. No, decided Dupuy, if Marks had left the place of his own free will, he must have gone boldly through the hall and out through the great front door. It could be done simply enough by a resolute man. He inquired as to the clothes the missing man was wearing, and learned that they approximated to the dress of a waiter, except for the ridiculous hat. At all events it wouldn't be hard to play the part of a waiter—hadn't the man a reputation for amateur dramatics?—for so long as was needed to cross the hall and get away from the hotel. And after that? He might walk through the neighbourhood in evening dress without exciting attention, but when morning came, what then? Was it all part of a deeply-laid plan, and had he a change of gear somewhere handy? Whom was he going to meet, why on earth—Dupuy came back at a boiling pitch of exasperation to the same question. Why? Why? Why?

You might argue that he'd be recognised before he left the place, but Dupuy had an answer there. Everyone expected Marks to be in the garden, somewhere in that tangle of roots and bushes, so they wouldn't expect to see him in the house; no, if he walked out on his own feet he could have done it, but why he should wish to was unfathomable.

He remembered a story by a master of criminal fiction, called *The Invisible Man*, that exploited the ease with which a man could move unnoticed among his fellows by being not physically but mentally invisible. Of course (he pondered), the clerk and the commissionaire and the waiters said no one like Marks had gone through the hall. But that means precisely what it says and no more. No one looking like Marks. It was part of their assumption that the Marks who left the hotel would be the counterpart of the Marks who was playing hide-and-seek in the garden. But who are we to assume anything of the sort? He was seen going into the garden and he was seen on the edge of the quarry. After that he may have been seen but he was not recognised. He had hurled his cap over into the firs, and, being light, it would be blown by the wind a considerable distance. There was nothing noticeable about his appearance; the addition of a moustache, a pair of horn glasses, a different gait, the assumption of some peculiar mannerism, all these would help to convince those who saw him that this was not Julian Marks whom they had seen dining not many hours ago. " Let me at all events," he said cheerfully," follow up this hypothesis. I do not, of course, insist that I am right. But at least it is an explanation and some explanation there must be." It occurred to him to send word to station-masters and ticket-collectors, though it was hard to believe that so acquisitive a man would voluntarily leave behind him so many valuables. " The man cannot have flown," continued M. Dupuy, " or have dissolved into dust. Therefore, sooner or later, I shall find him."

2

So soon as it was light enough for investigations to go forward, Dupuy and his men were at work searching the grounds of the hotel, making, it must be admitted, remarkably little headway. Far too many feet had trampled the slopes and paths for any one footprint to be distinguishable.

But for one moment during the long and exacting search on that sultry 1st November it seemed as though the element of pure sensation might be going to win the day. That moment came when Dupuy discovered that someone had been tampering with the opening of the well. This well had never actually been sealed down, though experts had protested against the condition of the water, but bindweed grew thickly round the rim of the heavy wooden slab that covered it, and Potain had adopted the sane policy of his nation—when Nature does something for nothing, why throw good money away? Dupuy tripped over the rotting branches of a tree that had fallen half across the mouth of the well, and it was in rising that he discovered the severed stems. These had been cut with a sharp edge, most probably a knife.

" Surely," exclaimed the bewildered man, sitting back on his heels, arrested for a moment in sheer amazement at so obvious a solution, " they—whoever they are—would not be so crazy as to deposit the body here?"

" Oh, no." For the second time he was almost thrown off his balance by that dry, unemotional voice, " I shouldn't think so. I know Marks was quite a small man, but not so small he could go through a crack. If you look, you'll see the tendrils are only cut about half-way round."

Dupuy rose to his feet to face this ubiquitous pursuer. " I do not know who you are, monsieur," he opened politely.

Mr. Latymer, with no change of expression, drew an engraved card from his pocket.

" Mr. Paul Harrison," the Frenchman read, and an address in the Strand. He looked up, still perplexed.

" You do not know the name, monsieur?"

" No, monsieur. It is yours?"

" Professionally."

Dupuy looked down again at the card. "Private Investigator," he read. "You have some reason for not using your own name?" Frankly he was suspicious.

"It would be so difficult," sighed Mr. Latymer. "Mr. Increase Latymer. People would laugh. The English have the reputation for being a sober nation. Besides, it is so awkward—I'm sure you have discovered this for yourself—so awkward to be a marked man. One has much more liberty if one can just wear a cloak, so to speak. I don't know if you remember the case of the Clancarty diamonds, the Sanderson Divorce case—there were some rather—er—delicate letters there. . . . You'd prefer me to keep out of the way, no doubt?"

Dupuy refused to commit himself. "Monsieur, I am the servant of Authority. It is not for me to choose my colleagues." And then, with no change of expression, he continued, "To return to the well. You say, and I agree, that the lid could be lifted not more than, say, three inches. But no body, not even sections of a body, could be pushed through that. And then there must be blood. . . ."

"More important still, there must be time," Mr. Latymer pointed out. "And that's what seems to me so short in this case. I think this cutting of the stems is fairly obvious. I should say that murder was intended from the start, and then the well was the place selected for depositing the body. Then X—let's call him X, shall we?—found the idea impracticable. You know, I don't know what your ideas are, but personally I'm looking for a corpse."

Dupuy's brows shot up. "I trust you may be wrong, monsieur. But I admit the well rather shakes my confidence. I wonder when these branches came down."

Latymer bent over them. "This has been hauled

off the parent tree, cut clean. Oh, it's obvious why it's here. We've had no storms recently sufficiently heavy to account for this coming down; besides, it's very new; look at the whiteness of the wood. Of course, whoever arranged it across the opening of the well hoped no one would notice the broken stems."

He stood up, dusting a greenish deposit from the dead boughs from the knees of his trousers. " I wonder if he was an economical chap. If so, the knife he used to cut these boughs may have come in again later. . . ."

" I think," said Dupuy abruptly, " I will see M. F——, the proprietor of the Cordon Bleu, and find out if he can help us." It may be, he thought, that this is a blind to delay us, that, while we waste our time over the well, M. Marks is being removed farther and farther from us. And, like the criminal, we have so little time. He straightened himself, pulling the sharp needles of the conifer firs from the sleeves of his suit. " How these things prick," he said. " I believe they can draw blood."

3

In the car that drove him to the Cordon Bleu, Dupuy's active mind continued to brood on the peculiarities of the position. Not only had a comparatively well-known man been spirited away in the midst of a party of watchers and listeners, and not only did no one know what had happened to him since his disappearance, but practically nothing was known of him during the years preceding the event. Nothing of his family, his relations, his domestic life, nothing of his business hostilities, his religion, his politics, his intellectual sympathies, little, in short, beyond the obvious facts that he was a rich man, that he had found a world-famous diamond, and that he had disappeared in a manner calculated to draw the utmost attention to himself. Who, the little Frenchman asked himself, are his enemies? Was he married? Had he a particular mistress? An enemy? Someone he had defrauded? He was a mystery in life and it looked as though he were going to be a tough mystery in death also. Whom was he going to see at the Cordon Bleu and could that man throw any light on the affair?

"But how should I be able to answer these questions?" demanded Dupuy dramatically, beating his clenched hands together. "I, who know nothing of the man? What is his past? His future? What, indeed, is his present, which is most completely our concern? Why was he going to the Cordon Bleu to-day and whom did he propose to see?"

That question at all events, he thought, he should soon be able to answer, and leaving the hotel and its grounds in charge of an able assistant, he drove down to the Cordon Bleu Hotel. Here he asked for the manager.

"I am from the Sureté, monsieur, and I am inquiring into a very unhappy affair, namely, the disappearance of a rich man in the late hours of last night. Now this gentleman, M. Julian Marks, an Englishman, staying at the Hotel Fantastique, made an engagement to come here to this hotel this morning at 11.30. Can you, perhaps, ascertain whom he was to see?"

"That should be easy, monsieur," said the proprietor at once, and sent for a clerk.

"A gentleman, a M. Marks, is expected here at 11.30," he said briefly. "Please to find out whom he is seeing."

A few minutes later the clerk returned to say that

M. Auguste Salomon, of No. 15, was expecting the Englishman at the hour named.

"So," murmured Dupuy, "Potain was right, then. But how cautious he was. Now, I wonder how much Marnier has learned. It would be a pity to approach my man with no cards in my sleeve."

Probably no police force in the world can get its .acts more quickly than the French; they keep the most extensive records, and when Dupuy telephoned Marnier for the second time he was presented with a wealth of information as luxuriant as buttercups in spring. All this information bore out his original impression.

Salomon was a diamond merchant, well known in Paris, Amsterdam and Hatton Garden. A number of reputable firms had had dealings with him for many years; but of late a disquieting rumour had gone round that he was rapidly approaching rock bottom. This rumour was, so far as could be learnt, confined to trade circles. The merchant was a man of divers interests; he had a large, very handsomely decorated house, with a fine collection of books; he entertained a good deal, though, of course, not on the same scale as Marks. For thirty years he had slaved and pinched to attain his ambitions, and now for four or five years they had been within his reach. The man was alert, suave, cultured, deeply interested in politics, in the drama and in literature. He had established a certain position for himself, had built up a circle, not perhaps very influential, but intelligent and to some degree exclusive. He valued his social standing very highly; he had no sons and this personal life of his was the limit of his wealth. During the past eighteen months, however, like numbers of others in his profession, he had suffered acutely from the slump in diamonds. It was well known, of course, that diamonds had always been restricted as to output, in order to maintain a certain price level. Marnier, who picked up all this information for his chief, spent that morning going in and out of public-houses and shops and offices, picking up a hint here, an incident there, till, piecing the whole situation together, it became obvious that, whatever his intentions, Salomon was in no position to make a bid for so extravagant a stone as the Marks diamond.

"What then?" Dupuy questioned. "To any jeweller such a stone is in the nature of a speculation. He may not be able to sell it, at all events not at once. Money is still fairly scarce, and then diamonds have not the chic they had once. Other stones are being preferred. My friends in the trade tell me that the tide is perpetually changing. And, in any case, when it comes to large stones, a perfect ruby would fetch more than a diamond. It is more rare, perhaps, but I have known of rubies fetching fifty thousand pounds and even more, when a diamond of similar perfection and size would fetch a bare thirty. Of course, if you have a buyer waiting on your doorstep to relieve you of the stone at a handsome profit, then you are not speculating, you are investing, what they call betting on a certainty. Now, was Salomon in that position? The only way to discover that would be to see him. Then I had better arrange to do so at once."

Salomon was still at the Cordon Bleu, and when his visitor was announced he sprang to his feet in a state of much perturbation.

"M. Dupuy? I know your name, of course. But I don't know why you come to me. I am much distressed, monsieur. I had an appointment with M. Marks. . . ."

"I know. I am, in a sense, here in his place."

Salomon's brow furrowed. "Comment! You know what has happened to him?"

"I know nothing. Indeed, I am going to ask you to help me, monsieur. It was in the hope that you might be able to assist me that I am come here this afternoon."

Salomon, a plump, shrewd figure, dark-skinned, with wings of brown hair standing away from either temple, stared; his hands had begun to tremble.

"You cannot mean—but no! There is nothing I can say. Why, I did not even see M. Marks. But what has occurred?"

"That we have yet to learn. All I can say as yet is that he has disappeared. Now. He was to see you here at 11.30 this morning in connection with the Marks diamond?"

"That is so, monsieur." The short, powerful hands still held the back of the chair he had been grasping when the detective arrived, for it had not yet occurred to him either to sit himself or to offer a chair to his visitor. Now, however, seeing the movement of Dupuy's head, the unmistakable suggestion that they should conduct their conversation with rather less formality, he said in abrupt, troubled tones, "Sit down, monsieur. I still do not understand why you come to see me." He spread his hands in protest. "I have told you, I know nothing, monsieur, nothing. Why, I have scarcely ever seen M. Marks. I would not know him if we met. I do not know what has happened to him at all."

"Neither do we," repeated Dupuy patiently, and proceeded to outline the position in much detail. Salomon's face turned pale, his jaw dropped.

"Then, monsieur, the diamond is gone also?"

"Beyond all doubt. Of course the diamond is gone. It is not M. Marks' body that is worth a fortune."

"But it isn't sense," protested Salomon. "Why should he wish to disappear like that? Or do you suspect foul play? And can a man be murdered and carried off in the midst of a crowd?"

"It seems possible." Dupuy's tone was heavy with a wasted irony.

Salomon sprang to his feet; it was as if he found this disappointment, this gross injustice that life was visiting upon him, more than he could endure.

"It is his own fault, monsieur. He is crazy. You knew he was coming here to-day. Perhaps others knew it also."

"And if they did?"

Salomon leaned forward; his brown eyes burned. His manner was eager yet wary; he was labouring under some apprehension of whose nature as yet Dupuy knew little. Professional curiosity might account for it, a hope that after all the diamond would find its way into his possession; or he might really have something to hide.

"Monsieur, a man who carries a diamond as Marks was carrying one, takes more than a stone in his hand. He takes his life also. Such a man is never absolutely free. Always, like beasts in a jungle, there may be others on his track. When he crossed to France, when he stayed in Paris, when he reached the Hotel Fantastique, at every step of his journey he might be followed. If it became known that he was to part with the stone to-day, then last night or early this morning was the pursuer's only chance. For why should he wish to disappear of his own will? That is too fantastic for us, monsieur."

"Perhaps, though the fantastic is often also the true, as I above all men should know. As to what is impossible here and what is not, of that we can scarcely speak. We know too little. And now, monsieur, I would be glad if you would tell me all you know of the Marks diamond, and of any connection you had with it."

Salomon seemed a little surprised at the turn of the question. "The diamond? No more than another, monsieur. There is always some excitement when a diamond of that calibre comes on to the market. I fancy two or three dealers were after it, but I wanted it in particular. I had a client, a difficult but very lavish man, who fancied it, not for a woman and not to wear for himself, but for something to keep. His house is like that, full of beautiful things. It is like a museum. It is very wonderful."

"For those who care to live in museums, no doubt," assented Dupuy politely. "And the name of this gentleman?"

"M. Sinclair Roden. He is an American settled in Paris. All the city knows him. Whenever there is anything special on the market, something more rich, more exquisite, more unusual than is common, he has the first offer. Money, monsieur, is of little value to him. He will not bargain with you; he will give you your price, if he likes what you have to show him. Naturally, monsieur, one is glad to keep such a client. Now I knew that the Marks diamond would please him, and so I was anxious to be first in the field. M. Marks asked £50,000; I knew that M. Roden would pay more than that. I made an appointment with M. Marks. He was to have come this morning."

"And you would have bought the diamond at that figure?"

"Exactly, monsieur."

"And M. Roden would have bought the diamond off you—when?"

"I had an engagement to see him this afternoon."

"And if he had not liked the diamond?"

72

"I had little doubt, monsieur."

"But—if he had not?"

"There are other purchasers."

"But perhaps not soon enough."

"Soon enough?" Salomon sounded haughty, but beneath that surface composure his mind was darting like a rabbit seeking a safe burrow from a pursuer. He could not be sure what his companion intended, how much he knew, in what direction this conversation moved. But his mind was full of apprehension.

"Soon enough to save you, M. Salomon."

"I do not understand."

"I speak in confidence, of course. You must realise that we of the police know many things; we have records of which you could not be aware. We know a great deal about all our prominent citizens." He smiled, but without malice, into M. Salomon's troubled face. "We know, for instance, that you have been unfortunate of late. You need money and you need it desperately. It would not be pleasant to be declared a bankrupt. Yet how are you to satisfy your creditors?"

"My creditors, monsieur?"

Dupuy sounded a little impatient. "This is wasting time," he declared. "It is known to me at all events that things are in a very bad way with you. Your credit at the bank is . . ." He opened his hands in a characteristic and expressive gesture. "You are being pressed for money. That is so?"

Salomon, who a minute or two earlier had leaped to his feet in a burst of rage, now sat down again, his face sullen and defeated. "It is that swine, Steinbaum," he exclaimed bitterly. "He always meant to ruin me if he had the chance. He knows my circumstances. That as soon as I can I shall pay him. But he will not wait. He is a fool." His voice gained in intensity as he spoke. "Where is the sense in making me a bankrupt? Will that pay his account?"

"But if he chooses to do so you can't prevent him?" insisted Dupuy gently.

"He could," the other acknowledged in grudging tones. "Both of us know it, but if he will wait a little and keep his head shut, I shall repay him. In any case, he has his interest paid regularly. If he takes this action he threatens he will not get even that."

"A moneylender," thought Dupuy triumphantly. "That should not be hard to trace. And clearly he was pressing hard for the money." Aloud he continued, "Perhaps, monsieur, you have already reassured M. Steinbaum as to payment?"

"I have promised him a substantial repayment within a week. He has agreed to that. I have told him that if he gives me this week—for it may be a day or two before Roden gives me his cheque—I will ask for no more indulgence. And now, it seems, he has been trying to ruin me. You realise, monsieur, that if it is known that I am heavily in debt M. Marks will refuse to sell me the stone. It is above all things important that that shall not be guessed now."

"But Marks was no fool," Dupuy pointed out. "Nor, M. Salomon, am I. Do you suppose that he would hand over the diamond without assuring himself of the value of your draft?"

"By the time he came to present it I should have Roden's cheque, and all would be well," Salomon insisted.

"A gamble," murmured the detective. "And he might not agree with you. You have told M. Roden of the position?"

"He sees the papers as well as I," retorted Salomon, half-sullen, half-absent. "Monsieur, tell me, have you no notion where Marks is?"

74

"Not yet," said Dupuy. "Even we of the police cannot work solely on intuition."

"In any case it will be too late," the dealer sighed. "I am done for, monsieur, ruined after all these years, and by a fool without sufficient foresight to understand his folly. Here was my chance . . ."

"It is certainly very inconsiderate of M. Marks," Dupuy agreed smoothly. "And perhaps, after your conversation on the telephone with M. Marks, you assured other creditors also?"

"They are not such fools. They are content to wait. It is Steinbaum . . ." he broke off, muttering savagely under his breath. Suddenly he turned eagerly to Dupuy. "Monsieur, you truly don't know where this Englishman is? It means everything to me. Oh, why was he such a fool?" He beat his fist softly on the desk. "To tell everyone about the diamond, to let them know how short the time was . . ."

CHAPTER VII

1

DUPUY left the Cordon Bleu and went by car to Marseilles, where he would catch the night train to Paris. First thing in the morning he would see Steinbaum and add his evidence to the slowly-accumulating pile. Presently he would be able to sift it and see where the conclusion pointed.

Steinbaum's offices were on the first floor of a handsome block of buildings in the Boulevard N——
It was a clear, vivid morning and the sun shone on fine carpets and comfortable chairs, on a bowl of flowers on a luxurious-looking desk, and on the tall ruddy man of middle age who came to meet Dupuy as

he entered. Nothing less like the popular theatrical and fictional moneylender could be imagined than Jacob Steinbaum; rather did he resemble the pictured heroes of Ouida's novels, freshly-washed and curled, moustachioed, with a plump smiling face and very quick long-fingered hands.

Dupuy presented a card, and Steinbaum looked up, smiling and non-committal. Here, thought Dupuy immediately, is a man accustomed to a crisis, a man who will not easily betray himself, a man shrewd, intelligent, versed in every way of gaining advantage. In short, a man with whom it would pay to be frank.

"Yours is a confidential business, monsieur," he began, setting his hat close to the bowl of blue and yellow blossoms. "It is, of course. That speaks for itself. And the same applies to me also. Sometimes, you will understand, it becomes necessary for us to make inquiries about some of our citizens. You will above most men realise the need for discretion. Of course, monsieur. Now, there is reason to suppose—indeed, I have his own admission—that M. Salomon, of Rue de Brie, is a client of yours."

Steinbaum bowed in silence.

"He is, in fact, your debtor for a considerable sum?"

"Considerable, monsieur."

"You will perhaps recollect the amount?"

Steinbaum's bland brows lifted. "He omitted to tell you himself, monsieur?"

Dupuy shot him a glance of admiration. Discretion personified, he thought. And then: but an ugly customer, and the word blackmail slid noiseless as a snake through his mind.

"I did not ask him," he replied simply. "The amount, perhaps, is not of any great importance. It is enough that he has acknowledged you have it in your power to ruin him, if a large sum is not repaid by the week's end."

"That is so, monsieur."

"And he has, of course, reason to believe that he will be in a position to repay this amount."

Steinbaum shrugged slightly. "One has heard before of these great coups that are to earn so much money for men. Unfortunately the money does not always trickle in the right direction."

"Trickle, my good fellow," thought Dupuy. "Why, it would need an avalanche to satisfy you." And aloud he added, "There is an English proverb concerning unhatched chickens. I commend it to your meditation."

Steinbaum smiled. "You do not think my farm-yard will be very full at the week's end? Well, monsieur, it is useless for Salomon to ask for further time."

"And to what purpose?" Dupuy demanded, cordially.

"So this source of revenue has dried up?"

"Disappeared."

"That is unfortunate indeed, for M. Salomon. For myself, I have no option. A million francs is a great deal of money."

"You have, I think, been pressing for the amount?"

"The debt has been outstanding a considerable time."

"You had recently written to M. Salomon?"

"About a week ago."

"You have, perhaps, the letter here?"

He had anticipated some slight difficulty at this point, but Steinbaum merely pressed a bell under the ledge of his desk and told a clerk to bring him a certain file. From this he took a flimsy carbon copy that he handed to Dupuy. The letter was short and written in a detached and forcible vein:

"MONSIEUR:

"Once again I must write and demand payment of the million francs so long outstanding. I have myself heavy charges to meet and cannot permit this debt to remain undischarged any longer. I would point out that, in spite of repeated promises and pleas for extended time, nothing has so far been repaid of the principal. Unless the money, or a considerable part of it, is forthcoming within the next 24 hours, I shall be compelled to take the only alternative.

"JACOB STEINBAUM."

"And in reply to that M. Salomon said?"

"He sent me this letter. You will see that he promises quite definitely to repay the money by the end of the week. He urges me to postpone action until then. Of course, insolvency has an unpleasant sound, and he has a great deal to lose."

"You agreed to his suggestion?"

"I gave him till the end of the week."

"And then you intended to put your threats into action?"

"One must live, monsieur."

"And M. Salomon realised that?"

Steinbaum's teeth bared for an instant in a queer, uncomfortable grin. "Oh, yes," he replied slowly. "I think that was quite understood."

2

Leaving the moneylender's office, Dupuy made his way to the amazing house that belonged to that peculiar man, Sinclair Roden. Everyone knew the name well enough, though few had met its possessor.

He was, indeed, more like a legend than a human being. All his affections were centred on the lovely treasury he had amassed during a long and critical life, and that he spent his remaining years in guarding jealously from every eye. He was supposed to be mildly insane, but since he was very rich and a hermit, that troubled no one; he wasn't likely to harm anybody who didn't interfere with his collection. Even burglars made few attempts on his house, that was reported to be fitted with every kind of police device. In addition, Roden was a first-class shot. He could be seen sometimes on the terrace of his house with his pistol, executing patterns of marvellous exactitude and intricacy on targets set up for the purpose. He made no secret of the fact that he would repeat the pattern in flesh and blood, if necessity arose.

Dupuy sent in his professional card, wondering if he would be admitted without a storm, but within a minute the door opened, and a tall, gaunt man with black, blazing eyes and a twisted mouth came into the room. He was like some blackened tree-trunk, struck by lightning long ago yet by some miracle continuing alive. The vitality that poured from that dried-up body gave Dupuy a queer sense of shock.

"You're from the papers?" he demanded, not troubling to look at the card in his hand.

"The police," Dupuy corrected him. "We do less harm, I think, though our profits are smaller."

"And what have the police to say to me?"

"I believe we have a mutual interest in the Marks diamond."

"And since when have the police become interested in art?"

Dupuy smiled. "A diamond has many facets, monsieur. It can also be regarded from many points of view. M. Salomon regards it as an object of barter, of profit; to you it is pure art; to me," he shrugged, " it is one more case of crime."

Roden's face changed. " Crime? It's been damaged, stolen?"

" As to damage, monsieur, I can't say. But stolen— yes—and the owner with it."

Roden made an impatient gesture. " Marks is nothing to me. But the diamond! How came he to be so criminally careless?"

" That, monsieur, we can scarcely enter into now. But I understand that you were proposing to buy the stone from M. Salomon?"

" I had an appointment to see the stone. If I had liked it, yes, I would have given him whatever price he asked."

" And that was?"

" Seventy thousand sterling, I believe."

Dupuy exclaimed involuntarily, " That's a large price for a diamond to-day, isn't it?"

" Perhaps. I should give him what it was worth to me. Am I a tradesman to bargain? My possessions are my life, and is it reasonable for a man to rate his life at the lowest possible figure? I can't understand these men who boast they've bought a thing worth a thousand pounds for nine hundred. What's that but cheapening and defaming the beloved object? Personally, I would rather give more than less than the value of a thing. I don't measure life by cash."

Dupuy's eloquent eyebrows rose as he glanced round the room. At every turn he saw something rare, beautiful and costly; and it was by these materialistic symbols of beauty that the man before him measured his life. A scene from one of his favourite English short stories came into his mind.

" Were there not things less perishable to possess; things that of their own nature would be less inclined to bid you good-bye? . . . I perceive here no faintest sign of life. And by life I mean a happy freedom of the spirit rather than mere amusement of the body. A life delighted in."

He had a sense of the complete unreality of this scene. These ornaments, some massive as iron, others frail as blown shells, this jade and crystal, the copper heads of ancient alien gods, all bespeaking their inanimate sense of a humanity that could never be altogether quelled so long as they, its descendants, continued to exist, oppressed his spirit. Suddenly he yearned for the homely, the sordid, even, so long as it maintained some hold on actual life. He moved quickly towards a window, but here also he was baulked. Some magnificent mediæval glass, in flashing scarlet and blue, had been introduced into the frame, so that he could obtain only a partial glimpse of the traffic of existence passing beneath him. But even that glimpse brought reassurance. Crime, planned and duly executed crime, had always appeared to him abnormal; and he reminded himself now, and found satisfaction in the thought, that he was dealing with the unnatural, that the whole sane world awaited him when he left this house that resembled more actively a cage, a prison of the spirit, than anything short of a real gaol had ever done. Meanwhile Roden placidly, even indifferently, was answering his questions. He had seen Salomon, he said, on the morning of the 29th; Salomon had come into his house before setting out for Monte Carlo; there seemed a little uncertainty as to the actual time of Marks' arrival. Salomon would reach Monte Carlo on the morning of the 30th and await Marks' pleasure. He would bring the diamond to Roden as soon as it was in his possession.

3

The more he considered the point, the more perplexed did Dupuy become. No man, however unsophisticated, could believe that a shrewd dealer like Marks would hand over a priceless diamond without reasonable security, and the most casual inquiries must elicit the fact that Salomon was on the verge of bankruptcy. Marnier had had no difficulty in getting details of the man's financial débâcle, and Marks was no eager innocent, or a man to take the smallest risk where money was concerned.

When he reached headquarters Dupuy found Marnier awaiting him in a state of considerable excitement.

"Here's news," he exclaimed, as his superior entered. "Salomon is not only heavily embarrassed for money; he is in danger of arrest for fraud. He must have £10,000 and at once."

Dupuy whistled softly. This put an even worse complexion on the position. Ruin was enough; disgrace of this kind was unthinkable. Hitherto Dupuy had been inclined to think Salomon's motive the weak point of any case he might put up against him, but this fresh information supplied motive and to spare. It justified him in following up Salomon's movements during the forty-eight hours following his arrival in Monte Carlo.

"Suppose him to be involved," he ruminated. "It was a question between prison for certain and a possible re-establishment, of course, taking a tremendous risk. So far as one can learn, the diamond was his final hope." Marnier had produced proof of his statement; Salomon had committed forgery and, unless he could lay his hands on sufficient money by the week's end, would inevitably go to gaol. He acted as trustee to a young woman and her brother, living in Paris, and had made use of their funds in an attempt to salvage his own affairs. He had to give account of his stewardship within a few days, and he must have been like the proverbial trapped rat.

Salomon's own account of his movements since leaving Paris gave the detective little upon which to work. The jeweller stated that he had reached Monte Carlo on the morning of the 30th and had spent the day in the hotel, expecting Marks to ring up and make an appointment for that day or the following morning. He added that Marks had been a little uncertain as to the date of his arrival, but had promised to communicate with the witness so soon as he arrived. At eleven o'clock on the morning of the 31st Salomon, having heard nothing, telephoned to the Hotel Fantastique asking when Marks was expected, but not mentioning his own name. He learned that the man had reached the hotel the previous morning.

" So that we must have travelled by the same train," Salomon explained.

" And you asked to speak to him, perhaps?" Dupuy suggested.

" No, not then. I did not wish to appear too anxious or to exasperate M. Marks. No, I thanked my informant and was disconnected before questions could be asked. An hour later M. Marks telephoned, saying he would be with me the next morning at eleven-thirty."

" And that suited you?"

" To tell you the truth, monsieur, it did not please me at all. I had all my business in Paris to attend to, and I had anticipated returning that same night. I hinted to M. Marks that I had kept the whole day free for him, and that as a business man this delay was irksome to me, but I did not wish to quarrel with him, and the matter remained as I have said. Later I got in touch with my office in Paris by telephone and gave certain instructions, warning them that I should not be back until the morning of the 2nd. In the afternoon I went for a walk alone, since I had met no friends here on this occasion, and in the evening I went into a cinema."

"Was that after dinner?"

"No, no, before dinner. Later, of course, I went to the casino."

"And you arrived there at what time?"

"About nine o'clock and remained until midnight or a little later."

He added that the commissionaire there would remember him; he was a constant visitor to Monte Carlo and the rooms, and though it was some time since he had been here, he would not be easily forgotten.

"Besides, I stopped to speak to the man," he added.

"Was it your lucky evening?"

"Emphatically no. I lost money steadily. I left the rooms about midnight, went for a walk, for the rooms had been very hot, and I was obsessed by thoughts of the diamond, and got back to my hotel between two and three o'clock. I couldn't sleep and I asked for my shaving water about seven and went out. I can't explain why I should have been so restless. Generally when I'm at Monte Carlo I lie in bed late. I have to work hard in Paris and I appreciate the change. I walked for some time, and presently I came to a café called the Trois Mousquetaires. I wanted, you understand, to fill in my time until my appointment with M. Marks. I had coffee and rolls at this café, and then suddenly I felt panic-stricken. Suppose there had been a telephone message saying that Marks was coming earlier? Suppose he came and, finding me not there, cancelled the appointment altogether? I began to think I had been mad to go at all. I can't explain why this should be. I can remember no other occasion of recent years when I have been so moved."

"It was a critical occasion," Dupuy suggested sympathetically.

"But I am not a boy, monsieur, eager about his first employment. I am a man accustomed to similar dealings. No, it seemed to me, before I heard anything, very strange that I should feel so troubled, though I had no notion that anything really had happened."

"You wouldn't say you had premonitions," murmured Dupuy.

A hot flush swept over Salomon's face. He drew himself up and said in haughty tones, "I am not an hysterical woman, monsieur. I returned, then, to my hotel about half-past ten, and waited for M. Marks. At half-past eleven he was not here, nor at noon. I rang for a waiter; I asked if there had been a telephone message; I mentioned his name. The man's face changed and before he spoke all my doubts had crystallised. Then I knew that disaster was upon me. Then he told me an amazing story. There was a gentleman of that name missing from his hotel, the Fantastique, since last night. All the town was talking of it. Monsieur, I was almost mad."

Dupuy looked at him sharply and a dull colour crept over the heavy, swarthy cheeks. "You think that strange? With so much at stake? Here was a great diamond, a diamond of which the world was speaking. It was not only the profit to be made from the sale of it, though that was a great consideration; there was the . . ." he snapped his fingers irritably, "the *empressement* of the position. To be dealing with the Marks Diamond—that is an affair that commands respect from other dealers. And I worked hard to be first in the field. I had spent all this time I could so ill afford to be in Monte Carlo when M. Marks was there. Of course, I had no notion that the police were involved, any more than I could guess why Marks should behave in this extraordinary fashion. I thought naturally he had left the hotel to meet someone—a woman, that is—and had not yet returned. But he has a name for a business man; I was perturbed and, as time went on, the position became increasingly serious. Then I learned that you, monsieur, were on the scent; that seemed final. I saw my hopes disintegrate. I wished to go to the hotel in person, but I felt they would tell me nothing. I must wait. I could not, I thought, return to Paris without more definite news."

4

It was on this statement that Dupuy now got to work. As the fast train took him back to Monte Carlo he mapped out his programme. Already the newspapers were humming with the story; enormous headlines flashed at the most casual passer-by; every detail that could be raked together concerning the missing man was given the greatest possible prominence. Political and social news was crowded into side columns. Dupuy's rapid glance swept the headlines. A woman had fallen from a fourth-floor window in Rue de la Rose in Monte Carlo at one a.m. and had lain for two hours on the pavement before anyone discovered her; there were threatened changes in the French Government; there had been a tremendous Blackshirt demonstration in England; fresh financial crises were prophesied from Germany; the world was threatened with new discoveries in the realm of light.

Dupuy creased the paper and flung it away. "And this one little man has ousted all that from the front page," he reflected with a wry humour. "And if he had not disappeared no doubt the suicidal lady would have taken his place. It was scarcely tactful of her to fall out of her window on the same night as Marks disappeared." As for the political situations, no one really understood them and very few people even pretended they did.

Arrived at the Cordon Bleu next morning, Dupuy found the first part of Salomon's story easy enough to prove. The manager agreed that the diamond merchant had arrived on the morning of the 30th and had spent the greater part of the day in the hotel, wandering about "like a forgotten soul, monsieur." There was a record of a local telephone call put through from his room during the following morning, and a long-distance call to Paris, lasting almost a quarter of an hour. Before lunch he had told the management he was expecting a gentleman called Marks next morning at eleven-thirty. No one recollected precisely how he had spent that afternoon, nor could Dupuy check any detail of the man's story. No local cinema attendant would identify him, and though Dupuy checked up the title of the film being shown, and the names of the principal players, this really advanced him no further, since a man could learn so much by studying the advertisements in the local press. Or the hotel could supply him with the programmes. In any case, it was a small point. The significant hours were not the afternoon of the 31st, but the late evening; Marks must have been alive long after Salomon's reputed visit to the cinema.

The Casino offered much more scope for examination. The commissionaire on duty remembered Salomon at once; he was a constant gambler, though it was true he had not been to the rooms for some time; he had paused as he entered and asked the commissionaire some question as to his family affairs. Lebaudin, the man in question, was touched that Salomon should remember what was only a triviality to the outsider for so long. They had spoken together for two or three minutes, and then Salomon had said he hoped he was going to be lucky, he could do with some good fortune. Lebaudin had agreed that times were difficult; he also said he hoped Salomon would wake things up a bit; there had been nothing outstanding or sensational for a long time, no stupendous gains or losses, chiefly the same monotonous crowds with their steady, dreary limits, on the whole losing steadily, but so unobtrusively that they could deceive themselves into thinking they were at last on the track of the perfect system. Salomon had laughed and passed in. The commissionaire could not recollect at what time he had left, but it had been earlier than was his wont, for there had been a small sensation later in the evening, and the word had gone round that Salomon was wanted. Search had been made, but the jeweller was not forthcoming and presently one of the habitués, who had recognised the man, said he was sure he had seen him leave the rooms early in the evening.

As to the sensation, it was merely this. An English girl, with the cool independence of her nation, had entered the rooms alone and had at once sat down to play; it was obvious that she was depending on no system, and was probably in the rooms for the first time. Very likely she was trusting to the famous but treacherous theory of beginners' luck. At all events, in her case it failed to work; within half an hour she had reached the end of her resources, but she remained where she was, watching the spin of the wheel, the eager, ruthless hands of the croupiers as they moved forward, clasping their rakes, collecting money from all sides.

Embarrassment seemed unknown to her; she sat with her hands folded until at last, looking up, she discovered a man staring at her, as if fascinated, when immediately she showed signs of distress. It was not, apparently, that she had said anything, but she moved as though to leave her place, then threw back her head and returned the stranger's stare, and when he at once dropped his eyes she relaxed again. But a few minutes later, when she looked in his direction, she found his gaze still fixed upon her, but now, she realised, it was not she herself, but a rather fine diamond drop pendant that she wore round her throat on a chain of platinum that held his interest. Involuntarily her hand went up, and she covered the stone; then hastily she stood up and began to move through the room. Before she reached the door she felt a touch on her arm, and there stood the man who had virtually driven her from the table. He was a Frenchman, swarthy and rather short, with dark, keen eyes. He apologised for alarming or annoying her; he said it was her diamond that had interested him, explaining that he was a diamond dealer; he thought it a remarkably fine stone. Probably only an English girl would have believed all that and not been offended, and probably no one but Diana Freyne would have turned on him, crying warmly: " If you think it's as good as that, and you're a dealer, will you buy it and give me another chance? I haven't had a scrap of luck to-night."

Salomon seemed rather taken aback. " I'm in earnest," said the girl, watching him intently. Several people had been distracted by the incident, and they listened, smiling or with lifted brows, according to their varying temperaments. Salomon seemed to hesitate; then he named a figure. The girl nodded indifferently.

" I suppose that's fair; I don't know much about diamonds, and you have to allow for your commission, don't you?"

The blatant candour of that almost overwhelmed Salomon, but he recovered himself sufficiently to say that the price was a very fair one, and the lady could try other dealers in the morning, if she wished. Miss Freyne, however, still free from embarrassment, shook her head.

" I'll be glad to have it. Could I have some at once?" She took the money and went back to another table. Here her luck changed almost at once, and she retired an hour and a half later with a bag heavy with her winnings. Before she left, she looked round for the dealer from Paris, but could not find him. She sent a page-boy to discover if he had left the rooms, and it seemed he had, since no one could discover him. A man standing by said he thought he had seen him leave comparatively early in the evening, before ten.

" If we can prove that," thought Dupuy, " it'll be a nasty blow for M. Salomon. But can we? And where shall I find the lady?"

The commissionaire did not know her name, but could supply that of the hotel where she was staying. Dupuy drove there immediately; it was not difficult to place his quarry. No sooner had he spoken of an English girl who had been fortunate the previous night than the clerk exclaimed: " Ah, Mlle. Freyne. She is in, I think." He lifted a house-telephone, and a minute later Dupuy was shown into a room where a girl, looking younger than her twenty-two years, was kneeling in front of a suit-case packing clothes. She stood up as Dupuy came in; she was small and rather round, with a gay, resolute face and an air of being quite undisturbed by any combination of circumstances that might either bring her into the limelight or involve her in humiliation; a face with a good deal of character, but not, thought the experienced Dupuy, the kind of face one would care to see across the breakfast-table every morning. One wanted something more placid and commonplace.

"M. Salomon?" she said, in reply to his question. "No, I didn't know his name at the time, but he paid me the money on the spot so references weren't required. I didn't see him go, but he went before I did. I wanted to find him and thank him for being the foundation of my luck. If he hadn't bought the diamond I'd have left the rooms a ruined woman." There was a wilful flamboyance about her speech that made Dupuy revise his opinion of her a little; not that he would have exchanged Mme. Dupuy at any time for this reckless young woman, but as a daughter, perhaps . . .

"And you left the rooms, mademoiselle?" He pulled himself up sharply.

"Oh, about half-past eleven."

"Do you recollect seeing M. Salomon after the transaction?"

"I don't recollect anything but watching the numbers and the change of colours, and seeing my pile growing."

"But you are sure he was not in the rooms when you left?"

"Oh, absolutely. I had every nook and cranny examined. Besides, some man said he thought he'd seen him go quite early. I couldn't wait there all night."

"I see. You are leaving the hotel, mademoiselle?"

"I'm going back to England, before I blue every penny I made. This is a chance I've been wanting for two years. Kennels," she explained cheerfully, pushing back her short, fair hair. "Only you need a good lot of capital. I never thought of anything so marvellous as this. What's happened about M. Salomon? Is he lost?"

"It's rather important to establish when he was last seen at the rooms," returned Dupuy evasively.

The girl nodded without interest. "Some beastly mess, I suppose," she murmured. "Well, I can't say he was there when I left because he wasn't." But all her heart was in her prospective kennels; she didn't really care what happened to the jeweller. Dupuy found that effortless impersonality rather chilling.

"Now why did Salomon lie about the time he left?" speculated the detective, walking thoughtfully in the boulevard and moving instinctively to avoid passers-by. "Of course there may be half a dozen reasons. He may have come to Monte Carlo intending to kill two birds with one stone; perhaps he had a friend here. Perhaps it is as well that people in general should not know how he spent last night. But the police must know."

At the Cordon Bleu he was told that the jeweller was out; he was returning to Paris that night and his room was already let to another gentleman. The management had no notion where he had gone, but he would assuredly be back later as he had left his luggage.

"He hasn't stayed long?" commented Dupuy idly.

"No, monsieur. Generally he stays here for a week, but then he comes on pleasure. This time he came on business."

"Oh, yes. Very unfortunate business, too, as it turned out. He seems to have been unlucky at the Casino into the bargain. Did he seem very gloomy when he came in last night?"

"I did not see him, monsieur. I do not remain here all night."

"So he was very late?"

The clerk shrugged. "When a man has only two days, and Monte Carlo has much to offer . . ."

Dupuy nodded. "There's a commissionaire or someone on duty even at night?"

"If he recalls. You will understand, monsieur, that this hotel is never locked. One never knows at what hour parties will return. They were dancing here last night until four o'clock and then some of them went out in automobiles."

A wild sort of place for Salomon to have chosen, if he was the sober man of business he liked to appear, was Dupuy's reflection; and he asked if it would be possible to see the commissionaire. This, it appeared, was quite simple. The commissionaire, however, said he wouldn't like to be sure of the time M. Salomon came in, but it wasn't till the morning. He recollected that, because the thought had gone through his mind that it would be an education for middle-class wives if they had any notion how their husbands employed their holidays. He had seemed dazed or drunk, the commissionaire wasn't sure which, had looked pale, and moved in a stiff spasmodic manner.

"And that seemed odd in the circumstances?"

"Odd to me, monsieur, though I did not know the circumstances, because I had never seen him like that before. But it was not bad, you understand, only a little noisy, breathless . . ."

"That admits of various explanations," Dupuy reflected grimly. "Breathless, eh? As though he had pounded along hell-for-leather. Perhaps it is true, he was drunk; or he was involved in some liaison and had escaped an angry husband by the skin of his teeth; or he may have been murdering Marks. But if so, how did he spend the remainder of the night? A man does not take so long to dispose of a body, unless he is burning it, and that is no easy thing to accomplish when you have no house in the neighbourhood. Besides, the police would have discovered something. Tremendous heat is needed; and the odour attracts attention. Perhaps it would be best to hear M. Salomon's own story in these changed circumstances."

5

Back at the hotel he found the jeweller fretting to return to his work. He turned passionately on the detective as he entered. "You understand my position better than most, monsieur," he cried, flinging up his hands. "That I should be in Paris at this moment is of the utmost importance. And yet I am compelled to remain here when I have told my story. . . ."

"Your first story," interjected Dupuy softly.

Salomon stopped dead; that wary apprehensive look once more obscured his face. "I do not understand, monsieur," he rapped out.

"And neither do I. I mean to say, I do not understand why you should tell me you were at the casino until midnight, when it is known that you left quite early, and yet did not return to your hotel until after daybreak."

He watched his man pitilessly as he spoke, and now he thought he could detect a pallor in those dark cheeks, swift attribute to fear. So that he was confirmed in his original impression that the man had something to conceal; not necessarily murder, but something he wished to keep hidden, at all costs.

He waited, therefore, for Salomon to speak, but the

wretched man, presenting every aspect of guilt, the bloodless countenance, the trembling lips, the downcast eyes, said not a word.

"Come, monsieur," Dupuy urged him. "There is some explanation. You cannot so soon have forgotten."

Salomon rallied himself. But when he spoke his voice was heavy and apprehensive. "And if I say, monsieur, that, troubled by my private affairs, rendered practically without means because of my transaction with the young English girl in the casino, knowing no one intimately, and not being in heart for casual acquaintanceships, I walked from the moment of leaving the rooms until my return to the hotel, what do you say then?"

"You walked for eight hours? In Monte Carlo? And there is no café that will recall you?" Dupuy's voice and expression were alike derisive. "Monsieur, you must not think the police are completely fools. Why, there would be some café."

Salomon shook an irresolute head. "I stopped at no café, monsieur."

"Then what?" Dupuy spread his hands to show how reasonably he was behaving. "You did not walk for so long—all through the night, mark you—without saying a word to a person, without meeting someone—recollect, monsieur, that you are well known here; you would meet someone whom you knew—without stopping, entering some place of entertainment. No, that story will not do."

Salomon had been standing beside the table, one hand pressed on the shining polished surface. Now abruptly he sat down. "Monsieur, you do not know what you ask. If I swear to you that I know nothing of M. Marks' disappearance you will not believe me. If I take oath . . ."

"I am a police officer," said Dupuy dryly. "Monsieur, you are wasting time. You must explain your movements. To refuse to do so renders you open to suspicion of the gravest character. You know that only such facts as are relevant to the affair will be made public; if you were engaged on private business you have but to recount it, and if the police are satisfied that your story is true you will not be troubled further. But to take a man's oath . . . why, all our criminals would go free if justice were so simple as that."

Salomon stood up and began to walk nervously up and down the room, his hand, a large powerful hand, short-fingered, acquisitive, buried in his trouser-pocket; through the thin material Dupuy could watch its nervous motions of clenching and unclenching. Whatever the issue, it was clearly of the gravest import to the tormented man who paced up and down, up and down, now and again opening his mouth to speak, then closing it, as though he dared not take the risk, and continuing his feverish gait. Dupuy said nothing; that silence, and well he knew it, imposed a definite compulsion on the man at his mercy. At length the jeweller turned and, with a ferocity that surprised his companion, exclaimed, "No, monsieur, I can do nothing to help you. It is true that I left the casino early. I had lost my money; the diamond I had bought from the young English girl left me nearly penniless; I could not afford to stake more. I left the rooms intending to return to my hotel immediately, but on the way I met a woman—I don't know her name—she was nothing to me, but like myself she was out for whatever the hour promised. I doubt if I would know her again."

"Her address?"

Salomon shook his head. "I do not remember. She

was an affair of the moment. But she was kind and she filled in the hours of waiting."

"So that's how you spent your time? I wonder why you didn't tell me the truth at first."

Salomon was suddenly angry. "It pleases you to be facetious, monsieur. Consider, if you will. Here is an Englishman spirited away, murdered perhaps. The police are on his trail; they examine so many witnesses. Presently they will come into court, and those witnesses will perhaps come with them; they will hear their statements read aloud. I am a married man, with three children. Is that the kind of thing I would wish them to hear of their father? Moreover, there is my wife . . ."

"She would rather hear you accused of one wild night than of murder."

"Women are strange," said Salomon. "If I were accused of murder she would leave no stone unturned; she would tear the throat from any neighbour who dared affirm the charge to be true. But the other— no, she would be my enemy then."

Dupuy regarded his companion speculatively. "You are sure you wouldn't prefer to put your cards on the table?" he suggested. "It might save time in the end."

Salomon turned on his passionately. "I can tell you no more," he cried. "No more. That you must believe."

At that date Dupuy was sceptical as to the truth of this, but afterwards, when the whole dreadful truth was known, he said to Marnier: "He was right, you know, though I didn't believe it at the time. He literally couldn't have told us more, told us the whole truth, as I implored him to. No man living could have done that."

CHAPTER VIII

1

At the hotel the party was becoming restive. During the first day boredom had been forestalled by a kind of shocked but pleasant excitement. The fact that the missing man was a millionaire, that his story was as mysterious as his disappearance, added spice to the situation; on the stairs, behind closed doors, in letters to friends and relatives, in conversations and in private thoughts, the minds of all those concerned were fixed on this perplexing affair. Personal concerns were buried with personal prejudices: Miss Hoult talked quite pleasantly to Mrs. Fellowes, whom she considered a fool; and Fellowes, who had frequently been heard to remark that the trouble with Sarah Blaise was that she hadn't been smacked enough when younger, now walked amiably round the grounds with her, airing his views and listening to her comments. He was even heard to remark that young people were sometimes sharper than their elders, qualifying the admission with a laughing comment about their having left school later. But when the 1st November gave place to the 2nd, and then the 3rd dawned and still Dupuy had not returned to the hotel nor lifted his embargo on visitors' departures without permission, a kind of petulance, an irritable patience, began to manifest itself. The only person who remained completely placid was Miss Hoult. A natural ghoul, she was in her element. She collared everyone she could—even Montstuart's slippery courtesy was overwhelmed in the end—and talked endlessly and boringly of psychological clues, and the mistakes that hang criminals; she said it was a man's

temperament and habits that were of first importance, not his actions. No, no, his actions depended
on his personality, and when Sarah asked impatiently
and rudely how you discovered the personal habits of
an invisible man, she replied sweetly that the clues
would provide a trail from which the police could
deduce certain habits, and from these they could
build up a character; after that, all they had to do
was to find a man with such a character, like the
Fairy Prince looking for the girl with the right-
shaped foot. Sarah said, "How sickening," and Miss
Hoult thought how fervently she agreed with Mr.
Fellowes, whom she found in the grounds and vic-
timised once more.

"A chain's as strong as its weakest link," she observed with a brisk sententiousness, ignoring Mrs.
Fellowes who had been standing by her husband, with
a bland assumption that they were alone; in fact, Mrs.
Fellowes nearly slipped away, she felt so strongly that
she didn't really exist. "I wonder," Miss Hoult continued, still addressing herself solely to the politician,
"if you remember a book of mine—or perhaps you
didn't read it; I really don't know why you should—
but in this story, *Innocent Alibi*, I had a position
very like this one. There the man had been murdered by a wife."

"Mr. Marks hadn't got a wife," said Mrs. Fellowes,
resolutely determined not to be ignored.

Miss Hoult looked politely surprised at discovering
her there at all. "I didn't say his own wife," she
pointed out rather loftily. "As a matter of fact, very
few wives are enterprising enough to do away with
their husbands. It's lack of imagination, I think; or
perhaps I should say extreme egotism. I think the
last. Because they know their husband's habits, and
would instantly draw deductions from any given set

of circumstances, they suppose that everyone else has the same knowledge. They're like the souls in the hymn that lingered shivering on the brink. They'd love to get rid of their husbands, poor dears, but they're afraid of the risk. I believe that's the answer to the tremendous problem why there aren't more domestic murders. Because, goodness knows, the motive's easy enough to find. I dare say there are a lot of husbands who murder their wives, but women are so loyal; they'd never tell the police they'd been murdered, whereas a poisoned husband wouldn't have any compunction."

Mrs. Fellowes suddenly discovered that her husband was preparing an excuse to leave them together, and this, she decided, was more than she could bear, so without a word she slipped silently away. On the verandah she found Montstuart reading a book by Mr. Wills Crofts; he put this down with an alacrity that was complimentary to the newcomer, if not to the author.

"That frightful woman," said Mrs. Fellowes, sitting down. "I really don't know what she's talking about. I don't believe Percy does either. I only know this is the most uncomfortable holiday I ever spent. This kind of thing never happened at St. Leonards or Folkestone or Cromer. I must say I'm rather disappointed in foreign hotels. I thought they were quite out of the ordinary, but they can't make you proper tea, and they never seem to have heard of those delicious little scones with currants in them that anyone will give you at home. And the people here are different. I always used to pick up such nice recipes from the visitors at the Hydro, and here no one seems interested in that kind of thing. I suppose it's all very modern, but I like the old way. Anyhow, people didn't get killed after dinner and spoil everyone else's holiday."

"I expect it's rather spoilt his," suggested Montstuart.

"He should have thought of that before he came," was Mrs. Fellowes' unexpected comment. "Do you think they'll ever discover what happened to him? It seems so dreadful with all of us quite close by. I wonder the gardeners didn't hear anything, but Percy says that people of the lower orders really haven't got any intelligence, only instincts like animals."

"I don't agree with your husband, and, even if he were right, instinct should have warned them there was something wrong."

"What's that about instinct?" demanded Miss Hoult, coming over and plumping herself into their conversation. "As if it were a cushion, Percy," Mrs. Fellowes complained later. "She bounced into it; she'd leave an impression on any cushion she sat on. And she squashed it quite flat. Mr. Montstuart and I had been getting on so very well up till then."

2

When Dupuy came in late that evening, tired and not very well satisfied with the day's activities, he found Latymer in the bar drinking a final whisky and soda. He invited the detective to join him.

"Wants to pump me, I suppose?" thought the latter suspiciously. But Latymer asked no questions. He only volunteered information. "Mrs. Fellowes was wondering whether the gardeners could help," he said.

"The gardeners?"

"Yes. While the search for Marks was going on— the preliminary search, I mean, before there was any idea of tragedy—she saw two gardeners working in the kitchen garden."

"But I have not seen them," cried Dupuy in a fine state of indignation. "Why did not Potain tell me of them?"

"Well, that's the trouble," said Latymer mildly. "Potain doesn't seem to have the slightest idea who they could have been."

3

For a moment there was an appalled, an incredulous silence. Then Dupuy said, "Do I understand you, monsieur? There were two men on the premises that night, whom no one has identified?"

"That appears to be the position. Potain assures me that he has never employed a gardener who would be at work at that hour, and certainly he wouldn't permit it on a gala night."

"And they were by the kitchen garden?"

"In the kitchen garden, Mrs. Fellowes says, gathering leaves."

"A peculiar thing to be doing at 10.30 in the evening."

"Well, I don't know. That might depend on your purpose. It seems to me an odd thing to do to fry bacon and eggs at 3.30 a.m., but if you're going to eat them I suppose it's all right."

"And they were gathering leaves . . .?"

"For the same reason as certain well-known songbirds."

"To cover the corpse?"

"It's only a suggestion," said Mr. Latymer hastily.

"And that woman actually saw it being done and suspected nothing?"

"I think you can hardly blame her for that. There was no reason why she should suspect them. She has seen—we have all seen for some days past—Potain's gardeners moving in and out of that part of the grounds."

Dupuy frowned. "It was a daring crime. To carry the body from the ridge—doubtless they were waiting there for the unsuspecting Marks to approach—across the lawn. But, of course, they had localised the interest of the party. That was clever. I wonder how they got in."

"I think I can tell you," offered Latymer. "Of course, you will wish to verify what I say. But here is my version. You know that a broad road, much frequented, bounds the bottom of the grounds. This runs through to the town itself, but there is a branch road that skirts the side of the hotel, making a right angle with the road that runs in front of it. Thus:

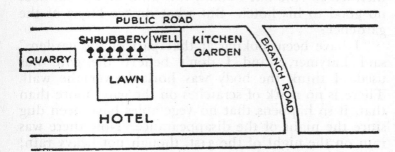

I think our murderers—I am assuming it was murder, and I think we may shortly have proof of that—entered the kitchen garden over the wall—there would be very little traffic on the side road at such an hour—stunned or killed their victim, laid their false trail (the stone in the spinney), and came back to the kitchen garden."

"One moment. There is a gate to this garden leading into the grounds?"

"Yes. A gate of which there are only two keys. One belongs to Potain himself, the other to the chief gardener. Both keys are in Potain's charge when the gardener goes off duty at night."

"And both those were in Potain's possession that night? I wonder?"

"So he says. But that means very little, since this is clearly a premeditated crime."

Dupuy nodded. "Wax impressions are easily made. You agree with me, monsieur, that this is the work of a gang of men."

"Obviously there were at least two at work, whom Mrs. Fellowes saw. There may have been others. There's the question of the disposal of the corpse."

"Supposing the gate to have been used, that appears to implicate either Potain or the gardener. I'm inclined to rule out Potain; this kind of scandal does no good to his hotel. But what do we know of the gardener?"

"I have been looking at that part of the garden," said Latymer, "and I don't believe the gate was used. I think the body was hoisted over the wall. There is no mark of scratches on the gate; more than that, it so happens that no vegetables have been dug since the night of the disappearance. Now there was rain on the night of the 31st, though not heavy rain; but the gate does not fit very well, and if it had been moved since the shower, that is, since 7.30 on the 31st, some impression of the lower bar would be left on the wet earth. In fact, there is no such impression. But on the top of the railings near the gate I found this," and from an envelope he shook into Dupuy's hand a fragment of black cloth of the kind of which dress trousers are made.

Dupuy stood nodding his head like a mandarin, after the fashion that had brought Bertha Hoult to the verge of hysteria. "So!" he murmured. Then he seemed to take a decision. "Monsieur, you offered me your help a day or so ago. I could give you no certain reply. But now, you have rendered me a great service, and I should be glad of your further assistance. I must acknowledge that I had not hitherto heard your name, but my experience of English private detectives is small . . ."

Latymer silenced him hastily. "It is by no means well known, monsieur."

"That, let me assure you, will prove but a question of time. You have much experience?"

"A little. But only as an amateur. Crime is my hobby; dissuade yourself from any notion that I am a member of the British police force disguised as a tourist." He touched Dupuy on the raw there; the little man had had his suspicions and coloured to hear them put into words. "It is a natural bent. I believe it goes with a mathematical tradition, that desire to put figures together and achieve unexpected results, to be faced with an apparent blank wall of incomprehensibility and to arrive at a solution. At all events, there it is. I have inaugurated a Crime Circle at Harrow—I live at Harrow," he added gently, "and we meet fortnightly to attempt to solve cases —French, German, American as well as English— that have not been solved by the police. We do nothing spectacular and we do not write to the papers. It is, as you might say, a hobby. It pleases us; we find it instructive. And a few years ago I was fortunate enough, in reading a case of a very brutal crime —robbery with violence, as it seems possible this may turn out to be—to notice a quite minor incident that aroused my suspicions in a hitherto unexplored direction. I could, of course, do nothing myself, but a friend of mine, a journalist, went down to the spot and contrived to extort a confession from the real criminal. After that, I thought I might act perhaps as adviser in criminal cases. I work on a quite small scale; I am not dependent for my livelihood on the work I do and the fees I draw. Not very many people know of my activities, but there have been cases of recent years—the Harpenden emeralds, the pearls Lady X lost at the charity ball at Clements' Hotel last year, an occasion where it is perhaps more discreet to avoid mentioning names, where a young man of family and position was accused of embezzling certain funds. I enjoy my work, monsieur. I do not claim to be an expert, but if I could be of assistance I am at your disposal."

There was neither energy nor ardour about the flat voice, nor any particular emphasis noticeable in any part of the smooth sentences; but Dupuy was impressed by some indescribable sense of vigour concealed in that lank body, by that melancholy voice, behind all the unimpressive lack of elegance of the languid personality. He thought, "This man has intelligence, he has foresight, he has application. His attitude to life and to persons differs from mine. So much the better. Trifles that I may overlook will impress him; together we may discover the truth." And he said impetuously, "Monsieur, I should be very glad. This will prove, I think, a hard nut to crack." Latymer straightened himself. "I will do what I can to help you, monsieur," he said, and he held out his hand. "But there are things about this case I do not like." Behind the mild words stirred a wealth of human feeling, rigidly restrained. And Dupuy thought with a shock of amazement, "What does he suspect? I believe he's afraid," and a fresh tingle of exhilaration spread throughout his body.

4

They went first of all to the kitchen garden to discover what more it might yield their trained observation. For they had agreed already that, whoever the two gardeners were, it was improbable that they had entered either of the obvious entrances to the hotel.

"They could hardly have walked through the front hall without being challenged," urged Dupuy.

"Unless they wore the usual evening dress that wouldn't distinguish them from anybody else," Latymer agreed. "But if so they'd have to disguise themselves again when they got to the garden. And that would be infernally dangerous. You see, they couldn't reach the grounds without going through one of the private rooms, or through the verandah. And you've made inquiries, and I've made inquiries, and no one can recollect one stranger being on the premises that night, let alone two. And then even if they got in, they might find the hotel like those old-fashioned mouse-traps; they'd be hemmed in, couldn't get out, and it was important that they should be able to get out; not only that, Marks had got to get out too, and I very much doubt if he could have got out by himself. I think he'd need at least one hand, probably three or four."

"I think you must be right," Dupuy acknowledged. "At first I believed that M. Marks left the hotel of his own free will, that it was he who flung that stone to distract the attention of you all. But now that we have found this piece of cloth I believe I was wrong. I think he left the hotel via the kitchen garden, and I think he was lifted over the gate from the grounds.

He may have been dead even then. One cannot tell. There may be traces. You have examined the garden, monsieur?"

" I haven't been near it. Curiosity took me as far as the gate, but though I hungered to poach I realised it wasn't my case. It wasn't even my country's case, though I suppose Marks does count as a British citizen. In any case, I'm sure Potain wouldn't have given me the key if I'd asked for it. He'd probably have suspected me of being concerned in the murder, and wanted to take the opportunity of your being out of the way to dig up the diamond from its hiding-place."

" I will get the key," said Dupuy. " I have been thinking. Mrs. Fellowes, you remember, spoke of the wheelbarrow. Since that was being used it can have been for one purpose only. In that case, perhaps some trace will remain."

" A blood mark," suggested Latymer solemnly.

" A button, a piece of a cuff-link, a few hairs," Dupuy spread his hands artistically. " Perhaps nothing at all."

But in the barrow they found something that proved beyond all doubt the purpose for which this had been used. Caught in one of the cracks were three or four strands of a bright cherry-coloured silk.

" Marks' cap," said Dupuy triumphantly. " The inference is obvious. Horrible though it sounds, it is clear from the size of the barrow that the corpse must have been crammed, doubled, into it, his head between his knees, perhaps, though he was not a large man. It was dark, with only occasional flashes of moonlight, so it would not be easy for anyone, certainly not a lady so short-sighted as Mrs. Fellowes, to understand why two men should be shovelling leaves so energetically at half-past ten at night. And, of course, they did not expect anyone to see them. The whole party should have been on the ridge at the head of the quarry. You will remember how immediately they despatched Mrs. Fellowes thither when she asked for directions. Why should gardeners know the whereabouts of any guests?"

"It is a pity Mrs. Fellowes was too much agitated to see the man's face," remarked Latymer. "He was in the shadows—well, naturally—and she noticed nothing distinctive about the voice. No doubt, in any case, that would be disguised."

"That makes no difference," said Dupuy in dry tones. "I do not think that Mrs. Fellowes is a lady who would notice the timbre of a voice at any time. Now, this is what I think happened. The criminals hoisted the unfortunate fellow over the wall, concealed him in the barrow and wheeled him to the second wall. That was for caution's sake, lest, after all, they be seen. How, I wonder, did they get him away?"

They were eagerly searching the ground as they debated the points at issue. It was useless to try to trace footprints, as the men had been in and out of the garden since the night of the 31st, but the two men examined the ground with minute care for any possible clue. A dropped button, a spent match, a scrap of material caught on a bush, any of these might help them to bring home the crime to its perpetrator. But here, at least, they found nothing at all.

Latymer came back to his own question. "I think they must have had a car," he speculated. "They took him out of the grounds over the wall—that seems obvious, since the body isn't here, and anyway there's no cover we haven't examined. And they couldn't carry him. But in a car they would have little enough to fear."

"That is true," Dupuy agreed. "A car standing in this lane for an hour or more at night would attract no attention. I understand that it is not used very much, except by those who prefer the darkness; and if the lights were extinguished an obvious inference would be drawn."

Latymer nodded. "Lovers and criminals like the dark," he quoted. "All the same, monsieur, I confess I don't think we've got the thing quite right yet."

"So?" Dupuy's brows lifted politely. "You have another theory?"

"Not another theory precisely. But I don't quite see how your criminals got into the garden from the lane. Oh, I know we agree they must have come over the wall, but how did they get to the top? Did they bring a ladder? I doubt it. They'd have aroused attention at once, and they simply couldn't have banked on the lane being empty the whole time. The crime would take—I hardly know how long; but say twenty minutes (I dare say it would be more)—and during that time any one might come along, and they'd be bound to be suspicious of a ladder leaning up against the wall. It would be most unfortunate for the criminals if an alarm had been raised. And I don't see how they could have climbed it. It's ten feet high, and being made of smooth stone it doesn't give any footholds."

"A rope perhaps?" Dupuy leaned over and examined the surface of the wall. "No, hardly that. There is no place. Even if they stood on the roof of the car, that would seem strange."

"And then lowering the body in afterwards." He frowned.

Latymer was still examining the surface of the inner wall; now with a mutter of triumph he detached something minute from a roughened edge of stone.

Dupuy took it eagerly. "A morsel of fibre," he exclaimed, and his face brightened. "Ah, that makes it easier to understand. Of course, the unfortunate M. Marks was dragged up this wall by a rope, probably fastened under his armpits."

"And the rope was fastened—where, monsieur?"

Dupuy looked grave again. "That is a difficulty. I do not see a single place where a rope might conveniently—or even with awkwardness—be tied. No, one of the 'gardeners' must have stood on the car and hoisted, while the other remained in the garden to guide the melancholy burden."

"And when they had got him to the top of the wall they lowered him on the other side, into a waiting motor-car? That was taking an incredible risk. If they were seen . . ."

"Would that matter? It is not they but their burden that must not be discovered."

"They must bring the body over. What do you mean, monsieur?"

"I agree they must bring it over, but must it still resemble a body? They used leaves in the barrow; and when they hoisted the corpse over the wall they may have so disguised it it seemed to any passer-by no more than—shall we say?—a sackful of sand."

"A sack? Of course. That would answer all the points; and if they were seen from the grounds, it would look as though they were storing leaves for manure next year. I believe you're right." All the excitable Gallic blood in the dark little man's body seemed burning and leaping as point after point was smoothed out. "Oh, they were taking no chances, but fortunately their time was short; at any moment M. Marks' absence might be discovered, and so they could not search too closely for clues; otherwise they might have found those silk threads. Now, they have the body in a sack, they have hauled it up the wall and placed it in the car. But suppose they are seen? —one man standing on the roof of an automobile receiving a sack from a second, standing in a garden. That would be strange, would it not?"

"I don't think that's how it happened. I took exception to the car from the outset, you'll remember. Why shouldn't it have been a lorry—an open lorry, loaded perhaps with other sacks to allay suspicion? This is all guess-work, I admit, but a single sack on a lorry would arouse doubt in the mind of a hen. But with other sacks aboard, filled how you please— no one would notice such a load. Even in England we don't inform the police simply because we see men working with a lorry by night."

"But of course. I think you are right again, monsieur. It would seem natural enough for two men to be standing on the floor of a lorry whence they could easily scramble to the top of the wall, watching their opportunity. There is a screen of trees at the bend there that would help them, and the wall at this point commands the lane in both directions. It would not be hard to choose the perfect moment. For instance . . ." he gesticulated a little, the natural actor in him blinding him to everything but the dramatic value of the situation. "Up comes the sack, I take it, I dump it in the lorry. You ascend the wall—how do you ascend the wall?"

"I'm not sure," said Latymer slowly. "Perhaps I jump on the barrow. I wonder if any one remembers where the barrow was found the next morning. It wouldn't look strange for it to be on the path there. Or perhaps I am very agile and haul myself up by the rope. At all events, here we are, all three of us in the lorry, X and Y and the dead man—what next?"

"I think you drive away at once. You have presumably some place in mind. It would never do to leave a dead body somewhere casually. There have been so many French crimes of violence traced because the murderer has been careless in his disposal of the body. No, you have a plan. Probably the body is to be taken some distance, perhaps a considerable distance, perhaps as far as the sea."

"That isn't very wise as a rule, unless you're going to take a boat and weight your corpse, and even then luck's often against you," objected Latymer. "I should think they're more likely to be marked down some disused quarry or some place well protected by bushes. You remember the Eyraud murder, of course? That body would never have been found but for the smell of decomposition. I suppose our next move is to try to find people who remember seeing a lorry laden with sacks travelling in this neighbourhood at about 11 p.m. on the 31st. That may prove difficult."

"The lorry itself may help us. I hardly think the lorry would belong originally to the murderers, though, of course, they may have bought it in order that they can abandon it the more easily."

"Even abandoning lorries isn't really satisfactory. The man who sold it can generally recognise it, and may be able to furnish a good working description of the man who bought it."

"No doubt," agreed Dupuy. "Of course it may have come from Paris or the coast. It may have been travelling for some days."

"So far as I remember, from notes in the gossip-columns of the English papers, it wasn't generally known that Marks would be at this hotel until practically the day of his arrival. I believe Potain only knew on the morning of the 30th."

" But he stopped in Paris en route?"

" That's true. I dare say his movements would be known there."

" And then would a man planning murder hire a Paris lorry? The Parisian numbers are different from those in this neighbourhood, and though no doubt they'd change them they very likely wouldn't do that at once. There are always enthusiasts noticing the different letters of various towns, whereas a local number would pass without comment."

" That is a good point, monsieur," said Dupuy approvingly. " I think perhaps you have been too modest over your detective abilities, and perhaps you have more experience than you will allow."

Latymer coloured a little. " It's largely theoretical, I'm afraid, just as one's explanation of this case is. Suppose, then, having disposed of the body, they abandon the lorry also?"

Dupuy shook his head. " There's no reason for that, monsieur. They could change the number, even repaint the lorry, if they wish, and later sell it to some dealer. That would be safer than leaving it where it would be bound to be found, provided, of course, that time did not cheat them. For instance, if they knew a lorry was being sought for, then they might part with it immediately. But it is now three days since the murder. They may be anywhere. But we might perhaps circulate the lorry-dealers, in case they remember selling a lorry, or buying one. And we should take the public into our confidence. True, that means warning the criminals, but it is not as if the scent were very warm. And we must hope now for someone, some stranger, some passer-by, to remember the lorry, perhaps to give us some description of it. So much in these affairs, monsieur, depends on chance."

"And of course some man may recall selling a load of gravel or sand to a man whom he did not know but can describe—remote, I know, but not impossible."

They finished their examination by entering the lane and investigating the wall from that side. On the top they found a lump of dried mud, similar to that on which thew now stood, and in this were implanted a number of blades of short grass. But when they attempted to get footprints from the ground, they found that the grass, though trampled on the night in question, had sprung up since then, leaving no useful impression behind.

"This would seem to show we're on the right path," said Latymer. "This earth clearly didn't come from this side of the wall. That would be right. They'd drive up, and their boots would be clean. But when they roamed through the garden they'd have collected a little mud, and that rubbed off while they climbed the wall. Besides, the earth in the lane is of a different quality. Potain had his soil prepared for his vegetables."

"I am inclined to believe, monsieur, that whoever is responsible for this crime knows the hotel from the inside; he has perhaps been employed there some time. You note the position of the lorry—we will for the sake of argument assume the lorry. It stands at the one place where a man mounting it would be least visible from within. That is because of that thin belt of trees. Another place might have been chosen, and the men been seen from the gate. I think, too, they must have an accomplice who described for them the lie of the ground. They would scarcely risk blundering about in the garden; it would be too dangerous."

"Except that, of course, the garden was very dark, and there's plenty of cover. Marks apparently kept to the ridge because it was the safest place, the most overlooked from every part of the grounds, and even there, when the moon was covered, he was practically invisible. If they had been prowling round the garden and any one had cannoned into them, they'd only have been taken for members of the party."

"I think they wished to take no unnecessary risk. There was, for instance, this man who was inquiring for M. Marks—the advance guard, I believe. He was to learn when Marks was expected; he would learn the plans for that night, the 31st; he was also seen lingering in the neighbourhood, he had to see all that was possible."

"And, of course," agreed Latymer, "there must be the element of risk in every crime." The wooden voice, the wooden face, so sharp a contrast to the ardour of his companion, masked heaven only knew what excitement and speculation. Dupuy, who had co-operated on two occasions with the English police, recognised the symptoms. "He sees a great deal farther than he will allow," he decided. "But he is cautious, he won't throw out suggestions, as I myself would. But he will be a help, oh, a great help." Aloud he added, "I was hoping to find traces of blood, perhaps in the grass or in this ditch. There is an appearance as though oil had leaked here; if the exhaust of the lorry was defective—but of course it may have nothing to do with our case."

"Perhaps nothing," Latymer agreed. "Yes, I, too, am sorry about the blood. Blood-stained grass might have implied a blood-stained lorry. It is these things that help the criminal investigator. But we are dealing with clever criminals, M. Dupuy. You have, I suppose," there was a shade of diffidence in his voice, " men watching out for the diamond?"

" Like bloodhounds," said Dupuy with satisfaction. But Latymer looked less pleased. " They have had so much time," he exclaimed. " And once the stone's out of the country, why should you ever hear of it again? Or this American, Roden? One's heard of him. A lunatic in his own line. Would he, do you think, be capable of buying the stone and asking no questions?"

Dupuy considered. " It is most probable. But it would be foolhardy, I think. No, no. I am more inclined to believe that one of them drove the lorry and the other caught a night train, perhaps to Amsterdam, perhaps to Marseilles. The diamond may have been on the high seas for two days."

" I suppose ships have been warned, in case any ship's safe is asked to accommodate the thing?"

Dupuy looked amused. " All precautions are being taken, monsieur. Rest assured of that."

" Yes, I'm only making conversation really," agreed Latymer. " It is so interesting."

" It was very daring," said Dupuy soberly. " To carry that body from the foot of the quarry, with the whole party just above their heads, to take that risk. They might so easily have been seen. Did they know the moon would be extinguished just then?" He seemed to be asking the question quite seriously, but Latymer had nothing to say. And suddenly Dupuy stopped and flung back his head and began to laugh.

" But, of course. The imbecile that I am not to have seen it before, I that had the evidence in my hands. Monsieur, you see it, of course. There was my central problem, and now it is no problem at all."

" No?" murmured Latymer, mystified but polite.

" How the body was taken from the foot of the quarry to the kitchen garden. How it perplexed me. And it is so simple. Now at last, monsieur, we can begin our work."

He whirled round, laughing into Latymer's mildly astonished eyes. Dupuy went on ahead to the hotel, forgetful of his companion, busy with his calculations, and as he went he talked rapidly to himself. "Why did I not think before?" he marvelled. " Is is because one takes so much for granted. I wonder if he has kept that box," he wondered a moment later. " I think perhaps he may. The French are a thrifty nation."

CHAPTER IX

REALISING the impossibility of preserving secrecy in a case that was attracting so much attention, and whose witnesses included both the servants and the guests of a famous hotel, Dupuy resolved to take the public wholly into his confidence, and appealed for the assistance of the community in tracing a lorry believed to be in the neighbourhood of the hotel between 10 and 11 o'clock on the night of the 31st. He sent out an S.O.S. from headquarters, circularised all police stations and invoked the aid of the broadcasting faculty. Then he settled down to wait with a greater patience than might have been expected from so eager a man. He took a room at a modest hotel at Monte Carlo, preferring this to Paris, since his informant would probably be a local man; and for two days nothing happened. He occupied himself in trying to trace down the (probably mythical) woman with whom Salomon had spent the night, but, of course, met with no success. If the man were arrested, the woman might come forward, if she recognised the prisoner's identity, but Dupuy did not for a moment suppose that the jeweller had given her his real name. Indeed, in such encounters names are not interchanged. He also sought for the man who had made himself so conspicuous at the hotel just before Marks' arrival, being convinced that he was an accomplice, but news of the lorry was received before he had met with any success in either direction.

Dupuy was actually discussing certain details with Latymer when the first news came through. " If the stone is already out of the country," he was saying, " it is quite improbable that it will ever be seen here again."

" Except by chance, or by the discovery of M. Marks' body."

" If we find it in time," Dupuy took him up. " The murderer may have left clues there, and by those clues we may track him down. But, if I am right, there are several people implicated in this affair, and they will tangle one another's traces. If we could find one and pin him down, we might wrench the truth from him, but these jewel thieves, as you know, are the cleverest people we ever have to deal with. The average murder for passion or revenge is child's play by comparison."

" It is all a question of time," Latymer repeated. " If decomposition has reached a certain stage, though identification may not be difficult, the medical details may be wiped out. We have no alternative but to wait, I am afraid." Even as he spoke a page came in with a letter on a tray. It was from a man who signed himself Raoul Paul, and stated that he had been driving his motor-cycle along the main road, that is, the road running past the grounds of the Fantastique, at 10.15 or 10.20 on the night in question, and had been almost run down by a motor-lorry without lights, that had turned out of a side-road, travelling at considerable speed. The lorry swayed dangerously as it turned into the main stream of traffic, but he thought this might be due as much to the bad surface of the dark side-road as to careless driving. Nevertheless, he gained the impression that the man found the lorry almost more than he could manage, but of course, added the writer ingenuously, it may just be that he was intoxicated. He, Paul, had stopped his machine and turned to shout after the lorry, that was, he considered, a public danger, but the driver, instead of retaliating, drove straight on without reply, without even lifting his head. Paul added that there were two men in the front seat, and the driver seemed rather bowed over the wheel; he had not in that light been able to see either of them at all definitely. The lorry was loaded with sacks, seven or eight, he thought, that he had supposed to be grain, but the matter, of course, was not his affair and he had wasted little speculation on it.

" I think we may say that Marks was dead by that time. Otherwise one of the men would have been seated among the sacks," was Dupuy's comment. " How and when he was killed we have yet to learn. I think we should see this man, M. Latymer. Does he give a telephone number?"

But the address was that of a street of small villas where telephones were little used, so Dupuy wrote a letter and sent it by hand, " though probably he works all day, and cannot come before night in any case," he added to his companion. At about nine o'clock that evening the young man turned up. He was tall, clean-shaved, very young, probably not more than nineteen; he described himself as a mechanic, and repeated the story he had told in the letter.

Dupuy questioned him closely, and was satisfied with the answers he received. The young man replied briefly and with promptitude, only pausing now and again when some point concerning time or a particular direction was in question.

"I was visiting the family of the girl I hope to marry," he said. "I stayed till 10 o'clock. I remember the time particularly because I left earlier than usual. The young lady lives with an aunt, and this aunt has the influenza and Lucille is nursing her. At 10 o'clock she told me I must wait no longer, as her aunt was supposed to be settled for the night by half-past nine, and she certainly would not settle so long as I was in the house." He entered into all this detail with an intent gravity that even Latymer, accustomed to discount ninety per cent. of all impressions and characteristics, found disarming.

"And the distance from the young lady's house to the point in question?"

Paul calculated; he offered the result in kilometres to Dupuy, adding, "I can't be sure within a few metres, but it takes me about fifteen minutes as a rule. I got held up in some traffic soon after I left the house, and that probably made a difference of three or four minutes."

"And the lorry came sweeping out of the lane?"

"Yes. She bumped badly; she was an old lorry. She didn't carry a number. I remember that because I looked carefully. I was angry, and I thought of reporting her to the police. Afterwards I thought it was very strange, and then I began to wonder if there was something wrong."

"And you didn't notice the drivers at all particularly?"

"Only that it was odd they took no notice of what I said. I didn't mince my words. Afterwards, again,

I thought perhaps they had their reasons, didn't want to be recognised. The driver was a man of medium height, with a black hat pulled well down over his eyes; I really didn't see the other one; there was nothing frightfully noticeable about either."

" If that lorry was turning out of the lane at 10.20 I doubt if there'd be time to look for the diamond," was Dupuy's conclusion when Paul had taken himself off. " I think they drove that lorry to a deserted place, and got on with the job there."

" They may have done anything there," said Latymer in an impersonal voice. " They may have thought it would be inconvenient for the body to be found and recognised at once. There are ways and means . . ."

" If they defaced the corpse to prevent instant identification, they would have to use a weapon of some sort; that increases their danger. Because you must either destroy the weapon afterwards, or be sure to remove every trace of evidence against you, and restore the weapon without any one noticing it has ever gone. Of course, they could dismember it, but that's a long job, and not one it's easy to do in the open."

" But have we evidence that it was done in the open?"

" We know that the body was in a sack; there are not many places in our sophisticated civilisation where a man can carry in a body over his shoulder and proceed to chop it."

" Unless there is a shed in some lonely, deserted place . . ."

" But think of the danger, of the blood. There would be blood everywhere, on the floor, on the man's clothes. Then, too, pits must be dug to conceal the body; that takes time, and they are not always safe.

No, I think we must try to follow up our lorry. It is obviously nothing but speculation at the moment."

Further inquiries were made for a lorry travelling in a specified direction, last heard of at 10.20, with neither number-plate nor lights. Various answers in reply to these came in, many of them quite misleading and not connected with the right lorry at all. The task of getting on its track proved a tedious one. It appeared to have been seen at all points of the compass within a few hours of the murder. For some miles it appeared to have been driven due west; then at midnight it was heard of on the farther side of the town; there were two blank days, and then the police picked up its spoor about eighty miles from the Hotel, travelling towards Marseilles.

That gave Dupuy the direction the lorry had taken, but after that it seemed to vanish into space. No one recalled seeing it; no police had attempted to arrest a lorry without lights. It and its contents and its human freight had simply disappeared.

CHAPTER X

1

In the early hours of the morning of the 8th November, Dr. François Cellier was driving back after a protracted confinement from the house of a peasant in the neighbourhood of F——, some sixty miles from Monte Carlo. It was a chilly damp morning, and he had spent the last nine hours alternating between anxiety and boredom, but eventually he had saved both mother and child. He was wet, tired and wanted a hot drink; it was after three o'clock and he had eighteen miles to go over one of the worst roads in France. This was not a motor-road in any sense of the word, and only a weary provincial doctor with no heart for his car, that indeed looked as if she would fall to pieces at every jolt, would have risked her springs by taking this short cut. The locality, so far as eye could reach through the fine drizzle of rain that didn't seem to have stopped for days, was void of any form of life; three derelict trees stood up starkly against the grim horizon; a deserted wooden hut, a relic of the war years, when the Americans had their rest-camps in the neighbourhood, was the only mark of human habitation you'd get for three miles. Practically no one used this road; even the farm carts shunned it.

" But it saves me that intolerable main road with its lights, that I always forget to notice, and the market carts'll be out already, and last time I got caught up in that block I crawled like a hearse for miles," reflected the exhausted doctor. Faint and shrill as a cockchafer's cry a clock chimed somewhere. Three. " I'll be in bed before four," he thought, " and I won't stir till nine, whatever comes through. All the prospective citizens of France can pass out before they've had a chance to realise the tribulations of this present world for all I shall do to prevent them." A minute later his back axle snapped. At the same time the rain increased in fury, so that within a few minutes it was driving through the unseaworthy hood of the car, and threatened to flood it long before any help could be obtained.

" This would have to happen here," reflected Cellier savagely. " Even if I can bribe any one to send in a car to tow her, we shall both be pulped before it arrives. And I suppose I'm miles from a telephone. I shall probably get pneumonia—and God help all married men with three kids, and nothing saved." Anxiously he scanned the horizon. He was still scanning it when the church clock chimed the quarter.

"I wonder how often I shall hear that before I move on," Cellier muttered, looking through the back window of the car in case Providence was exerting itself on an insignificant doctor's behalf. But there was nothing in sight.

"This may be a damn rotten car, and most people would say it is," Cellier continued, lighting a cigarette. "But it's the only car I've got or am likely to have for a long time yet. And this delightful road will soon be a mudbank, and she'll be hitched up here with the slush drying round her wheels three inches high, and it'll be nearly as cheap to get a new bus as dig her out. Point is, could I shove her as far as that shed—it can't be more than three hundred yards—and shelter us both?" He considered the point critically. He was young and athletic, and, though he was tired, it was not really too much of a strain for youthful muscles. "What's thirty-six?" demanded Cellier, and the answer came back to him, "About half your life, if you don't perish from pleurisy and so forth in this confounded downpour. I suppose I'd better have a shove at it."

The shed stood some thirty yards from the edge of the road, a black derelict affair, with a flapping gate. They said it had been used in the war for stores, but Cellier thought that unlikely. Much more probably it was a shelter for sheep before this part of the world went out of cultivation, before even this rotten road had been cut through the common land. He had passed it often enough, without paying much attention to it; he supposed it might serve as a shelter for tramps if any of them were fool enough to come this way.

Turning up the collar of his coat, and wrapping a shabby mackintosh round his shoulders, he climbed out of the car, and began to ease her along the road towards the shed. It would be a shorter journey to run her straight on to the grass, but he doubted whether he could push her on that uneven surface, though she was light enough as cars go. So he levered her forward steadily for about a quarter of a mile, and then urged her over the edge on to the bumpy common land.

"Poor devil!" he thought resignedly, meaning the car, not himself. "This will probably be the last straw. But I can't afford to have her shored up all to-morrow and perhaps the whole of the week after. Oh, to hell with this rain. I'm drenched already."

As he progressed he noticed that someone had been over this way recently; there were signs of some heavy weight traversing the field; clumps of a wild golden flower had been trodden down, leaving the stems split and the leaves bruised and black.

"No foot would do that, bar a giant's," reflected Cellier. "Perhaps some other chap's been smitten with the notion of using the shed for a temporary garage."

The door of the shed hung an inch or two open as it had done ever since he could remember. It was a long shed, pitch dark, with no window, and no ventilation, except through the door. Cellier pushed the car slowly in, and then crept inside himself, panting, soaked through, feeling for his matches. He stood in the doorway staring at the streaming rain and wondering at the utter desolation of the landscape.

"Good place for a murder," he thought automatically. "No one would see you here, and I doubt if any one would hear even if you shrieked. And that's a jolly thought to start a day like this."

He pitched down his match and instantly a tongue of flame leaped up behind him. He jumped away quickly, but the flame burnt higher.

"Here, dammit, stop that," he exclaimed, stamping at it. To his surprise the flame merely hissed at his sodden trouser-leg, and seemed to gain strength from his efforts. It took him a minute or two to beat it out, and then he wondered what on earth had caused it.

"Let's see, I chucked down the match and fire started, as if I'd pitched it into a pail of paraffin. I suppose it wasn't paraffin? It couldn't have been. But it was something inflammable, all the same. Let's explore a bit." Gingerly he lighted another match, holding it high above his head, but it only threw a small distorted shadow that confused him and did little to illumine the prevailing darkness. Then he remembered that in the car he had a torch; he never went out at night without one. When a man was his own chauffeur that kind of thing came in useful. You never knew when you mightn't have to lie prone and examine the creature's least accessible parts. He found the torch and pressed the button; after a moment he became aware of a gleam on the floor, the soft shine of light on a wet surface.

"Water? Oil? Blood? Heaven knows." He stooped. "No wonder the flame shot up. Turpentine. But who would want turpentine in a place like this? It can't have been there very long, or it would have dried up. Someone taking shelter here, perhaps." That might be a plausible explanation, but a man seeking cover from the rain need not bring his equipage with him, and anyway, why spill turpentine inside an empty shed? The beam of the electric torch enlarging the range of his vision, he now saw that the shed was not completely empty. At the far end, no more than vague shapes, was a number of sacks.

"Wonder how long they've been there," he thought. In no investigating spirit, but as a matter of idle curiosity, he strolled across the shed and laid his hand on the nearest.

"Straw, I should say. Did the man who brought the turps here bring the straw too? What on earth's the idea? You don't, outside a lunatic asylum, mix the two." He opened one of the sacks, that was dry and crisp, and found it stuffed with straw to the mouth.

"And it hasn't been here long, either, or it would be mouldy. There's nothing damp-proof about this old barn. But if a man simply wanted to protect his sacks from the rain, why lug them to the very end of the shed? And why leave them here anyway? You don't generally buy half a dozen sacks of straw and decant them, and then apparently forget all about them." The idea of arson went through his mind, but he dismissed that. The shed wasn't worth a brass half-penny, and for years, as everyone knew, it had stood there, ownerless and undesired. Then a far more sinister idea occurred to him.

"Suppose the turps and the straw are here together for a specific purpose? Suppose someone means to burn the shed, and burn something else with it?"

For some time it seemed to him he might have struck the right solution. A student of human nature and of detail in animal processes, he didn't believe in the haphazard mingling of ingredients to no purpose. He remembered a story he had once read, a book by an English writer (being himself a Frenchman he could not, of course, make the very important dis-crimination between English and Scots authors). Two characters had been discussing the art of the detective novel. "They are too easy," said the first. "It's simply that the author writes the story inductively, and the reader follows it deductively. If you want to write a story of this kind you begin by fixing on one or two facts which have no sort of obvious connection. Imagine anything you like. I may take three things a long way apart. Say, an old blind woman spinning in the Western Highlands, a barn in a Norwegian sæter, and a little curiosity shop in North London kept by a Jew with a dyed beard. Not much connection between the three? You invent a connection—simple enough if you have any imagination—and weave all three into the yarn. The reader, who knows nothing about the three at the start, is puzzled and intrigued, and, if the story is well arranged, finally satisfied. He is pleased with the ingenuity of the solution, for he doesn't realise that the author fixed upon the solution first, and then invented a problem to suit it."*

"But it's equally true in reality," argued Cellier. "Whoever put the turpentine and straw here knows the reason, that is the solution. I'm the reader, trying to discover what it is. Well, suppose my last idea was right? Something's going to be brought here to be destroyed? But is there enough straw? And that little pond of turps isn't going to be much good. It's the turpentine that troubles me. There isn't enough of it. Or else there's too much. A drop like that isn't going to start a fire; and if there isn't going to be a fire, why is there any turps here at all?"

And then he thought, "I might as well make sure there's straw in all the other sacks. There's something very odd about this."

The first sack and the second were full of straw and so was the third. But the fourth, that was concealed by the barrier made by the first three, clearly contained something quite different. Its shape was peculiar, as if some hard substance had been thrust

* *The Three Hostages* by John Buchan.

129

out of sight behind the brown canvas. For a minute the doctor thought it was stolen silver, and then he realised, from the appalling stench that seemed suddenly to flood the whole hut, what it was. It was amazing that he hadn't detected it immediately; he could only suppose that a slight cold, his drenched condition, and the fact that he was smoking strong tobacco, had combined to distract him. No thought of waiting for the intervention of the police passed through his mind; he pulled the sack forward, realising as he did so that its contents had been there for some days at least. There was a thick cord knotted round the mouth of the sack, and this he cut with his pocket-knife. The edges of the sack instantly fell apart, revealing a head to which a good deal of dark hair clung. The weather had been oppressive during these latter days of rain, and the work of decomposition had made some headway, but it would be possible to recognise the man by his features, and the false teeth he still retained would provide an additional clue. A pair of tortoiseshell rimmed glasses fell out on the floor, but Cellier paid no heed. With his knife he ripped up the rest of the sack, and a minute or two later he saw the whole man lying before him. Even then it didn't occur to him what his find must mean.

In these grim circumstances his professional sense came to his aid. He decided that his victim was a man in later middle-life, probably sixty or sixty-two; he was slightly below average height, was well-dressed in evening clothes, of which the collar and tie were torn open, as if some struggle had taken place before death. He was clean-shaved, dark, an elegant figure of a man in life. There were slight marks of bruising round the throat, but certainly not enough to have caused death. On the finger of one hand was a remarkable ruby ring. One of the waistcoat buttons had been forced into its wrong hole, so that the waistcoat looked shapeless. Rather sick, Cellier bent over the head. "Someone bashed him all right," he reflected grimly. "I wonder if that's how he died." Then he turned the body over and knew that the blow had only been a preliminary. For there was a deep knife-thrust between the shoulders, and the weapon was still in the wound. It was a long, thin knife, as Cellier knew from its appearance, though he didn't attempt to remove it; the haft was made of black wood. It was the kind of knife that can be bought for a few francs at dozens of shops in every town in France.

2

The rain ceased abruptly at five a.m. For almost two hours Dr. Cellier had been alone with his dreadful companion, wondering what on earth was his next step. Clearly he could not move the car; yet he was anxious not to leave the body unguarded. The man had certainly been murdered; probably the body had been here for some days, so there was little likelihood of the criminals returning to the spot. All the same, Cellier felt responsible. He wondered how long it would be before any one passed whom he could hail. Laboriously he pushed the car out of the shed, shut the door and scanned the road. There wasn't a soul in sight. Eventually he decided to leave the car blocking up the entrance—the police could move her when they arrived—and trudged back to the road. After walking a mile and a half he came upon a telephone and rang up the police.

"My name's Cellier," he said. "I'm speaking from a road telephone box. I've found the body of a dead man in a shed on X—— Common. I should say he's been dead some days." He described the position in some detail. "I've been up all night myself," he added, "and my car's smashed up, a broken axle. Do I wait for the police to arrive?"

He was told that he did; they'd want a statement. "I want my breakfast," said Cellier, reaction taking the form of extreme irritability. "After all, this dead bird's nothing to me."

He next rang up a garage and explained his position; then wondered if he'd been precipitate. Because the police could give him a lift back, and probably they wouldn't want strangers falling all over the corpse and fouling any clues he himself hadn't obliterated. The garage said tepidly they'd send a man as soon as they could, and Cellier told himself, as he faced the return journey, that he could say good-bye to his breakfast. He'd be lucky if he got any lunch.

He was, however, overtaken by the police before he reached the shed, and told his story as he was driven back. The sergeant in charge looked at the body, snapped his note-book shut, and said in a calm voice, belied by the blazing excitement of his eyes, "This had better wait for M. Dupuy."

"Is he another policeman?" asked Cellier patiently. The exhausting ache for food had subsided now in a gnawing feeling to which he would soon grow accustomed.

"He's the inspector in charge of the Marks case, monsieur."

"Good heavens! And you think this is the man? Well, why not, after all? What could be fairer? What about the diamond, though?"

The sergeant said they had better await Dupuy's arrival; he asked Cellier to take the police car and drive back to the telephone; he himself wouldn't leave the body. His weariness forgotten, genuinely moved by this chance participation in a mystery that had thrilled and perplexed the public of two countries, Cellier went back as requested.

"What compensation do I get from a grateful civic authority?" he asked the police, who grinned. "Oh, it's no laughing matter, I assure you. I've got a wife and three children to support and this is making hay of my day's work." But he wasn't seriously aggrieved, and he lighted a cigarette, offered one to the sergeant, and persuaded him to talk about the Marks case.

"We must pass the time somehow," he urged. "I don't know whether your lords of the Sureté are immune from the laws of the road, but the average driver couldn't do it under an hour or more."

"In a case that has dragged on so long the circumstances aren't likely to be affected by an extra hour or so's delay," was the dry retort.

"You aren't forgetting that I'm a professional man, who's paid on time?"

"Your car has broken down," was the sergeant's serene reply.

"Yes, confound her. I'm waiting for the garage to send a man to tow me. Or perhaps your estimable M. Dupuy will do that for me, seeing how much inconvenience I'm enduring for his sake."

So Cellier sat and smoked and stood about in the sodden mud outside the hut, saying he had had enough of stenches for a twelvemonth, until the arrival of Dupuy in a high-powered, dark-blue car. He came across the common, a small, forceful figure, his head bent forward, his steps light and firm. Cellier received the impression of tremendous nervous strength; the detective's glance was keen and penetrating, his manner cool. He looked once at the body lying on its torn sack, and then asked Cellier for his story.

He nodded persistently as the doctor added detail

to detail, then asked, "And you have examined the body?"

"Not thoroughly. As soon as I realised it was a case of murder I thought it was a job for the police surgeon."

"Whom I have brought with me." Dupuy beckoned to his companion. The police surgeon was a tall, stout man, with a good deal of dark hair on his face; his report was the same as that Cellier had already made. The deceased had died of a knife-thrust in the back, following a heavy blow that had fractured the bone without breaking the skin. He had been dead six or seven days.

"Was the blow powerful enough to kill him?" Dupuy asked.

"In my opinion, no."

"But it might have stunned him."

"Certainly it would have stunned him."

"Then probably he was killed before he recovered consciousness."

"There is nothing against such a notion, though again there is nothing to prove it. That open collar and tie are puzzling. It looks as though they might have been torn off in a struggle, but if I were reconstructing the case I should say that the stab followed quite soon after the blow."

"And I should agree," said Cellier promptly, to whom Dupuy had silently turned.

"And there is the question of time," the detective contributed. "There was clearly not an instant to spare. I think he was stunned, stabbed, carried away, thrust into the sack all in a few moments. You would not expect a great deal of loss of blood with such a wound?"

"So long as the knife was not removed there would be scarcely any effusion of blood at all. I see that the sack is stained; possibly the floor of the vehicle, a lorry, I believe it is, would show similar evidence."

"That, you may be sure, will not remain to assist us."

He then began to examine the hut in great detail, while Cellier remained unobtrusively where he was, making no sound lest he be curtly dismissed from the scene. In the middle of the floor lay the grotesquely crumpled body, stiff, like clay baked in an infamous shape; the doctor was not more sensitive than most men of his profession, to whom death early becomes a commonplace, but even he was a little shocked at the ease with which all three men disregarded that travesty of humanity sprawled in their midst.

"I am wondering if an effort was made to throttle the man before he was struck," said the police surgeon presently, but Dupuy said sharply, "No, no. That would be taking an unjustifiable risk. And this criminal is far-sighted; he did not work haphazard. M. Marks' death was not the first of a series of incidents; many had preceded it. He would not give the man an opportunity to scream, to utter a sound of warning; he would leap on him from the dark and strike at once. No, no, I agree, I do not understand, but then," he wound up magnificently, "I understand so little as yet. And now, monsieur," he turned to Cellier, "you have handled the knife?"

"No, not consciously. It is important?"

"For prints, though so shrewd a murderer will have remembered that point. The detective writers," he added gloomily, "have made crime more difficult for the police; every story they issue is a warning against the blunders that criminals perpetrate. It is not good citizenship. . . ."

The police surgeon, Lemaitre, threw up his hands. "What would you, monsieur l'inspecteur? It is their bread-and-butter. To be a good citizen—oh, it is a fine thought, but it is an abstraction. But the stomach, he is always with you."

There were not many marks likely to help the police on the clothes of the dead man. Dust was there, a fine reddish dust, particularly noticeable on the knees; and there was more dust and some earth under the finger-nails. There were also traces of a whitish dust that perplexed them until Dupuy exclaimed, " Of course, the sack. Now for what was that used before it became the unhappy man's shroud?" He carefully shook out the corners, and more of the whitish dust scattered on the floor.

" Flour," said the sergeant triumphantly.

" That is clear," Dupuy snubbed him mercilessly. " Now for the remainder. The dust is from the ground of the hotel, the earth in the nails . . ."

" The stone, monsieur l'inspecteur," exclaimed the sergeant. " He had, you will remember, moved the large stone with which he deceived the party."

" And now for the contents of the pockets," continued Dupuy, who seemed unwilling to allow the sergeant any credit in this affair. " Will they prove of assistance?"

Beyond the fact that they established beyond all doubt the identity of the dead man, the contents of the pockets were disappointing. There were two or three letters, none of which threw any light on the tragedy, an empty envelope bearing a Californian stamp, a pair of long nail-scissors, the blades a little stained, a handkerchief, some knots of string, a platinum cigarette case, a gold propelling pencil, some notes and coins worth about six pounds sterling, a pocket calendar and some stamps. Dupuy swept this heterogenous collection together, saying decisively,

"These can be dealt with later; there is nothing here that concerns us now. The body has told me many things, confirmed my suspicions, given me a new opening on to the crime. And that, you will agree, is much." He smiled suddenly at Cellier, as though to include him at last in the scene, but the doctor looked back at him, weary and bewildered. Now it didn't seem to him to matter who had killed Marks or why. Men who lived such lives existed outside his sphere and he wanted desperately to be back in familiar surroundings. He was tired of mystery and policemen and their fussy, self-important ways. "I'm glad," he told Dupuy heavily. "I confess it didn't convey any of that to me, but then I'm not a professional."

"Ah, but consider." Dupuy leaned towards him, eager and instructive. "Now, what was it that attracted your attention? The pool of turpentine that you discovered by an accident. Now why, arson apart, that seems unreasonable here, should there be turpentine in a shed that no one uses? You cannot think? Then I will tell you. See here, monsieur." He moved a little farther up the shed and drew the doctor's attention to a patch, dark and sticky, near the base of one wall.

"Blood?" asked Cellier in astonishment. But Dupuy shook his head.

"Smell, monsieur. Paint. You see. No? Then perhaps you have not heard that, when one wishes to paint a thing that will dry quickly, one adds turpentine to the paint. This thins it out, and it dries within a very few hours. Of course it spoils the quality of the paint; it does not dry glossy and even, but patchy, dark green in one place, and a much lighter green elsewhere. But it serves. A man seeing a lorry, for instance, thus painted, pass him on the road, will notice nothing but that the surface is new, is shining.

The fact that the paint stares, as you would say of a dog's coat, will probably escape him, unless he is a professional himself. Now this paint is a dark one, so that most probably what we must find is a dark-green lorry. Of course, there is the possibility of its being repainted to confuse us further, but I think the murderer did not expect us to learn of the repainting, and will remain satisfied with the single operation. And now, when was this work done?"

Cellier said, "It's been raining pretty well without a break for the past week. But none of these sacks is damp, and the straw isn't mouldy. If it had got wet through it would be bound to have deteriorated; this place is like a vault in itself."

Dupuy straightened himself, dusted his hands and turned to his attentive audience, with all the ardour and perception of a professor about to address an appreciative class. "Let us figure this out together. They have killed the man, they have the body in the sack, it is late at night and at any moment the hue and cry may be raised. They have very little time; they must act with despatch and courage. Two alternatives are theirs. One to abandon the lorry somewhere, in which case it must be traced at last; or two, to stop at some filling station for more petrol. A lorry of three tons, which is how Paul describes it, though it seems a very large lorry for the task, will run perhaps fourteen or fifteen miles to a gallon of petrol, and such a lorry can carry about twelve gallons."

"And how do you find that out?" demanded Cellier.

Dupuy flung up his hands in an extravagant gesture. Probably the dead man was no better actor than the astute little inspector, when occasion demanded. "We observe, monsieur; we keep our ears open and our mouths shut; we have thousands of eyes, thousands, monsieur. At every corner, in every station, in auto-

138

mobiles, in trains, on tram-cars, we have our representatives. Presently we shall find the first straw to
point the direction, and as we proceed we shall find
others. That is how criminal cases are built up, atom
by atom."

The sergeant, who was listening impatiently, now
leaned forward and cried in urgent tones, " But the
diamond, monsieur l'inspecteur, the diamond. What
of that?"

Dupuy stared at him. " Well, where did you expect
to find it? On the body? Or do you think that men
commit murder as an after-dinner game for no better
reason than to perfect themselves in the art? This
murder, my good Perichet, was committed because M.
Marks owned a diamond that another man or many
men desired. As for where it is now . . ." he shrugged
his shoulders, stooped and jerked into full view the
dangling end of a cut steel chain.

" You see," he told them, smiling, " is was not so
very strong after all."

CHAPTER XI

1

Dupuy was discussing this latest development with
Latymer. " And now," he said briskly, " let us see
what we have learned up to the present. As to the
driver—not very much, perhaps, but this: He was
accustomed to driving, though not necessarily so large
a vehicle, or he could not have manipulated the lorry
over that heavy ground or in the narrow lane. We
need not say he is a professional, but we can say he
must be skilful and experienced. The ground on that

night was hard, for there had been little rain up till then; also the lorry must have been driven into the shed, but the door was not damaged; there is no new splintering there."

"Didn't Paul say he drove the lorry as though he weren't altogether familiar with it, even though he had it under control? For I gather the danger of his driving lay in the fact that he was reckless, not that he was inefficient."

"I think that is right. You see the same thing in horsemen sometimes; they are good riders, but when they have an unfamiliar beast between their knees they are not quite easy in their seat. Now, still following up our driver, I have here a number of replies to our inquiries as to second-hand lorries bought recently; in most cases we have traced the owners, and know they cannot be implicated. But there are one or two still." He frowned. " There is a man called Rodolphe. He has sold a lorry to a man we cannot find. The address is an accommodation one, and the lorry was driven off as soon as the bargain was made. The buyer, whose name is not known, claimed to have an whole-sale rubbish business. That is, he collects quantities of old tins, packing-cases, old iron, etc., and delivers these to a factory that can make use of such mer-chandise. He is paid by both sides, by the first to remove the rubbish and by the second for whatever value it may have. Now there are a number of men following this profession, and we cannot trace the lorry-buyer as identical with any of them."

" He may only have just started in business," Latymer suggested.

"You might expect him to come forward, if he is innocent, but, though he can scarcely have failed to see our appeals, he remains obstinately hidden."

" There's one other solution," suggested Latymer,

a little diffidently. " The gentleman may not exist anywhere but in M. Rodolphe's imagination."

" I had thought of that," Dupuy acknowledged.
" But what motive would Rodolphe have? He might
be mad, certainly, and wish to attract notoriety, or he
might be implicated in the crime. We can provide
ourselves with no evidence as to the first, and we have
complete alibis as to the second. Moreover, there is
the ledger entry. The whole affair of the sale seems
clear enough. I think myself we should continue to
seek for this man. Even if he has no connection with
the crime we should at all events have solved the
mystery of that lorry; it would be one avenue definitely
closed; and when you have eliminated all other possi-
bilities, as your greatest of English detectives has
observed, what remains, however improbable, must be
the truth."*

" And you will spend countless hours examining
lorries that have nothing to do with the crime,"
Latymer said, and sighed.

Dupuy looked at him in some surprise. " Is it your
experience that things are so simple that one loses no
time in wild goose chases?" he asked in dry tones.

But Latymer refused to be snubbed. " The public's
so unintelligent in matters of this kind," he said, " and
enthusiasm isn't a good makeweight for discrimina-
tion."

" Nevertheless, I favour publicity," returned Dupuy
with a great air of decision. " I grant you that
numbers of people have apparently no faculty for
observation; but there are the few who are different,
and they are the men and women who will assist us to
clear up this mystery. You know the kind, their
apparent irrelevance—a man selling flowers, a woman
walking her dog—it will be someone like this who will

* Sherlock Holmes.

141

provide the coup d'état. Women in particular are useful in criminal cases; they have a genius for details that men regard as insignificant. It's no question of training, it's an instinct, like road-sense, something you cannot explain, a kind of gift from on high. Women will notice some trifle about another woman, the width of her wedding-ring, her jewels, the way her clothes are made or her hair done, whether she's made up a lot, the shade of the paint she puts on her lips, the quality of her shoes and stockings, an unusual kind of handbag, all things that men take for granted and don't, unless they are specially trained, recall. For instance, if that lorry driver had drawn up and asked a woman his direction, she could tell us a good deal about his personal appearance, whether he were clean-shaved, the kind of manners he had, whether he was shabby or neatly dressed, the kind of stratum of society from which he came—women are very quick on such points as these—even the colour of his eyes, and certainly the colour of his hair."

"Allowing that a lorry-driver would be likely to pull up and ask a lady the way."

"We must allow for all manner of improbabilities, monsieur."

"And you are not afraid of putting the criminal completely on his guard?"

"But that is our winning card," cried Dupuy in astonishment. "So soon as our murderer knows that we have learned of the painting of the lorry then it will be obvious that he must abandon it at once. It will be a cynosure for all eyes. He will be afraid to drive through any large town, for everyone will be looking for a newly-painted green lorry, with a patchy appearance. He will not dare try to sell it (unless, of course, he has done so already, in which case we should immediately hear from the purchaser, for all dealers will have to be warned that the police want it); so he must abandon it, and he must abandon it with secrecy. And that, monsieur, is less easy than perhaps it may seem to you. It is possible to put a lorry in a garage, but that involves speaking to the proprietor, possibly to an assistant, answering questions—all possible clues if you are a criminal. You can't leave a lorry by the roadside as if it were a car. You have to show perpetual ingenuity, and all the time you know that the whole of the public is watching out for you. That is why I say that is the strongest card in our hand."

Latymer still looked puzzled and stubborn. "You seriously mean that you believe we serve our interests best by warning our man that we're waiting for him."

"But surely that is common sense. If you are being watched, that will be an added strain to your nerves. You are more likely to betray yourself through over-caution. You have noticed, I dare say, how frequently criminals are arrested because they are so anxious to obviate every risk. If a man does not know he is being followed he will take more risks, and very possibly defeat us in the end. No, no, monsieur, my mind is resolved. We will tell everyone about the lorry."

2

It was Dupuy's habit, when he was perplexed as at present, to get as far from crowds as possible and turn over in his mind the various points he had made, in an attempt to co-ordinate them into an intelligible whole. He worked best, he found, out of doors and alone and he always returned from these solitary excursions with a fresh zest for companionship and the sharpening of his mind against another's. But those delicate processes leading from intuition to deduction, they must be followed up in silence. He concentrated

now on the criminal's opportunities of disposing of
the lorry. Apart from selling it, there were other possi-
bilities. He might have taken a risk and left it in a
yard or garage, but, if he were as intelligent as Dupuy
supposed him to be, he would realise there are other
more anonymous ways of ridding himself of the incriminating object. He recalled a case some years
earlier, where a man had quietly left his lorry along-
side three others working on a down, where chalk was
being quarried; this had been late on Saturday night,
and Monday being a drenching day, the additional
lorry was not discovered until the next morning, by
which time the criminal had left the country. And
there was a second case that came into his mind, where
a man had attended a market day in a country town,
driving up in a lorry that he parked just outside the
ground, remarking to a neighbour that he hoped to
take a fine young calf back in it. That comment
proved his undoing; for though the criminal had provided himself with a quantity of mesh netting, the
other was too good a farmer not to realise that it was
by no means strong enough to hold out against the
alarmed creature's frantic plunges and rushes.

"If anyone had found a derelict lorry you might
expect him to come forward," he murmured. "I'm
inclined to fancy the man sold it as soon as the paint
was dry. So many questions get asked about a lorry
that's left ownerless. By this time a garage proprietor
would have informed the police, in case the vehicle
was the one we're after. Besides, X knows we're looking for a lorry; he won't do anything conspicuous. He
would not suppose that we should know he had repainted the lorry; that was chance, hazard, what M.
Latymer would, I suppose, call an act of God. Therefore he will sell it in a place where he is not known;
he will sell it in a false name, with, I think, a false

history. Now we must tell the public all we know and wait for results."

He did not have to wait long. Within a few hours of the publication in the papers of the sensational story, a garage proprietor communicated with the police, saying that on the 3rd November he had repaired a lorry answering to the description given, so far as this was available, whose exhaust was defective. The owner of the lorry had been a little indignant, saying that he had only just bought her, and it was hard he should have to pay repair charges so soon. "But," he had added, "I might have suspected something of this kind. A man who paints his lorry in such a hurry wants to get rid of it; I should have been more careful, but the price was reasonable, and I needed the lorry." The proprietor stated that he did not know the man in question, whom he described as being small, stout, dark-skinned, with a quantity of rough reddish hair. Before the police could start inquiries for this person, the man himself turned up, "a tennis ball on two vestas," with rough, sandy hair and a voluble manner. He gave his name as Pierre Simon, and said he was the present owner of the lorry that he had brought with him. He invited Dupuy to come and examine it. Dupuy approached with some eagerness. He did not suppose that the murderers would have been foolish enough to leave anything behind that would help him; nevertheless, for the first time he felt he was really on their track. An unjustifiable view, of course, but he felt his spirits rising and, being a man of exalted temperament whenever the luck seemed to turn in his direction, he placed an unwarranted reliance on this easy discovery of the lorry. Almost, his thoughts ran, we have them. We have their corpse, we have their lorry; soon we shall have their description. And, before he had finished his examination, he had something else, too; a pearl stud from an evening-shirt that had rolled into the right angle formed by two of the sides and had slipped down into a crack.

" This may be chance," he said with some excitement to Latymer, who accompanied him, gaunt, silent, preoccupied, from stage to stage of the case. " This may have been here for some time. And yet—is it likely? Is it even probable? Since when have lorry-drivers worn pearl studs in their clothes? No, no, this is a trace left by the criminal. It follows, then, that he was in evening dress. Well, that is not impossible. He may have covered it over with a coat, concealed everything with a great scarf. That is guess-work. But it does help us. It shows that we are up against a certain type of thief; this is no work of the Apaches, in spite of the absurd rumours to that effect in the papers. This man may have actually been talking to Marks, have beguiled him to that place where he was set upon. There were many people in the hotel that night who were not playing this ridiculous English game. We must make inquiries as to them. Presumably the proprietor will have a record of their names. And we have to bear in mind that story of Messieurs Jekyll and Hyde. A most respectable person may turn out to be the thief; a priceless diamond is very tantalising. Now, is it too late for us to find out if a pearl stud was missed by any gentleman? It will be a discreet work. We must send men to the homes of all those who might be involved, to question valets, parlourmaids, anyone who would be likely to notice. Or perhaps Potain himself has received inquiries. And now for the rest of the lorry."

This, in fact, revealed very little; there were no bloodmarks, but the floor had been vigorously scrubbed, and it seemed to Dupuy it might be possible to establish the fact that blood had been spilt there. It would have to be a recent stain, as otherwise it would have resisted all efforts to dislodge it. Dupuy next asked for a detailed description of the man who sold the lorry.

Simon said, " He was a stranger, monsieur, much like another. He had no scar, no strange manner. We were at H——, a town where I go sometimes for the market. I was, in fact, wanting just such a lorry if I could get one at not too high a price. I have a little removal business, and I am branching out. Often I have orders I cannot fulfil, and I thought if I had a second lorry I would hire a man to drive. I saw a number of second-hand lorries at a dealers at H——. on the 1st November, and I went in to ask if he had one that would suit me. But unfortunately he had not. I was just going away when a man touched my arm and said, ' I've got a lorry outside, I was going to see what I could get for it. I've had to go out of business, times are so bad, and I've got a job as driver to another man, who doesn't want my lorry. I've painted her up a bit to make her look fresh, and you'll find she's a good worker.' I inspected the lorry, monsieur, that was painted a brightish green, and it seemed all right; the tyres were good, and the price was moderate. The man who sold it to me said he knew he was not getting the value of her, but he had to pay for her garaging each week, and he had some small children and high expenses; he would rather get something down and be rid of the expense. I paid him what he asked, and drove the lorry away. It seemed all right at first—we did not drive it very far, but at the end of the first day's work my employee came to say that the exhaust was unsatisfactory, and he thought the lorry should be overhauled. I examined her, and agreed with him;

I did not then think the price so moderate, though I still thought I had done quite a good bargain."

" And the appearance of the man? Did you notice him particularly?"

" He was a man like another," repeated Simon. " A Frenchman who knew Paris. He spoke of the city, of the position there; he knew streets and businesses and the names of manufacturers. I have lived in Paris myself at one time, and I should notice any mistake. He was brownish, a little thin in the throat, perhaps, he wore a brown moustache; and—there was one other thing, monsieur, though I did not think much of it at the time. His hands. He had spoken of being a mechanic and driver, but you know their hands, monsieur, they are out in all weathers, they are working hard, they become roughened and tanned and calloused; the nails, too, are often deformed. Now this man had not hands like that. The nails were not very clean, but they were not broken; his hand had not the hardness one might expect. I recall saying to the dealer who witnessed our bargain that I was not surprised he found it difficult to get work, a man who was shy of his wheel. No, I thought little about it. So many men think they will win easy bread by driving a machine; they don't know how early you must be up getting orders, cutting prices, being in the field before anyone else."

Dupuy nodded. " That is very helpful, monsieur. Now, you are sure of the story he told you. He had work with another driver, he had been using the lorry for removals?"

" That is right, monsieur."

" And the dealer who saw him, perhaps he could help? You will give me his name and address? And I am grateful. You we need not detain, monsieur, but we must keep your lorry. Oh, be assured you shall be fully compensated. But it will be necessary to see if this lorry can be traced to a particular buyer."

Simon nodded eagerly. "I understand, of course. Then," curiosity overcame his discretion, "you believe it to be a fact, monsieur, that the body was actually carried in that to the shed?"

Dupuy's brilliant smile flashed out. "How can I tell you, monsieur? Why, I may not even tell the press, who would give me a picture in the paper, and perhaps something in addition, for the news. But wait a little." He nodded confidentially. In his own mind he had very little doubt. This lorry had clearly been painted in a hurry, there were little splashes of brightish-green on the wheels, there was a scratch on one side where the lorry had run against something. And the colour was precisely the same shade as the patch found on the floor of the shed.

The dealer who had spoken earlier of selling a second-hand lorry to a man who wanted to cart old tin for a profit identified the vehicle at once. He said he knew the exhaust was not very satsifactory, but the lorry was not of a recent manufacture and he had sold it very cheap. It would not be necessary for such a cargo to have a very expensive or high-powered machine. Asked about the buyer, he could recall little; he had been a bit shabby, and he (Rodolphe) had been glad to see the appearance of the notes. He had for some minutes been afraid his client was going to suggest some instalment plan, and that, he said, I never have believed in. Besides, with a lorry—it would be absurd.

Dupuy agreed a little absently that it would. He knew the rest of the story, that the address had been a false one, and that nothing more had been heard of the buyer. "And that in itself," persisted the amiable dealer, "is unnatural. A man comes round to complain at all events when he finds something he has bought is not perfect. But this man never returns. It is strange."

"It's criminal," Dupuy pointed out, and asked for a description of the man. But this the dealer could not supply. He said he had a good many men in and out and it was impossible to notice anything but outstanding peculiarities, and this man, so far as he could recall, had none.

CHAPTER XII

THERE being as yet no likelihood of tracing the purchaser of the lorry, Dupuy left that matter in the hands of his colleagues and returned to Paris, whither Salomon had preceded him by some days. The jeweller still looked haunted and nervous; when Dupuy was announced he jumped to his feet, the quick colour flaring into his face.

"Monsieur?" He kept his hands pressed to the table and did not advance to meet his visitor.

"There is a little discrepancy—a little matter about which I must speak to you," said Dupuy.

"In connection with this murder? Monsieur, why will you try to confuse me with Marks' death? I tell you, I never saw the man. That night . . ."

"You have explained how you spent that night, I know." Dupuy's voice was leisurely, too leisurely for derision, nevertheless the remark stung.

"And you—you have made my name a byword, I dare say, with your inquiries and your investigations, and my photograph shown to every woman of the type in a ten-mile radius?"

"He's not very clever, if he's guilty," thought Dupuy. "For a hundred francs or so he could easily have found a woman who'd have supported his alibi. Or is he more afraid of Madame Salomon even than of the police?"

"You come to me when I am half-frantic," Salomon continued. "You above all men know my difficulties, though doubtless by this time all Paris knows of them too. You hope to entrap me, to make me contradict myself. I tell you, I know nothing of Marks' death. I am the last man to wish him dead. What use is his diamond to me when he is dead?"

"Well, diamonds don't lose their value when their owners die," murmured Dupuy reasonably. "They're not like race-horses."

"And it would not lose much value if it lost no more than the man himself was worth," Salomon exclaimed. "He was harder than any stone. He would cut and run from any ship if so much as a teacupful of water splashed over the side. I know. I have dealt with him before. Of course, nothing I can tell you of our relations will be new to you," he added, with a hideous forced courtesy. "You have been nosing into my affairs ever since our first meeting. You are aware how precarious is my position; I have a business, a wife, children to support, liabilities, a position; I have Steinbaum pressing me every instant till I feel I shall go mad. So, of course, what a fine motive I have to commit a murder, so fine that everyone will remark on it—too fine, monsieur, too fine. It would be asking to be arrested to kill M. Marks, a man in my state."

"There is another thing I would wish to ask you. This lady who should be your alibi—you had not an appointment with her?"

"I have explained that I had not."

"You had not intended to spend the night away from your hotel?"

"The thought never passed through my mind till I left the casino; then the emptiness, the lonely hotel where I knew no one, the suspense . . ."

"I see. I have a reason for asking."

"I think I can guess that, monsieur," cried the tormented man. His voice was very bitter.

"Not to harry you, as you suppose; no, no. But there is a custom in your hotel for a guest to hand in the key of his room as he leaves the premises, and to reclaim it on his return."

"Well, what then?" The sullen glare of the hunted man's eyes betrayed something of what he was suffering.

"You did not leave your key at the desk when you went out?"

"And if I did not?"

"It might occur to some people that you had a reason, that you did not wish anyone to notice the hour of your return."

"The world is full of suspicious people, it appears. Why should I wish to do that?"

"Ask your suspicious people. I think they might know."

"Ah, it is clear enough what you mean. But it is preposterous, this idea of yours, that I know anything of Marks' death. He was my only hope. I could have tided over . . ."

"Always supposing the deal had gone through. But we've had all that out before. And now . . ."

"There is nothing more to be said," cried the harassed man. "Nothing. I have told you all I know. I have no secrets left; you have pried into every scrap of my life. . . ."

Dupuy paid no heed to this semi-hysterical outburst.

"Not quite, M. Salomon. I believe it is true you wear studs like this in your evening shirt?" He opened his hand and showed the pearl he had found in the corner of the lorry. The jeweller put out his hand to take it up, but Dupuy shifted very slightly.

"It is an ordinary pearl stud, monsieur."

"So I perceive. But again—I do not understand. What is this new story you are trying to tell me?"

"It is all part of the one story. Do you wear studs like these, M. Salomon?"

"Possibly. But so do thousands of other men."

"Oh, I do not question that. But perhaps you would permit me to see yours. No, don't trouble to fetch them yourself. Your servant . . ."

"Do you think I keep my things about loose? I'm an orderly man, let me tell you, and I know the value of things. Only I have the key." He produced a bunch from his pocket and flourished them aggressively.

"You will let me accompany you upstairs?"

"As you will. I can scarcely prevent you," he added sourly.

They went up to Salomon's dressing-room, a well-furnished apartment on the second floor. A long drawing-room and a small boudoir occupied the long narrow space of the floor below. Salomon opened a little box with hands that were not quite steady.

"Oh, it wasn't locked after all," commented Dupuy pleasantly.

Salomon made no reply to the jibe. But, "These are my studs, monsieur," he explained, turning them out on to a table. "They are very similar, I own."

"They are identical," said Dupuy.

"But none is missing. You had observed that, I hope."

Dupuy picked up the studs and examined them carefully. Then he took a glass from his pocket and looked again, laying each stud in turn on the palm of his hand. Presently he looked up.

" I observe something else. One of these has very recently been replaced."

" Yes, indeed. I lost the head. It is an easy thing to do."

" You can recall when this happened?"

" Not precisely. Within three months, shall we say?"

" I think we should say a little more exactly than that. Your jeweller, who supplied you with the new pearl, he has a record, of course."

" I hardly think, monsieur, that a man makes a note of every small repair or replacement that comes his way."

" But he would remember you."

" I do not follow that argument."

" You will have bought other goods from him—perhaps these very studs."

" You misunderstand me, monsieur. I did not go to any particular jeweller for these. The studs are not of great value, it is not difficult to replace a single pearl. . . ."

" And you have often had to replace them, perhaps?"

" No. I believe this was the first time."

" But you cannot remember exactly when it happened?"

" Not absolutely."

" Nor where it took place?"

" Oh, it was after some party. I go out a great deal; and I do not always wear the same studs. Perhaps I left these in my shirt and my wife removed them and she might not remember to tell me for some days, or until I next wished to wear the studs, and then I would find out for myself."

"Then perhaps she would remember?"

"I do not think she does, monsieur. She has never spoken to me of this. And I did not speak to her, for women think men extravagant, luxurious. She would say, 'The pearl must wait; you have other studs.'"

"But it was in Paris that the pearl was replaced?"

"Oh, certainly."

"And you did not take the stud to the jeweller yourself, perhaps?"

"I took it myself, I remember. A servant may be careless. I wished to get as good a match as possible."

"Quite so, monsieur. And you have no notion whatsoever of the name of the jeweller, or of the date?"

"There are so many jewellers in Paris."

"There are, of course. That makes it more difficult to trace. But perhaps you returned to the shop where the studs were originally bought."

"They were a present, monsieur. That's why I can't tell you where they came from."

"A jeweller's name is normally in the case."

"I keep them in a little box. I don't recall that I ever had them in a case."

"They are good pearls," murmured Dupuy. "Such pearls as these should be returned to the makers, to ensure a good match."

"I have told you I don't know the makers."

"That was unfortunate. You keep accounts, monsieur?"

"Some accounts."

"You could verify the date of the purchase?"

"I'm sure I couldn't. I am a busy man." His face was livid with fear. He went on hurriedly, "But if you ask any jeweller of repute in Paris, he will tell you that he is constantly repairing studs like these. How can he remember one man . . .?"

Dupuy was still staring at the studs and frowning. "I am afraid he was not a very good jeweller," he said. "This is not a good match."

"It was doubtless the best that he could do."

"You wanted it in a hurry, perhaps?"

"I dare say I did. I haven't any other pearl studs."

"But you have other studs, monsieur. Why, only a moment ago you were saying that sometimes you do not use these studs for weeks at a stretch."

"I suppose I wanted the pearls particularly that night. I can't remember these trifles. No doubt I had some good reason."

"I don't doubt that," Dupuy assured him. "And now, perhaps, you will let me borrow this stud— both these studs—for a few hours? I promise you shall have them back safe." He lifted his sharp bland gaze to his companion's face. Salomon looked desperate and distraught.

"What do you want them for?" he exclaimed "My God, I know you're trying to prove something, and I'm in the dark. I don't know what you're getting at. Why can't you be candid?"

Dupuy shifted his gaze over the clear landscape beyond the window. It was a perfect day at last, windless and golden, with a blueness in the air that coloured the walls of the surrounding buildings. "I am a policeman," he said simply. "It is my duty to sift everything that comes my way. If you are seeking a place, and there are twenty roads leading in that direction, you may try sixteen of them before you are right, and then you can put up a notice NO ENTRANCE in the fifteen that are blind alleys. I must be sure they are blind, monsieur. That is all."

"And I suppose in a minute you'll be telling me that an innocent man has nothing to fear," sneered

Salomon. "My God, you people are the direct descendants of the Inquisitors."

Dupuy said nothing, but he carried away with him the little box containing the two pearl studs that didn't quite match.

So certain was Dupuy that he was on the right trail that he wasted no time examining the jewellers' shops of Paris; he bade his subordinate, Marnier, put through the necessary inquiries, and he himself returned to Monte Carlo, where he spent a day making the rounds. Suppose Salomon is lying, he argued, and this pearl I have found on the lorry is his, as I suspect, he would probably discover his loss as soon as he arrived back at the hotel, and the first thing he would do would be to try to replace the lost gem before anyone had time to discover the accident. He might have hoped for good fortune, that the pearl had dropped to the ground and been trodden into unrecognisable fragments; that it had fallen into a ditch or some thick bush where it wouldn't be discovered. But since there was the possibility that it would come to light in uncompromising circumstances—and none could be more damnably compromising than those in the case—then he must have the pearl replaced immediately; and he mustn't let anyone know who he was. There would be no time to write to Paris to the makers or to his own jeweller; and the fact of his profession and his frequent visits to Monte Carlo made it difficult for him to enter any jeweller's shop without being recognised. Therefore, argued Dupuy, he will search out some out-of-the-way little place, somewhere quite unfashionable where personalities are never recognised, and get the work done there. It has been well set, and the setting is curious, but the match is not good. That is strange, for one would have said the pearl was put in by an expert craftsman. There seems to me no explanation of the facts but that he wouldn't wait until the right shaded pearl could be secured. In any case, it would be too risky to write to Paris; the letter might be produced in court.

Dupuy began to examine the jewellers to discover which was the most probable for the purpose. There were the large shops where they couldn't possibly put a name to all their customers, but this course was attended by a double danger; that an acquaintance of Salomon's would come in and see what was going on and later set all the town by the ears by talking of what he had seen; or the shopkeeper himself would recognise the man. No, it was more likely that he had gone farther afield in one of the little shops outside the fashionable radius. Not, though, into one of the small exclusive shops, where conversation is an integral part of the ritual of sale; he would be too well remembered there, particularly in a place where he was already known. No, for him the large cheaper shops would be more secure, shops where a constant stream of customers obliterate the memory of one particular face as surely as a sponge wipes the record from a slate. Here his danger would be reduced to a minimum and a man trying to cover his tracks after a murder must expect to run some risk, argued Dupuy, suddenly vivacious again, setting out on his quest.

It was, however, at Menton late that night that his search ended, in an obscure little jeweller's shop in a side street. The proprietor was a small bald man, a Jew of mixed Continental blood, a figure difficult to forget, with his brooding eyes, in their deep sockets, and that air of weary watchful patience that stamps the race. There was nothing here of the vigilance that safeguards self-interest that Dupuy had found in almost all his earlier encounters; the little shop was dark, slovenly even, with stones of unexpected value winking from cobwebby cases; through long years in semi-darkness the old dealer's face had acquired a dark leathery tinge, and as he moved between light and light, from the sun-pierced shadow at the back of the shop to the counter where artificial light was already burning, it was as though an observant man could read from that network of lines and wrinkles, and in the deep expressive eyes, a long history of endeavour and frustrated ambition and woe. He looked up strangely as Dupuy closed the door and approached to the counter. It would be hard to say where that alien spirit had been roving since last the door clicked, but he was a man dwelling in his own mind that was a tent to cover him in any city, and a treasury of beauty and recollection even here.

Dupuy said, " I am wondering, monsieur, if you have lately replaced a pearl stud for a gentleman who wanted the work done in a hurry?"

As if those last words touched some revitalising spring in the old man, his face suddenly flashed into a brilliance so unexpected that even the level-headed Dupuy was startled.

" A hurry? Yes, monsieur, so much of a hurry that he thought it a little thing for me to supply him with an ill-matched pearl. ' People will not know,' he said. It was nothing to him, monsieur, that I should know. But he was impatient. He was to see a lady that night. He had no other studs. I would lend him a pair, I said. I could match his pearl perfectly. It hurt me that he should wear those studs in the wrong way. And it would only be a day extra. But he would not wait. He said he would go elsewhere. What could I do? I am an artist, monsieur, but I am a tradesman also." The long bony chin sank into the haggard curved palm that rose to meet it; the dark eyes stared beyond Dupuy, who had a peculiar impression of transparency. Already he had ceased to matter to the old man, since he openly allied himself to the man whose passion for order was so small that it did not even trouble him whether a job of work was done finely or expeditiously.

"You remember the gentleman?" Dupuy pursued. "I mean, you would recognise him again?"

"I would know the stud and the pearl," responded the other slowly. "As for the gentleman, he was tall, thin, impatient . . ."

Dupuy frowned; this was no description of the thick-set Salomon. Nevertheless, he produced the little stud and shook it out on to the counter. Gaugin took it up. "That is it, monsieur. I should know that pearl. It is not quite white, as pearls should be white, a pale colour, almost pink. One sees better when one puts it next to the other."

"And you can tell me the day that the monsieur called?"

Gaugin opened a large book written in a sprawling hand. From what he could see of the contents it seemed to Dupuy that Gaugin's bookkeeping system was extremely simple. He simply put down each day a note of what he had earned. He had no till; the money went into the drawer. Straining his eyes, Dupuy saw more than one gem of great beauty and value in the cases at the back of the shop, probably not even locked, simply asking to be burgled. This is the kind of place that sooner or later gets into the papers, he reflected. Old man found with his head bashed in, shop ransacked. Money lying about . . . and then politely, as Gaugin looked up with his strange far-sighted gaze, "Yes, monsieur?"

"It was on the 1st November," said the old man.

"And you are sure of the man who brought the stud?" persisted the detective. "Was he perhaps like this?" and he produced a picture of Salomon.

Gaugin laid the pasteboard down. "No, monsieur. That was not the man, but this is the stud. I recollect not only the pearl, but it is not a very usual fitting . . ." he wandered into technicalities.

"And did he give any reason, tell any story, about losing the pearl?"

"He said he had been out with a party of gentlemen and they had become rather riotous; there had been bear-fighting. When he returned home he found the pearl missing."

"And he inquired of his host?"

"He said, 'It would be useless to try to recover it. I must cut my losses.'"

"This other pearl, the one he wanted you to match, is quite a valuable one, isn't it?" asked Dupuy carelessly.

"It is a finer pearl than usually one sees in a stud," Gaugin acknowledged.

"And did the owner seem a rich man, the type to have this kind of stud?"

"He seemed to know nothing about gems. I could not understand how he came to have such a pearl."

"Obviously Salomon didn't come himself," Dupuy reflected. "And he didn't come till the late afternoon. Now we know there are two men in this, the two men who were in the lorry. Suppose Salomon to be one, then this man who brought the stud is very probably the other. He must at all events know Salomon and knows why it is imperative the stud should be repaired immediately. Now as to time." He produced a pencil and a scribbling pad. "He could do it well enough. The lorry was painted, I think, by both of them; then Salomon returned, breathless, later than he had intended; and X drove the lorry north and sold it to Simon. He could be back soon after midday," he consulted a time-table and saw that this was an accurate deduction, "and he would perhaps go at once to Salomon, whom he would find half-crazed with anxiety because of this unlooked-for disaster. I think Salomon was not built for crime; he hasn't the staying-power. A criminal must have nerves of steel. Now, will anyone remember a man coming to see Salomon at the Cordon Bleu the day after the murder?"

It was not very easy to establish this, so many days having elapsed; but at length Dupuy discovered a clerk who said he had been on duty for a few minutes on the day that the Marks mystery thrilled the whole neighbourhood; the clerk on duty had been called away for a short time, and this young man had taken his place. He said he remembered a man, whom he described very inadequately, coming in and asking if a M. Salomon was staying there; he said he had business with him, and the youth had thought it couldn't be much fun to a man of importance in the commercial world if you couldn't even keep your holiday free. This was shortly after his, Dupuy's, first visit to the hotel.

" I will be unlike the chivalrous English," decided Dupuy gaily. " I will give myself the benefit of the doubt instead of the man I intend to arrest. I will say, ' This man who came on the afternoon of the 1st was M. Salomon's accomplice.' I do not know who he is; all our efforts in that direction have utterly failed. But if I have one bird from the nest perhaps the other will flutter down. It is like catching white mice that have escaped. Secure the one mouse and leave the door of the cage ajar; the second will nearly always come home. And then I know a little about this man. He is not a jeweller, but he knows the neighbourhood. Gaugin is not a man Salomon would know; he is not sufficiently ambitious in the right way; it follows, then, that X has chosen him, and most likely X knows his Monte Carlo. Anyway, I, like the successful, cannot hope to pull off my coup without some risk."

Next day all sensation-mongers were astonished and excited to learn that an arrest had been made in the Marks mystery. The suspected murderer was a well-known Paris jeweller, Salomon by name. And excitement rose to fever pitch when it leaked out the same afternoon that the warrant for the arrest on a capital charge preceded by an hour a second warrant, coming from Paris, where the man was wanted for criminal fraud.

CHAPTER XIII

1

WITHIN twenty-four hours of the arrest, with all Monte Carlo buzzing with rumour and conjecture, with plump gentlemen in linen suits and panama hats meeting one another and crying anxiously, Have you heard about this fellow, Salomon? Scandalous, isn't it? meaning that it was scandalous he should have run amok with other men's dividends and not at all that he should be in sight of death for murder, with the police trying to guard the fact of his depredations and the press intent on publishing the story in every detail, with the wretch already condemned in thousands of hearts—still within that brief space there came to the Hotel Fantastique a woman of a beauty so striking that even Potain was awed.

"It is not natural," he told his wife. "So much excitement in one house. And she is divine. What hands, what lips, what shoulders."

The distinction of the stranger impressed far less vulnerable men than Potain. She had arrived at the hour when the English guests had tea, and there were a good many of them in the lounge. She sat erect on a small stiff chair, looking through some papers, her exquisite head in its closely-fitting black cap revealing only the faintest trace of pale gold hair, a black silk coat drawn lightly round a lovely figure. Montstuart, passing her, thought immediately, "Thank God I haven't got to defend her in a murder case. No one would believe a woman as astounding as that hadn't poisoned her husband."

Nicholas Marvell, entering a moment later, thought, "Why, she's like a tree in the way she stands and moves. That turn of the head, and lift of the arm," and he almost expected to see her draperies sway with her smallest gesture, as leaves move on a branch when the wind touches them.

Miss Hoult frankly stared, then said, "My dear, how magnificently she's dressed the part."

"What part?" demanded Sarah.

"The heroine, of course. Who's she waiting for?"

"I'm sure I don't know. Bertha, you remind me of vampires; you know, disgusting creatures that suck the blood of the living. What does it matter to us?"

Miss Hoult simply turned her back and asked a waiter. The waiter said, "M. Latymer, madame," and scurried away. Miss Hoult lifted her fierce brightly-coloured face on its long neck and exclaimed in a triumphant hiss, "I might have guessed it. What's she to him?"

" His wife, perhaps," suggested the modern-minded Sarah.

"His wife? Really, you'll never make a novelist. Wife indeed. But I can't say I'm surprised. No man could be as harmless as Mr. Latymer looks."

Then Latymer himself came in and stood aimlessly by the door, his pale eyes behind their tortoiseshell glasses roaming over the occupants of the lounge. A page appeared beside him and indicated the mysterious newcomer, and still without hurry, without any apparent pleasure in her beauty, he crossed to her chair. In his hand he held a card, and, looking at this, he said a name, without lifting his eyes. Miss Hoult was bitterly disappointed that she couldn't hear what it was. The woman, however, seemed oblivious to everyone except Latymer; her voice was perfectly modulated, clear and musical. She wasted no time, but plunged directly into the purpose of her visit. Degas, shamelessly eavesdropping at a table close by, overheard most of the conversation, and his interest in Latymer, that had hitherto not been great, was suddenly intense.

It was difficult, he thought, to associate so much charm and persuasiveness with that dry-as-dust Englishman with the absurd name; even now, as he stiffly seated himself, he betrayed no excitement at this astounding deal of fate.

" Mrs. Brodie?" he said. And waited.

Degas grinned. You didn't deceive a young man of his experience by that air of subtle indifference. No one, decided Degas, knew anything about this man. Most likely he lived a Jekyll and Hyde existence, and was famous from one end of Jermyn Street to the other—an assumption that credited Mr. Latymer with taste of the very worst kind.

" If I can do anything for you I shall, of course, be

delighted," the fellow was saying in his wooden way. "At present I am afraid I am in the dark."

"This is quite unconventional," she agreed at once. "I would not have come, would not have dared to come, if the matter were less critical. Believe me, I realise that I have absolutely no claim on you or your services. But I am helpless myself, and you are in a peculiar position."

"Yes," Latymer agreed, and Degas could have kicked him for the impassiveness of his manner. The young Frenchman was far from realising how much of his neighbour's success was due to his manner and appearance. Besides, Sarah Blaise had been more correct than her aunt would allow when she asked pertinently, "But how do we know he's dull? We don't know him at all. He's a mystery to every one of us. And that's something to have achieved in a community that does nothing but talk about its neighbours morning, noon and night."

Whereat, of course, Miss Hoult said, as was to be expected, "Still waters run deep, and his deeper than most."

Meanwhile the amazing Mrs. Brodie was saying to Latymer, with Degas listening intently to every word, "You must think it very strange my coming to see you like this, when even my name is unknown to you, but I hope you won't misunderstand me when I say you are the only hope I have." Her eyes clear and steadfast met his level uninspired gaze. He just said, "Yes" and waited. He didn't even warn her that what she said could probably be overheard; he believed that when women reach thirty, as this lady obviously had done, they were old enough to behave without being guided like children. A stranger could have felt the curiosity in that room like a naked flame. Latymer knew that all eyes were on him, and

166

that if Degas didn't hear everything and report faithfully to them, they'd have no hesitation in inventing a truth of their own. And "I stand for a minimum of lying," Latymer had once heard an old judge say.

"You're in a peculiar position," Mrs. Brodie went on. "Without being attached to the police, and so untrammelled by their precedents, you've had a great many of the privileges they presumably enjoy ever since this Mr. Marks was spirited away. You know what lies behind Dupuy's action in arresting M. Salomon. Of course, you may feel bound to refuse to discuss the subject, but since it matters rather more than my life to me, I hope you'll be generous."

"You want me to give you Dupuy's reasons?"

"I should be very grateful if you would. That's no treachery to him, because they must be given to M. Salomon's defence; but the sooner we can begin to refute them, the sooner he'll be released."

"You are convinced he will be released?"

"He must be. He isn't guilty. To me it's astounding that they could ever have connected him with the affair. It's infamous," the voice dropped to a whisper so that even Degas couldn't hear what was being said, "that they should have taken him."

Latymer said decisively, "Let me get the position quite clear. You represent M. Salomon's defence?"

"I hope, in alliance with yourself."

"I'm no lawyer," he warned her. "I couldn't undertake a defence even if I were convinced Salomon isn't guilty."

"I don't ask you to do that. I ask you to take up the threads where you dropped them, and see if they don't eventually bring you to another conclusion."

"I'm always open to conviction," he said slowly. "And I admit I should like to have this case completely cleared up. I could undertake to go on with investigations on your behalf. I should have to be quite impersonal, and if at any time I ceased to agree with your views as to M. Salomon's innocence I should have to hand in my brief."

"I couldn't ask more of you than that," Mrs. Brodie acknowledged. "And you will?"

"I've no authority to take particular action," he warned her.

"You're a private detective, I understood."

"Only an amateur one, so to speak. You could employ someone with an established name, if you preferred."

"But they'd come to the case fresh, knowing nothing. You've trodden every inch of the official road. That's why you're so immensely valuable to me."

"I think," said Latymer, "it would be as well to have a legal mind on this point. There's a very well-known barrister staying in this hotel. I'm not suggesting that you should brief him for the defence, or that he would accept it in any case, but at least we should know better the most important steps to take, and in my experience I have always found a lawyer a very useful guide, when one is unsure of the right direction. They know, you see, what a prosecution will stress, what questions it will want answered, the general line the law will take."

"I'm prepared to be guided by you," said Mrs. Brodie. "Who is he?"

"His name's Montstuart; he's a Scotsman."

"I've heard of him," she said at once. "He got an acquittal for the Ferrers widow two years ago."

"That's the man."

"And you think he'll be willing . . .? But I thought he was on holiday."

"He can no more resist the chance of a case than

a beetle can resist beer. At all events, you will let me ask him?"

"It would be very kind."

"And you have evidence that would clear M. Salomon? Or just a conviction that because he is such-and-such a type of man an accusation of this kind cannot be substantiated?"

"Evidence," she told him quietly, and to Degas' cruel disappointment he did not ask her what that evidence was.

2

Montstuart, approached by Latymer, said at once, "Busmen's holidays are the only kind I appreciate, my dear fellow. You need have no scruples about asking me to lend a hand. It's meat and drink to me—as I take it it is to you," he added shrewdly.

"Oh, it's my bread-and-butter or part of it," returned Latymer in such impersonal tones that Montstuart almost believed he spoke the whole truth. And yet could any man be approached by such a woman and not be moved, though it might be to apprehension or anger? It almost seemed as if some could.

"And presumably to Mrs. Brodie it's life and death. What is her interest in this man, do you know?"

"I should say the usual one. I haven't asked."

Montstuart frowned.

"That puts you off?"

"I loathe the cases that are complicated by this kind of thing."

Latymer's brows rose. "You must find yourself compelled to refuse a good deal of work."

"I don't say I refuse to do it. I only say I dislike it. As a matter of fact, we're making assumptions that may prove to be utterly unfair. In any case, whatever the circumstances, I'd give a good deal to be in at the death."

"It's a pity you're prejudiced against the lady at the outset," remarked Latymer in his candid way. "You've nothing actually against her, not at all events until you know the circumstances."

"On principle, I'm against her type. They're dangerous. They're the kind that get men into trouble. They're subtle, too, and I don't like subtle witnesses. Nor do judges. They have an unhealthy and often well-founded idea that they're being led up the garden by the nose, and that's bad for everyone, particularly for the man who's trying to get a verdict."

"I dare say you're right in saying she's dangerous. I'm not a particularly susceptible person, but she's involved me all right."

"I don't know how you make that out," replied Montstuart sharply. "You were involved before she came on the scenes."

"That was on the side of authority."

"And now you're involved on her behalf? And you call yourself insusceptible!"

Latymer let that go. "How do you feel about joining us?" he inquired. "What it really amounts to is holding a watching brief for Salomon and doing a good deal of the donkey work ourselves. Of course, you do understand you'd be definitely agin the Government."

"That's nothing new to me. I'd rather defend than prosecute any day. There's something horrible to my mind in the notion of the whole community ranged against one man. That fact alone prejudices you in his favour and makes you plead badly. I never accept a prosecution if I can help it, but sometimes temptation's very powerful. I suppose she's got the usual sort of evidence of Salomon's innocence. Point is, can she establish it?"

"I really haven't any details. She gave me her card, but what her relation to Salomon is—whether they're just casual lovers or whether there's some permanent relationship between them—I don't know."

"I'll do it," said Montstuart recklessly. "You bet I'll do it. I'm here for my health, you know. Overworked, threat of a nervous breakdown, says the specialist. Devil take the man. Doesn't he realise that what is likely to bring on senile decay is this hanging about in an hotel ten times too rich for me with nothing to do but watch another generation amuse itself? They make a water-tight compartment of it as we never did. We couldn't separate work and play as they do. And at my age, I confess quite frankly, I don't want to. So deeply wary as I feel about your mysterious lady, I'll leap at the chance of lending her a hand."

Latymer went back to the lounge to tell Mrs. Brodie that Montstuart had consented to help them, and to make an appointment for the three of them to meet with less publicity that same evening. As soon as he had done this she stood up, held out her hand, that Latymer touched for an instant, and went away at once, looking, like the seekers after truth, neither to the right nor the left, her head bent, her hands clasping a white morocco bag and a rose-coloured frilly parasol.

That night to an audience of the two Scotsmen she told them her story.

"I know Auguste is innocent because a man cannot be in two places at once," she said.

"Meaning he was with you?" That was Montstuart, blunt and conscious of the immediate return of his ancient prejudices. Why couldn't the woman say so outright, instead of being romantic and stupidly subtle? She'd have to face the utmost candour if she were going through with this.

"From about ten o'clock or even earlier until seven the next morning. It was like him not to tell the police."

"It's very bad law," growled Montstuart.

"He stands to lose so much if the truth comes out," Mrs. Brodie defended him.

"He stands to lose more by keeping his mouth shut."

"I suppose he knew that I should clear him by a public statement, if that's the only way. You're thinking me wholly selfish, I can see," she flung the unexpected challenge to the barrister, who coloured with chagrin at having been caught off his guard. "But he has a position I haven't, and it's his position I'm thinking of."

"I'm not sure that isn't true," thought Montstuart on a spasm of reaction. "Gentlemen may prefer blondes but it's the brunettes that last. It's funny, but I've noticed again and again you can't put them off with money, as you can the blondes. This one seems to have taken the whole thing pretty hard. Another shipwrecked marriage, I suppose. Women have no sense of proportion."

"I'd better tell you a little about myself," suggested Marcella Brodie. "I'm English and I have an English husband, but we have lived abroad for years. I grew up in France and really I've had practically no contact with England since I was a child. My husband represents an important firm, and that means he is constantly travelling about. Sometimes we are together for months, sometimes he is away for two or three weeks, sometimes for two or three days. At first I used to go with him, but I soon abandoned that. It wasn't really suitable; he couldn't always put up at the kind of hotels he thought right for his wife—he is a very circumspect man—and then he often worked late, and he didn't care for me to be alone. So after a time he went and I stayed behind." While she was speaking Montstuart's knowledge of the woman was deepening with unusual rapidity. He saw her as a rebel, a pioneering type for all her beauty and softness, someone with the hard core of the artist at the roots of her being, unsentimental, self-protective, a peril, an adventure, dissatisfied with narrow codes and conventions. He realised how she must appeal to a man like Salomon, that careful climbing social personality, how he had (presumably) crashed, casting his discretion to the winds, in order to keep pace with that flashing swift-moving personality.

"And how long have you known M. Salomon?" he asked, out of his experience of the divagations a woman will make in telling a story.

"About four years. I met him during one of my husband's absences. I have a flat here, and whenever Adam went away I used to come down, sometimes alone, sometimes with a friend. I had friends and acquaintances in Monte Carlo, and soon I began to look upon my husband's business tours as my own periods of release. I used to feel that without them my brain would snap. He was away a good deal, and I took up interests I'd more or less dropped during the first two or three years of marriage. Music, for instance. My husband is bored to death by it. If he recognises the National Anthem, it's about the only bit of French music he knows, while I'm passionately devoted to it. I have a number of musical friends, but he makes no secret of the fact that their conversation wearies him. He'll ostentatiously go out and telephone when they're here; oh, it was quite intolerable," she cried spiritedly. "And so I felt myself free to live as pleased me most, so long as it didn't openly make hay of Adam's life." She caught sight of a new expression, of a dry disdain, on the lawyer's face and she added at once, "Oh, nothing in those years that a husband need mind, nothing so long as we continued our lives together as husband and wife. That lasted about five years. Long before then I knew, and I suppose he did, that we'd made a frightful mistake. He thought my friends dilettante and insignificant, and I found his boring and uncultured. He reads nothing but detective stories and the daily papers and trade reports; he detests this place, doesn't gamble, doesn't walk, doesn't swim or play any games. He doesn't even play bridge. Our separation was gradual, but now to all intents and purposes it is complete. Of course, he very much resented my spending my time here, when he was away."

"What was his suggestion for you?" asked Montstuart. "That you should go to relations?"

"I have no relations living."

"To his relations then?"

"He thought so, but it was impossible. They were two elderly cousins living in the country—there was a married sister, but I never had any very pressing invitation from her—I don't know precisely how they spent their time, but it was unthinkable to me that I should go there. In any case, they didn't really want me. I was everything of which they most disapproved. In their eyes I was a Parisian, and worse than most, because I was of English birth. They were the type that is convinced that any Englishwoman who voluntarily lives in Paris must have immoral motives. Besides, after the early years of my marriage, when it became obvious that we were absolutely in-compatible, and equally obvious that we could do nothing to alter the position—my husband would not dream of allowing a divorce—I looked forward to his absences as times when I could be free. I used to shut the house up; it was his house, furnished by himself; they were my holidays. About five years ago I first met M. Salomon at the tables here, and later I was introduced to him by some friends. We used to meet at dinner-parties and again at the casino. I had very little feeling about my husband's rights and so forth. We had ceased living as man and wife for some time, and when it became clear that I should never be free to marry again I accepted the circumstances and eventually the only alternative; Auguste became my lover."

Latymer's flat voice said, "You knew he was a married man?"

"Yes, with a position to keep up, and children to whom he is devoted. His marriage was one of con-venience, and in any case his outlook is a reasonable one. He doesn't wish to break up his home. Be-sides, among sensible people these things can be arranged. At all events there it was. Auguste is a great gambler, so that his frequent visits to Monte Carlo aroused small comment. And for four years this has been going on. I don't think my husband ever suspected. I did my best to keep it quiet."

"Why?" asked Montstuart surprisingly.

"I felt I owed that at least to Auguste. I didn't want his home life spoilt. It's difficult, perhaps, to make people with the—the true-blue English outlook understand how the affair seemed to me. I didn't feel I was doing anyone any wrong by taking my happiness; but it would have been a terrible wrong to have broken up a household. And my husband is

a jealous man; he calls it pride. You know the type.
Perhaps I'm making too much of the affair. At all
events, my husband went to England for a fortnight
on the 27th October, and on the 29th I came down
here as I always do. On the 30th M. Salomon telephoned me from his hotel. He's a discreet person and
anyone could have listened in to both sides of the
conversation. He asked me if I would be at the rooms
that night, and I said I certainly should. He said he
was down on business, and told me to look out for
him. That was all. I knew from that we should leave
the rooms at approximately the same time and meet
in my flat."

"There's nobody else in the flat, Mrs. Brodie?"

"I have a maid, but she's the soul of discretion.
She's a French girl and devoted to me."

"To the extent of backing up your story in court?"

Mrs. Brodie turned to him in sudden passion.
"Mr. Montstuart, this isn't to come into court. It
mustn't. I won't have Auguste's life ruined."

"It wouldn't be your fault," Montstuart pointed
out reasonably. "It's just that the dice are loaded
against him."

"That wouldn't make it any better when the story
came out," remarked the lady dryly. "Now, what
hope is there of exonerating him?"

"You'll be able to prove your version?" said Montstuart. "This maid would recognise him?"

"She's been seeing him at fairly regular intervals
for four years."

"And she saw him come in that night?"

"She opened the door to us."

"She knows he spent the night in your flat? You
didn't go to any elaborate device of shutting the front
door and calling good-night in order to deceive her?"

"Oh, no. She brought up the shaving water in the morning. He came to my flat when he left the Casino, I suppose about a quarter or ten to ten. I knew he was troubled about money, but he said he didn't dare tell his wife. He'd got into the hands of some moneylender and he'd been hoping for a good run at the tables, but the luck was all against him."

"Did he tell you more than that?" demanded Latymer shrewdly.

"No. What more was there to tell?"

Latymer hesitated. Then, "I think it doesn't matter at the moment, and I'm a little unsure of my own legal status. After all, I was in Dupuy's confidence, and if he doesn't see fit to publish everything he's learnt he probably wouldn't think it suitable or necessary that I should. But Salomon was in about as tight a place as a man could be—except perhaps the one he's in now."

Montstuart crossed his knees, felt for his cigar-case, accepted a match from Latymer, murmured to his new client, "You don't mind? Thank you," and said in slow legal tones, "I ought to warn you that this defence is pretty thin—or perhaps I should be putting it better if I were to say that a French court of justice will find it pretty thin. It's so obviously the kind of story an affectionate woman would trump up. Even the maid doesn't really help. You admit she's devoted and she's been with you several years. That's Salomon's case for the defence, and against him he's got the fact that he's told several lies and the pearl stud has been brought home to him. We're going to have the devil of a time getting away from that stud. I know, of course, that circumstantial evidence can lie like the proverbial trooper, but I admit I don't at present see much light on the situation."

Latymer stubbed out his cigarette and said, "Yes, it's the usual puzzle. Find the murderer. The police have found one; we've got to cap their effort. The point is, who else is there who could be involved?"

"There's young Marvell's story of the man who was hanging about the hotel. There may be something in that, particularly as he seemed to have a shrewd idea when Marks was expected. The police, I admit, dismissed him pretty early from the case, deciding, presumably, that he was one of these lunatic busybodies who're out for free publicity."

"Ah, but if he wasn't, if there was something behind all that farrago of nonsense he talked? The police have written him down as very simple. Suppose, on the other hand, he's particularly subtle? He will guess the line the police will take, that no man who is going to be concerned in a murder makes himself conspicuous on the scene of the crime a few hours earlier. So they dismiss him. Any man with much foresight, certainly any man capable of planning this crime, would realise that's what they'd say. It's the old game of double bluff, and so far he's pulled it off. The trick's as old as the hills. Poe exploited it in the Purloined Letter. I'm inclined to try to find him myself. Suppose, when he came to the hotel—he was seen all about the neighbourhood, he was there to spy out the land? He hadn't been inside the hotel so far as we know. It's one of Dupuy's points that the criminal knew how the grounds were laid out, etc. Now the chambermaids wouldn't acknowledge it, but I dare say he was told he could come in, they gossiped with him. An astute man can pick up a lot of information in half an hour."

"You think he's the John the Baptist of the gang, so to speak?"

"I think it's worth trying."

"And how do we find him?"

Latymer looked up in astonishment. "Oh, just by work and inquiry, the usual way," he replied.

CHAPTER XIV

1

AFTER Mrs. Brodie had gone, Montstuart observed rather gloomily to Latymer, "This story of Salomon having spent the night with that woman may be as true as gospel, and it would probably be easy enough to establish the fact of their relationship; you can't fool all the people all the time, not for four years anyway, but that wouldn't show he was there between the hours she says he was. The maid doesn't really help much: she could so easily be squared. I dare say that little sideline of Mrs. Brodie's is worth quite a comfortable nest-egg to her. We could easily show, I suppose, that Salomon went to the flat, but I don't know how we're going to prove when he left it, unless we can find someone else who actually saw him go. Where does she live, by the way?"

Latymer looked at the card Mrs. Brodie had given him. "Rue de la Rose. We know he came back to the hotel about seven, which fits in with her story."

"But naturally it would. She's not such a fool as to tell a yarn in which at first sight holes can be picked. There's the question of the clothes he was wearing, though I doubt if that helps us much either, for if he went straight to the Hotel Fantastique when he left the casino he would be in evening dress, anyway. He kept the key of his room, by the way, didn't you tell me, so possibly he slipped in and changed before he embarked on the crime."

"You're inclined to agree with the police, then?"

"I'm arguing from their standpoint. That's all. I wonder if any one at the hotel would remember what he was wearing. But my experience of these luxury houses is that the waiters are too superior to notice their guests. I must say, if they must bring forward this kind of defence, I wish they'd staged their adventure at some hotel where it would be possible to get some disinterested witness to come forward. That maid won't cut any ice in anybody's mind. No, I think we're back at the old problem. Not—Did Salomon do it? But—Who did?"

"In a sense we start one point up. The police have eliminated one suspect."

"You mean Salomon? You seem very certain. I confess to an open mind. I'm not defending the fellow, I'm simply examining the position, and if, at any stage, I become convinced that this story is nothing but a hoax put up to get the fellow off, I shall withdraw. I suppose Mrs. Brodie understood that."

"I think your attitude was pretty clear," Latymer assured him, and, if possible, his voice was now drier than Montstuart had ever heard it.

Montstuart shrugged; then decided to admit the implication. "I don't mind telling you this is the kind of case I particularly detest. It's the needle in the haystack with a vengeance. This fellow's had about nine days' start, time to smudge out all his clues, and show a clean pair of heels. As for the descriptions we have of him, they'd fit roughly eighty men out of a hundred. We don't even know where to start picking up the trail."

"Whoever he was he knew a good deal of Marks' movements. It was known that he'd be on the Continent, but no one was supposed to know where he was staying. Even Potain only heard on the morning of the 30th, and the same day this fellow appeared. That seems to have been the first spark of wisdom Marks showed, and it came too late. If he hadn't bragged so confoundedly about the diamond probably it wouldn't have occurred to any one that he was carrying it about with him, and he could have gone strutting round the Fantastique as proudly as ever."

"I think he'd got to a pitch that successful men do sometimes reach, when he considered himself invulnerable. When there was all that talk about his crashing, I doubt if he spent a sleepless night, though I dare say a good many of his creditors did. I don't believe it occurred to him that he could go under. He took the diamond, his position, all the things you or I would call stupendous luck and be duly grateful, as the natural workings of providence on his behalf. Very likely he considered himself immune from the disasters that attack ordinary men. If he had time to realise what was happening to him, he must have had the most appalling shock when he was set upon that evening."

"Oh, well," said Latymer unsympathetically, "that's not a very different brand of faith from that of a great many pious people I know. You may have some plan of campaign to suggest, but my inclination is to trace the affair back to the beginning, try to discover if he was being trailed and, if so, by whom. There may have been a man following at a discreet distance from England onwards. We don't even know if this man who bought the lorry was French, though I admit everything points to it. But men like Marks have enemies and very bitter enemies at that."

"Are you starting from the day he left London?"

"I understand he spent a night at an hotel in

181

Dover. I'd be interested to know why he should do that. He could have driven straight down and boarded the boat without setting foot inside an hotel. We could get that address, perhaps, through the Paris hotel where he stayed. If not, his secretary would be able to tell us."

"I'm against all this publicity and advertisement the police seem to favour," Montstuart observed sharply. "The longer we work in the dark, the more chance we have of success. At least, that's how I see it."

"If we get our basic information we shall get our man. It's all a question of starting at the beginning of the trial," insisted Latymer.

"I will give you the end of a golden thread To roll it into a ball, It will lead you straight to Heaven's gate, Set in Jerusalem's wall. How optimistic the faithful are! Well, yours is the first move, I think. There's one thing, we've plenty of time. They don't put themselves out for little matters like trials in France, I understand."

2

Latymer decided that the most satisfactory course would be for him to take up the investigation in person, starting at Dover, where he would learn what had brought Marks to that place when he could so much more easily have boarded the boat straight from London. He had discovered the name of the hotel where Marks had stayed, and he hoped to find the answer to his question there.

"For though it's odd, and to us incomprehensible," he told Montstuart, "Marks wasn't the type that does things without a purpose, though I dare say we shall find some very queer things behind his purposes.

You'll be on the spot to deal with any emergencies that arise, and to keep in touch with Mrs. Brodie."

"She'll keep in touch with me. You can bet on that," returned Montstuart bitterly. "I can only imagine she displays rather more discretion in her husband's home than elsewhere, unless he's deaf and blind. Considering how anxious she is to preserve the sanctities of Salomon's home-life she's showing about as much wisdom as—oh, as you'd expect from her type," he wound up, with unusual cynicism. Murder for possession was all right, he thought, and if Salomon actually was guilty, then he could understand his motive, but it exasperated and angered him that a really intriguing murder should be complicated by a clandestine love affair; at the same time, he despised himself for his lack of impartiality, learning with a fresh apprehension that he grew less tolerant of this particular failing with each year of his experience.

Latymer was still speaking. "You've tested her story, by the way?" They had agreed that it would be unwise for Latymer to make local inquiries, since everyone knew he had been hand in glove with Dupuy. Latymer shrewdly suspected that the lawyer was rather pleased with himself in the new rôle of sleuth.

"Oh, yes," said Montstuart, "and with the obvious results. You pointed out yourself that she wouldn't tell such a story if she weren't backed up to the hilt. The maid remembers Salomon perfectly, has often seen him before, knew his name, said he telephoned to his hotel to ask if any messages had come for him, and added that he probably wouldn't be back that night."

"Didn't the hotel ask for a number, in case of some message coming through?"

"The maid swears he didn't give one. Just rang off without saying where he was staying or why he wouldn't be back."

Latymer played absent-mindedly with a jade-handled paper-knife. "I don't much like the sound of that. It looks as though he knew he might need an alibi. But that may be pure coincidence. Anything else?"

"The maid says she went to bed before they did, and she doesn't know what went on. She overslept a bit, and got scolded by Mrs. Brodie—who, I should say, has a tongue of vitriol when she pleases—and was told they wanted the shaving water at once. She took it up, and heard Mrs. Brodie being apologetic. Salomon was obviously a bit rattled. The girl heard Mrs. Brodie say, ' But why should Adam ever guess? You're being foolish, Auguste. We've protected ourselves for four years. Besides, I tell you he's in England.' She didn't hear anything else because she has to do something for a living besides listen at doors, and a few minutes later the front door slammed, and Mrs. Brodie came in in a very bad temper, and said, ' If any one should ask you, Marie, you realise that you have not seen M. Salomon. You understand?' and she gave her a tip, a pretty big tip at that."

"A picture of vice recoiling on its own head, if even vice can perform such acrobatics," remarked Latymer. "Having paid the girl to tell lies, I suppose she's had to pay her again to tell the truth. I wonder if the husband really is in England. I should say she was a reckless type of woman, and it's pretty clear who—er—wears the breeches in that establishment. Did you try the hotel?"

"I did." Montstuart spoke with professional emphasis. "And that's where I can't make the pieces fit quite. You see, the moment Salomon got in he rang for the chambermaid and asked for some shaving-water."

3

Excitement at the Hotel Fantastique raged like a furnace during the forty-eight hours of Latymer's absence. Everyone realised it had something to do with the mysterious stranger; everyone realised that Montstuart had been drawn into the affair. He was stopped and questioned and subjected to badinage, curiosity and even aggression, that he met with a blandness as impenetrable as ice. No one could so much as learn from him the lady's identity. Nor did she haunt the hotel or spend unprofitable leisure ringing up on the telephone, as Montstuart had been afraid she would. Having told her story and set the ball rolling, she seemed to have returned to her flat, whence she would not emerge until there was something more for her to do. Montstuart still eyed her distrustfully in his mind, but he liked her attitude. So many of his feminine clients would bombard him with senseless inquiries that, besides running their bills up to totals at which they would presently, quite unreasonably, protest, almost drove him frantic. He had by this time become definitely interested in the case. It was the first time he had found himself actually on the spot when a crime was committed, and he was more disposed than he had hitherto found himself to sympathise with the police.

Latymer, who had a head for heights and whom nothing could discompose, was flying to England, and returning in the same way, via Paris, if necessary. It was known that Marks had been at a Paris hotel immediately prior to his arrival at the Fantastique. He agreed with Montstuart that time was becoming more and more the essence of the affair. This man, whoever he was, was getting daily more opportunity for evading detection altogether, and Mrs. Brodie had made things as easy as she could by shouldering all financial responsibility.

On the 14th November, Montstuart received a telegram from Latymer saying he expected to arrive that night, and at about eight o'clock the three of them dined in Mrs. Brodie's flat. Montstuart had had some doubts as to the wisdom of this, but his companions urged the danger of eating anywhere in public, where their words might easily be overheard. " Everyone at the Fantastique is resolved to be posted as to the latest developments," remarked Latymer, who looked tired by his driving two days. " I admit this may be indiscreet, but it seems to me our only hope. I can't believe we should show more wisdom in engaging a private room, while here Mrs. Brodie's only servant knows the facts of the case, and isn't likely to catch stray phrases through a keyhole and distort them magnificently, as those people at the Fantastique would do."

During the meal itself he talked with an outward placidity, that seemed almost too much for his hostess's impatience, of the lack of comfort of the modern luxury hotel. " It's a bitter comment on the age," he said, helping himself to potatoes, cooked in a way that even the Fantastique couldn't have bettered. " More than novels, more than poetry even and much more than clothes do hotels mirror their time. I never feel completely at home in an hotel like the Fantastique, and the Sumptuous was very like it. I remember staying at an hotel at Dover many years ago where I really experienced luxury. We dined from a stiff white cloth on a long table, and afterwards we smoked in a parlour with painted glass vases on an overmantel and Landseers round the walls. And enormous photographs of relations utterly out of focus. I don't quite know the word I want. Perhaps cosy would be the best. Ball-fringe and ferns in bright-coloured china pots. Oh, it wasn't artistic and it certainly wasn't beautiful, but it hadn't the null, dispassionate effect of this modern luxury."

Then, at last, the maid left them, and they could get down to the subject of their meeting. Latymer was an adaptable person, more adaptable than people who didn't know him would have thought possible, and he had, apparently, found no difficulty in getting into conversation with the manager of the hotel.

"He's one of those super-beings who makes a point of coming round and assuring himself personally that each guest is satisfied. I wondered what he'd do if I said how much I disliked the hotel, which would have been true, but would have precluded all further conversation.

"I knew he wasn't likely to linger more than a few minutes," he went on, "so I said almost at once, 'You had Marks here, didn't you?' And he said, 'Yes, he'd been there for two days.'"

"Two days," said Montstuart, the little lines of perplexity deepening in his face. "Did you discover why?"

"I suppose, because the fellow he was going to meet didn't turn up till the second day."

"Who was this man?"

"That I haven't yet discovered, unless he was the same as hung about round here—the fellow whom we're holding responsible every time we find ourselves up against a difficulty. At all events, this is what happened. The manager was a bit suspicious; I suppose he thought I took rather a lot of interest in the fellow, so I said I was actually staying at the

Fantastique when the murder took place. That got him at once; he was all agog for details. It's odd how the laity is always convinced the authorities are suppressing all the more relevant parts of the story. I couldn't add much to his information, but at least it made him eager to talk. He wanted to know whether I thought Salomon really did it. I said I thought the police were on rather thin ice, but of course I wasn't in a position to sit in judgment. He talked about circumstantial evidence and I talked about lucky coincidence, and asked if Marks had given the impression of being nervous when he was there. I wanted to know if he guessed he was being followed, if he expected to be followed, or if he hadn't a notion. The manager, whose name is Bryant, said that if he was nervous he didn't show it. He seemed a bit impatient during the first day, but the next morning the stranger appeared. It appears Marks was expecting him. He'd got a private room at the hotel, and the two went up there at once, and were closeted together for so long that Bryant says he began to feel a bit apprehensive. Curious is the word I'd have used, though of course I didn't say so. At all events, he went up presently himself and knocked on the door."

" He might have used the house-phone," said Montstuart.

"That's why I substituted curious. At all events, he got no reply and he knocked again. Then, when nothing happened, he tried the handle and it turned easily enough and he opened the door, expecting to find an empty room, instead of which he saw both men sitting at the table staring at the diamond."

"Lucky chap!" exclaimed Montstuart. "I'd have given a good deal to see that."

"So would I," breathed Marcella Brodie fervently. "I love precious stones."

"What was Marks' reaction?" Montstuart went on, his professional interest instantly re-asserting itself.

"He was infernally annoyed. He jumped up and demanded what was the matter. Bryant—whom an earthquake would hardly discompose—explained the position, and Marks said they were both coming down. He didn't try to hide the stone or anything; he behaved as a well-bred person does when you break one of the crown derby cups; he just ignored the whole thing. I must say I'd have liked to see it myself, and now, unless I've got some amazing good fortune ahead of me, I suppose I never shall. But Bryant said Marks might as well have locked himself into a padded cell with its occupant as wander about a big city carrying that on him. He seems to have had the courage of his convictions because he told Marks—not blatantly, you understand, but . . ."

"With great respect," interposed Montstuart and grinned.

"Precisely—that his life wouldn't be worth half a crown to any insurance company so long as he had that in his pocket."

"Marks' answer seems to me a little strange. He said, 'Oh, but I shan't have it much longer. I'm assured that I'm lucky to have kept it so long.'"

"Which is the particularly strange part of that?"

"The last part—the bit about being lucky. And being assured."

Montstuart looked doubtful. "Just a habit of speech perhaps," he said judicially.

"It may be that I'm prejudiced by what happened later. Not at Dover, though. Afterwards, when he got to Paris. Nothing else of importance seems to have happened at Dover, except that he gave the chambermaid a five-pound note."

"No explanation forthcoming?"

" None, apparently."

" What does the girl herself say?"

" Unfortunately she was only a temporary worker, filling up a gap for a girl who'd sprained her ankle, and she left the same day that Marks did. She wasn't a girl either, but one of those elderly, respectable women whose rarity other elderly women, spending most of their time in registry offices, so often deplore. Marks seems to have taken to her. She valeted him, answered his bell promptly and wasn't, Bryant assures me, the type that tries to see a man's letters. Not that Marks had any incriminating letters, for all I know. Anyway, there it is. He rang for a drink and she went up, and fetched it for him, and came down blank and dithering, saying she'd seen the diamond, and how could anyone believe it was worth all that money? Anyway, who decided what stones were worth? and she'd seen plenty of things at the Cairo Jewel Stores that would be more becoming to a woman than that. Especially if she happened to be one of these sallow females. Another original mind, you note."

" Did she say that to Marks, do you know?"

" I couldn't tell you. I've seen two of the servants, who say she claims to have said something of the sort, but they don't believe her. They don't believe anyone would be fool enough to jeopardise the chance of a handsome tip—there's a pathetic belief in the generosity of millionaires in that part of the world—by being so outspoken."

" As a matter of fact, she probably delighted the fellow. That kind of honesty isn't very easy to come by, as I certainly, and you most probably, know."

Latymer nodded. " It's a pity I couldn't see her, in case there was some ulterior motive behind the fiver. But the manager hadn't any address for her—they don't bother much about a woman who only comes in for a few days—so I don't see how we can get at her. I don't know that it matters."

"We can leave it for the moment at all events. What happened at Paris?"

"He went to the Cosmopolitan. Much the same sort of place as this, and the Sumptuous. I learned that from Bryant."

"He must have been sorry to see you go," suggested Montstuart.

"Oh, I fancy he's got the idea into his head I'm a reporter or a detective writer, anxious to score off the French police. Publicity and all the rest of it. He said, 'You're one of these people who're engaged in crime? Is that it?' I said there were happier ways of putting it," Latymer's lips twitched at the recollection, "but that it could be expressed like that."

"I'm inclined to take seriously your suggestion that Marks' visitor at Dover was the man who hung about the hotel here," said Montstuart slowly. "We don't know his official connection with the deceased, but it's possible he was something to do with the mine—Marks' partner, perhaps, or a creditor who wanted to be assured he'd get his money. He may not have trusted Marks. I don't suggest in that case that he has anything to do with the murder. It's a pity we know so little. Did you find out if he'd appeared again at Paris?"

"He didn't come openly. In fact, there was no actual persecution at Paris."

Monstuart looked startled. "Persecution? That's an odd word to use."

"I employ it advisedly. I told you something peculiar happened at Paris. I didn't see the manager there. After all, we don't know who the murderers are—we know there were at least two of them; if it was a gang there may be several other people in the secret, and all of them know by this time, I expect, that I was going about with Dupuy, and my staying at the various hotels where Marks had been just before he came here would look suspicious. I wanted to exercise reasonable caution."

Montstuart nodded. "Life's sweet."

"So they say. Personally, I'm inclined to think Hamlet came nearer the mark. At least in life you can see what you're up against, but we have the haziest notions of what we may be called upon to face hereafter. Annihilation's a blessed conception for a large number of people, but no one can be absolutely sure of it. And it wasn't even that with me. It was curiosity. Just plain unvarnished curiosity. I want to know who killed Marks and I want to know where the diamond is. As I say, I didn't trouble the manager, but I got hold of the waiter, who remembered Marks quite well. He would, of course. He was a queer old man, bald, with a yellow wrinkled head, like a tortoise, rather short and unexpectedly sturdy—yes, like a tortoise in a lot of ways. Except that he had a knowledge of wines that was surprising in a human being and would have been miraculous in a reptile. He explained to me that he'd once been a head waiter, but he hadn't had good luck —drank, perhaps, or got into a mess with a client, goodness knows—that wasn't relevant—and it was easy enough to slip in Marks' name. This old chap spoke of him with respect. He said he had good taste —he knew about wine and he knew about ladies."

Montstuart's brows shot up; Marcella Brodie had not spoken a word since Latymer began his story.

"Ladies?"

"Yes. There's a lady here, too. I wondered rather about the Paris interlude. I mean, it seemed so ridiculous to hang about there when he was nervous already about having that diamond, in spite of his surface sang-froid—yes, he was, I'm coming to that—and yet he deliberately prolonged his danger by two days. He had some reason for that, of course."

"And you think the lady was the reason?" Montstuart's voice was very dry. This case became more and more distasteful to him. He agreed with a passage he'd once read in a novel—oh, years ago now, but a very good novel, and heavens knew they were rare enough. "Passion is such a hot, stupid, muddling thing, all emotion and no thought." And yet there were men who went in for divorce for a life job. He came back from his momentary reflections to hear Latymer say, "It's possible. Or there may be another explanation. He may have been trying to put someone off the trail."

"Then he was frightened?"

"Oh, undoubtedly. He didn't mean to give himself away if he could help it, but my waiter was no fool. He said, talking of Marks' death, 'It would need to be a very splendid possession to make that kind of misery worth while.' Yes, he said misery. He was talking English. I think he liked people to realise how well he could talk it. He'd been at an English hotel for years, he told me, not so much to learn waiting as to learn the right way to tackle the English. He meant to make most of his money out of them, you see. I repeated, 'Misery?' and waited, and he said, 'Yes. He was not at ease all the time he was here, except when he was actually with this lady. The rest of the time he was perpetually on guard.' It was so bad that he asked Jules if anyone had been asking for him. Jules said he'd inquire, and came back to say that no one had. Then he said had anyone rung up, but no one had done that either. Finally, he spoke of letters, but there were none waiting for him. At length he asked outright if any one had noticed a man skulking round the hotel. Jules wasn't surprised, exactly; a man who carries that treasure about with him must expect trouble. But he says that Marks really was alarmed. He knew there was someone after him."

" He wasn't suspecting the strange visitor of Dover?"

" One can't be sure. Of course his record doesn't help us much. He's a man of mystery, and I wouldn't be at all surprised to hear he'd got a lot of enemies one way and another. He used to go to Paris a good deal, but he didn't stay at the Cosmopolitan then. No one quite knew where he was. It would be an interesting story if only one could unearth it. But I dare say we never shall. Anyway, there he was, expecting to be followed. . . ."

" We assume that that was on account of the diamond, but it mightn't have been. It might have something to do with the lady."

Latymer looked sceptical. " Do you really think a man of his commercial outlook would run a tithe of that risk for any human being alive? There was one other thing. He spoke of letters; he didn't say anything sufficiently definite to give us a lead, but the waiter swears he was getting anonymous letters and that was getting on his nerves. And the next morning there was a letter for him in printed writing. A letter with the local postmark. No one knows what was in that letter. Presumably Marks destroyed it, since it wasn't found among his belongings. The police would have unearthed it if it had been."

" All this is very interesting," said Montstuart, whose spirits had gradually returned during the latter part of Latymer's story. " All the same, there's a discrepancy somehow. If you're planning to rob a man you don't go to the trouble of warning him first."

"We don't know that it was robbery. The writer may have been demanding justice—we know nothing about Marks, as we've already agreed. At all events, Marks was definitely afraid of him, whoever he may be."

For the first time Mrs. Brodie spoke. "Did you find out anything about the woman at the Cosmopolitan? Was she a friend of Marks'?"

"The waiter didn't seem to think so. He said he'd got a pretty wide experience, and that was a first meeting. I rather gathered that that was the lady's game. She was very attractive, one of these red-haired women, plenty of curls, the waiter said. She wanted someone to pay for her dinner and she was prepared to be companionable. She seems to have made the running. But suburban virtue appears to have been preserved. The lady acted with quite passable propriety. She got her dinner and her wine, and she gave her companionship. Jules thought the man was glad of company. That's all he wanted, and the next day he left the hotel, after making a second set of inquiries. Later—but this may be innocence overdone—she asked Jules who the gentleman was, and seemed astounded to know he was Marks and a millionaire."

"And did you learn when she reached the hotel?" asked Mrs. Brodie.

"She'd only come that morning, I think."

"From England?"

"She was an Englishwoman. I should think it's very probable."

"The visitors' book would tell you that. That would be easy to discover."

"And who she is? That might not be so easy."

"What are you driving at, Mrs. Brodie?" demanded Montstuart in blunt tones.

"I was thinking perhaps it's rather strange that just before Mr. Marks arrived at the Sumptuous a strange chambermaid was taken on, a woman of noticeable appearance, grey-haired, elderly. She disappears as soon as Marks leaves, and that night another woman, of whom nothing is known, turns up at the Cosmopolitan and makes herself attractive and lures him into conversation. Of course, it would be easy for a woman who was a chambermaid to see the name of the hotel a guest was going to; it would be easy, if you had the means, to fly to Paris, and arrive before Marks did. And I dare say it wouldn't be very hard to get out of him the name of the hotel in Monte Carlo where he was going to stay. This isn't a one-man crime, you see. And is there any reason why one accomplice shouldn't be a woman? Mrs. Fellowes didn't see anyone at all clearly."

Latymer stared at her in sheer admiration. "You're suggesting that this woman, who disguised herself first as a greyhead and then appeared—in her right colours?—no, you're right. She wouldn't dare look conspicuous in case she were recognised later and her movements traced—cleverly disguised, was following him, learning his plans? And then?"

"Sent a telegram to her accomplice."

"The lurking stranger? Let's see, when did he begin to lurk?"

"Some time on the 29th, according to all accounts."

"And Marks reached Paris on the 28th. And that was the night he dined with the red-haired siren. She learnt from him what his subsequent movements were to be, and sent a telegram presumably. Wasn't that dangerous?"

"Oh, she needn't send it from the hotel," Mont-stuart cut in. "Who's going to trace a telegram sent from some busy post-office?"

"The question is how to trace it. We don't know what it would be signed or to whom it would be addressed. But presumably it would mention the name of the hotel. Unless they used code. That would complicate things a good deal. If we could trace that telegram we should be a good deal nearer our solution."

"We'd have no legal proof that it had anything to do with poor Marks' death," the lawyer pointed out. "I don't suppose this woman is so simple she'd actually use his name."

CHAPTER XV

THE tracing of the telegram was extraordinarily easy. Montstuart, with all a Scotsman's superstition, felt dubious when he heard the result of Latymer's in-quiries. The private detective had gone to the large general post-office near the Cosmopolitan and explained that he was trying to trace a telegram that had gone astray. It had been sent from Paris on the 28th or 29th October, he could not say to whom, and contained a message about the Hotel Fantastique, Monte Carlo. He asked for a copy for which, he said, he would, of course, pay. The assistant looked uncer-tain, but Latymer went on in his faultless French, "I must insist. It was a telegram from a lady to a gentle-man." . . . And immediately the girl thought she under-stood. This queer, smouldering man had discovered that his wife had a lover, that she had sent him tele-grams making an appointment at the Hotel Fantas-tique. It was not difficult to look up the record of telegrams, and quite soon she found one dated October 29th, reading:

" Hotel Fantastique October 30."

There was no signature, but the telegram had been sent to a man called Michelet at a Parisian address.

"You don't recall who handed this in?" hazarded Latymer, but that, of course, was too much to expect. The young woman, keenly excited in this drama, urged her companions to rack their memories, but nothing was forthcoming. The record of the message was the proof that it had been sent, but any information as to whether it had been handed in by a man or a woman, and any sort of description, proved unobtainable. Nevertheless, Montstuart felt that they were a definite step on, though where, he wondered, all this is leading us, I've no notion.

He went round to the address given on the telegram to explore the neighbourhood, and found himself facing a well-constructed block of service flats, comfortable but probably not very expensive. So Michelet isn't particularly prosperous, thought the investigator. I wonder, by the way, where he is now, and where the diamond is, too. He discovered Michelet's telephone number and rang up from an adjoining office, without getting any reply. If there's a porter on the premises I might be able to learn something of the fellow's movements from him, Latymer thought, and a few minutes later he was speaking to a burly voice that assured him that M. Michelet— No. 49, he called him—had gone out a few minutes earlier and would not be back before the evening.

That gives me all the time I need, decided the satisfied inquirer, leaving the box and returning to the block of flats. One or two men were moving on the stairs as he turned in at the entrance, but he ran up briskly, paying no attention to them. There was nothing about his appearance to attract notice, and he had no intention of skulking guiltily round the corner until the hall and staircase were empty. This supreme caution had undone more criminals than the laity would ever guess. He found the lock on the door of No. 49 a simple matter to deal with, and with scarcely an impression of fumbling he was inside the flat. It was a neat, comfortable bachelor establishment, sitting-room, bedroom, bath and cloakroom, lobby and kitchen. Latymer closed the door and without any hurry began his methodical search. A number of papers and memoranda stood on a square writing-table, and Latymer went through these carefully. But they told him nothing of importance regarding the man he sought. The table finished, Latymer began to examine the contents of the drawers, and midway through the second one was brought up short by the original telegram he had been so eagerly tracing.

" Hotel Fantastique October 30th."

he read, and saw that the telegram had been handed in on the evening of the 28th. Even Latymer's poise was disturbed by that amazing discovery. It was, he decided, not merely an unlooked-for piece of luck, it was a miracle.

" I thought I'd saddle him eventually with the murder, once I'd discovered who he was," he observed aloud, " but I didn't think he was going to make it as easy for me as this. What in fortune's name persuaded him to keep such incriminating evidence? It was the act of a madman. But, of course, he never expected to be traced. And even now, we shouldn't find it very easy to go into court and get a jury to believe, beyond all doubt, that this telegram refers to Marks at all. An ingenious man could think of a dozen explanations, and it won't be possible for the most enterprising authorities to pin Michelet down without more direct evidence than this. This telegram is noncommittal enough. And I've no letters I can produce."

Latymer's original excitement was beginning to cool, when a second discovery caused it to leap up like a tongue of flame. He was examining the last of the drawers and here he found a sheet of note-paper on which someone had drawn a neatly-annotated plan. When he turned it right way up Latymer saw that it was a plan of the grounds at the Fantastique. The plan was executed with the thorough-going care of a draughtsman; it showed the entrance to the grounds from the side door, to which Michelet had been once at least, the path running down to the kitchen garden, the holy well, and the outside wall. At the foot of the sheet was scribbled in very tiny, neat writing, " A thief could easily get over here; the gardeners would have gone by that time, and no one would be likely to linger in this part of the grounds. Test outside wall for way in."

This second piece of luck was so stupendous that Latymer felt there must be a catch somewhere. No man, not even a lunatic, could have preserved a document for several days after a murder that would inevitably bring him to the scaffold. Or had he forgotten he'd got it? That seemed improbable. Nevertheless, there it was, and Latymer took charge of it, slipping it into a stout envelope in his portfolio, along with the fatal telegram. There was nothing else to interest him, though he took his time over the search. It was striking six when he left the flat and prepared to take up his position in a nearby café. He didn't mean to leave Paris until he could recognise his man. At about eight o'clock, walking slowly on the opposite side of the street, he saw lights burning in the windows of the sitting-room, and he went confidently upstairs and knocked on the outer door. A shortish, dark man, with a merry, unscrupulous face, opened it.

" Who d'you want?" he demanded.

" M. Michelet."

" That's right. Who are you?"

Latymer produced an attaché case and began a flood of commercial patter. Michelet listened for two minutes, then he said, " I haven't anything for you, and I'm not going to give an order. I can hardly pay my rent as it is."

Latymer kept him in conversation for a little longer, while he memorised certain minute details. His eye was remarkably quick and keen, and by the time the door was closed against him he was reasonably certain that he would recognise his man if he met him again. No matter how cleverly he was disguised certain physical peculiarities would betray him.

" If we're to fix up a case against him," he told himself in stern tones, " we can't afford to take any risks. In a matter as delicate as this one, the most insignificant detail may turn the balance."

Now he must find out as much as he could about his suspect, without attracting attention. So long as Michelet had no notion he was being followed there was little to fear, but, though Latymer did not yet understand his game nor why he had been careless enough to leave that map lying about in a place where it could easily be discovered, he realised that he might have almost insuperable difficulties to combat before bringing the crime home. " Even if we do persuade Dupuy that he's implicated, as likely as not he'll suggest that here is the accomplice they haven't succeeded in naming. Of course, they'd have to prove contact between Salomon and Michelet, and that might prove pretty difficult, but I'm inclined to think

Montstuart's right, and Salomon's alibi wouldn't hold water in any court in the world." So on all counts it was important to learn something of his quarry's manner of life, his friends, his means and position generally; if it became possible to learn where he ostensibly was on the night of the 31st so much the better. So far Latymer knew nothing of him beyond his address and the fact that he had received a telegram from Paris on the evening of the 28th, in reply to which, presumably, he had gone to the Hotel Fantastique. Latymer's knowledge of the world warned him that at this stage his best source of information would be the porter at the block of apartments. Supposing Michelet to have been there for, say, six months, he would be sure to have accumulated a good deal of gossip and certain facts. Latymer went back to his hotel, thought over what he had learned during the day, and went to bed early. The next morning he disguised himself slightly and put on a different suit: experience had taught him how unobservant is the average human being, and that men will travel daily in the same train with a neighbour without realising the colour of his eyes or hair, the type of collar he wears, the shape or size of his boots, any distinguishing marks, such as a ring or seal, anything, indeed, that might serve to differentiate him from other men: and he felt he ran little risk in taking no great pains to re-create his identity. On leaving his hotel immediately after breakfast he entered a telephone booth and rang up M. Michelet's flat. Michelet himself answered the call, giving his name. Latymer at once apologised for a wrong number and rang off. The flats were only a minute's walk, and he paraded up and down the street, mixing skilfully with the crowd, most of whom he approximately resembled, until he saw Michelet himself come down and turn sharply to the left. It was no part of Latymer's plan to follow him or learn his movements now. The great thing was to discover what he was doing on the 31st. The fellow was carrying an attaché case, so it was scarcely likely that he would return at once, so, with little fear of detection, Latymer entered the flats and turned towards the porter's quarters. He saw that he was not recognised, though he had actually seen the same man for a few moments on the previous day. Yesterday, too, he had spoken in perfect idiomatic French, but to-day he was the Englishman, careful, precise, stilted, making himself understood but without fluency. He asked if there was a M. Michelet among the tenants. The porter said, " Yes, Flat No. 49."

" M. Paul Michelet?"

" M. André Michelet."

Latymer was at once the self-conscious foreigner, fearful of a rebuff, anxious not to lose an opportunity.

" You are sure of the name?"

" Absolutely, monsieur. And you?"

" Equally so. There is not another?"

" Not in these flats, monsieur. This is the address?"

Latymer drew a slip of paper from his pocket. It was inscribed.

> " Paul Michelet,
> " Rue Jacquebord,
> " Paris."

and underneath: " I understand he has a flat there in a large block, whose number I don't know."

The concierge looked doubtful. " What is he like, this M. Michelet of yours?"

" Shortish, rather gay, dark, very vivacious."

" That seems the same. And yet—this one is André without a doubt."

" He is, perhaps, at home?" hazarded Latymer.

" He went out less than a quarter of an hour ago, and will not be back till after lunch."

" I am very unfortunate," murmured Latymer. " It is most important that I should see him, if indeed it is my M. Michelet. What does he do for a living, this one, can you tell me?"

" He is a partner in a jewel firm, I believe, monsieur."

" Then it must be he. And you say he won't be back for some time?"

" After lunch, monsieur." He thought this English-man was a trader of some kind, interested in stones, too, very likely.

Latymer softly beat his gloved hands together. Always wear gloves was one of his maxims. Hands betray you like nothing else, and you can't change them as you change a face.

" So this is the second time! I have a train at mid-day. I was to have met him at Monte Carlo a few days ago. . . ."

The porter pricked up his ears. " M. Michelet was at Monte Carlo not long since."

" You can remember the date? I was there for four days from the 29th October."

" I have a note, I dare say. Monsieur said there might come a message, very urgent. I was to telegraph him." He turned up a black note-book, flicked over some pages. " That would be the 28th, monsieur. I remember he came running down the stairs. . . ."

" He had just had a telegram?"

" Yes, I think he had. I think he said, ' This has just arrived. I must go at once.' He was not quite sure how many days he might be away."

" And was it the morning or evening?"

"It was the evening, monsieur. He said he hoped he might catch the night train."

"So that fits in," was the investigator's comment. "He wouldn't know then, probably, about the All Hallows party. He mightn't be sure which night . . . Oh, we can dispose of any objection he may make as to that." And aloud he went on, "This is all very strange. He was at Monte Carlo. I was at Monte Carlo. We should have met. I was at the Cordon Bleu. Was he not there also?"

"I couldn't say, monsieur. He gave me a telephone number."

"And what was that?"

Rogier told him. "Not the Cordon Bleu," said Latymer with decision. "So that was how we came to miss. I expected him there." Of course, he reflected, it would be a nuisance when Michelet returned if the porter repeated all this conversation. Michelet might get suspicious at once, but some chances have to be taken, he decided grimly, and went on to the crucial question. "And what day did he return?"

"It was on the 1st November, monsieur. He came in—oh, very exhausted, saying he had been travelling all night, very uncomfortable. He missed the express. He says he met a friend. . . ."

"I wonder if he could produce him," thought Latymer sceptically.

"These slow trains are very inconvenient," he offered. "He probably took twice as long to get back as he'd expected."

"He was back a little after midday, monsieur. He asked me if a message had come through, but I told him not. He seemed exasperated, oh, unreasonably so. He stayed in almost all the afternoon expecting a call, he said. That was the night, you will remember, when the great diamond mystery began."

"This Englishman, Australian, whatever he was—I know whom you mean, a fellow called Marks who had found an amazingly large diamond."

"That's it, monsieur. I recall reading the news and my wife, who is pious, said, 'What is the use of diamonds when you are dead?'"

"I suppose they might still be useful to someone else," observed Latymer callously. "I expect, since he's a jewel merchant, M. Michelet took the same view."

"He was very strange in his manner. Knowing him to be interested in the diamond—he had spoken to me of it, saying he wished he had it in his hands, and some people had all the luck, and that it was not for nothing that one used a corkscrew to open the wine and not a knife with a straight blade—I spoke to him of it. I said, I see this man with his diamond has vanished."

"He seemed shocked?"

"He laughed, monsieur. He said, 'The old fox.' And he said, 'Well, after all, why not give the police a run for their money?' He said, 'We shall have to be careful, Rogier. There will be a nice lot of gentry trying to sell us outsize diamonds for some time now.'"

"He didn't seem troubled about M. Marks' death?"

"We didn't know then that he was dead. Only, afterwards, he seemed more anxious. He said he was an old fool—Marks, I mean—and that he had asked to be murdered. He said he had been a nuisance to most people he had met when he was alive, and he was carrying on the tradition. He spoke very wildly."

"He hadn't been trying to buy the diamond himself, I suppose? That would naturally enrage him against the thieves."

"I hardly think so, monsieur." The concierge

laughed. "He is not a rich man, M. Michelet. There are times when I have to be very discreet about the rent."

"We all know about that," Latymer agreed confidentially. "And, for jewellers, times just now are almost impossible. They've shut down any number of diamond mines. I'm rather dreading going back to England myself. I don't know how many bills I shan't find to settle. Fortunately, there's no rent due till Christmas."

"Oh, well, I think he must have been lucky at the tables," the concierge laughed. "He seems to have come back with plenty of money. So if you wish to do business with him, monsieur, this is a good time."

Latymer looked at the plain gold watch on his wrist. "I shan't be able to wait, I'm afraid. No, it really wouldn't be any good leaving a name. He wouldn't know me. I heard of him through a friend in England, who thought he might be able to help me with a deal I'm trying to put through. But I've got to leave Paris at midday, and there's a second address I've got that I must try. Thank you for all your courtesy." A coin changed hands. "I'm glad M. Michelet is having some luck. They say, don't they, that when one person's happy the ratio of everyone else's happiness increases in proportion, and presumably the same thing's true about prosperity. I'm not so lucky as M. Michelet, unfortunately, and not for want of trying, either. By the way, if he ever comes across that diamond, I'd like to see it. By all accounts it was something pretty fine."

"I'll tell him so," promised Rogier jovially. "I must say I wouldn't mind having a hand on it myself. Good-day, m'sieu." He went comfortably back to his office. A good reward for half an hour's gossip.

"And now," wondered Latymer, coming out into the sultry street, "where does that lead us?" The weather, after several days of unusual brilliance, was blowing up for rain again, and the air seemed full of dust and discomfort. Irritability was expressed on innumerable faces; even the wind blew hot and comfortless through this endless area of dwellings. Latymer paused, fascinated as always by the conception of these thousands of homes, each housing so many creatures intent on their own aims, all blindly playing into one another's hands, thwarting, desiring, fighting one another, a whirlpool of human personalities, and his own blood warmed at the thought of the impasse in which he found himself. A man with a certain reckless tendency, despite his demure appearance, he was inspirited and stimulated by danger; not once but several times in his adventurous career had he carried his life in his hand; four times to his knowledge had attempts been made against that life. He knew that he had never been on thinner ice than he was now; a false step and he might find he was at the end of his career. He was accustomed, even when he was not engaged on a case, to think of the myriad windows he passed as the peep-holes of his enemies, men and women who had a grudge against him, people eager to see him out of the way. He recalled some of his more hazardous experiences before, with a characteristic shake of the shoulders, he set this absurd dreaming aside and applied himself to the difficulties of the present position.

"Where does that get us to?" he repeated, turning a corner and walking slowly close to the wall. "Michelet had a telegram saying that someone—presumably Marks—would be at the Fantastique on the 30th October, and immediately he goes down there. We assume that he's the man who made such a scene both at the hotel and in the nearest inn. I might be able to get that verified. There are some physical details I noticed. He's lost the top joint of the fourth finger of his right hand, though I haven't much hope that any one will have realised that. I've noticed so often that a small disadvantage of that kind almost always goes unseen; I remember that fellow, Smellie, to whom I went when I had a poisoned arm about seven years ago, telling me a story of a patient of his, one of his insurance cases, who wanted to claim some colossal sum, because of a road accident in which he'd lost the top joint of one of his fingers, and Smellie, showing me his hand and saying that he'd lost a similar joint years ago and it had never, he found, interfered with his work and practically no one ever observed it. I hadn't myself, but I've been more careful since then. But it might be possible to get one of those giggling servants to identify the man. Not that that's likely; he was wearing a red beard when he came to the hotel, and behaved in an outrageously conspicuous manner. I dare say he wore a red wig, too. Now, there's a point. Did he hire the wig? It might help us if we found that he had, because he's simply got to explain why he behaved in that extraordinary manner. To take a day's journey in disguise, play the fool at the end of it, and then just disappear, isn't the act of any one outside a lunatic asylum. There was some motive behind it, of course, and it seems pretty obvious that that motive had to do with Marks. I don't suppose he thought for a moment any one would be following his tracks in this painstaking manner;" he grinned as the words passed through his mind, " and he probably went to the nearest costumiers, one of those places where you get fancy dress, and hired the wig. A Trades Directory will give me the addresses, and I can try them myself before I return to Monte Carlo. If that telephone number he gave the porter is the number of the hotel where he was staying that's another source of information, and I ought to be able to learn when he arrived and when he left. He told Rogier that he missed his train; that would explain his late arrival. He didn't get in till midday. I should say he travelled on small connections, possibly with a wait at every turn. He'll have to explain how he came to miss the express. He may have an alibi—making a night of it, or something of that sort—or at the tables. That would be a difficult one to break, because in a crowd like that, if you go in alone and nobody knows you, it's next door to impossible for any one to trace your movements, unless you create a scene or you're outrageously successful. And our case has got to be that he wasn't noticed because he wasn't there. After all, there's this map of the grounds; that won't be very easy to explain away either."

He had plenty of time—he was a man who refused to hurry and he attributed his success up to the present to the fact that, though he could act quickly and intelligently when necessity arose, he never put a plan into action until he had tested it thoroughly, foreseen its weak points and guarded against them to the height of his ability. He wanted to keep this inquiry secret for as long as possible, though he knew that, once Michelet realised someone was on his track, he would discover the loss of the telegram and the ground-plan, and might act in a manner impossible to foresee, that would defeat all his (Latymer's) campaign.

There were three costumiers reasonably near the flats where Michelet lived, and Latymer made his patient inquiries at each in turn. At the third he was told that a red beard and wig had been hired out on the 28th October to a gentleman called Michelet at the Rue Jacquebord, Appartement No. 49.

So he'd been ready to start at a moment's notice, his plans all cut and dried, just waiting for the telegram.

" And when was it returned?"

" On the 1st November, monsieur. I recall it coming back, because it was the only one precisely like it that we had in stock, and a gentleman had been promised it for that evening. M. Michelet had said that he would return it without fail before midday. He said that if he could not be here himself, since he was a little unsure of his plans, he would send it through the post. At twelve o'clock we telephoned to his flat, but he had not returned. And then, at about two or a little later, he came in saying that he had been delayed."

" That's two people ready to swear he wasn't back by noon," Latymer reflected. " I wonder what his explanation will be, and what ground we shall have for asking him any questions at all. That's the disadvantage of being a private detective and not the police. I've no authority here at all. Not that I'd have any authority in England, except that of the ordinary citizen, to arrest a proven criminal, but I'd be more likely to get a hearing there. I don't think there's anything else to be done this end, but all things considered, I won't go back till the night train. I couldn't do anything at midnight at Monte Carlo, and as I generally sleep very well in a train I can get to work again immediately I arrive."

He spent an amusing and not unprofitable afternoon picking up scraps of information about Michelet. The other tenants of the flats proved friendly in more than one instance, and when a man appeared at their doors trying to sell them paste jewellery on commission they told him he had a competitor on the premises, a real jeweller. He returned to his hotel at six-thirty, ready for a bath, a shave, a good dinner with the kind of wine he appreciated, and a couple of hours' entertainment before his train went.

CHAPTER XVI

AT the instant of his arrival, Latymer's shrewd side-long glance assured him that Montstuart was simmering with excited anticipation of his return, although training and tradition alike forbade his putting his anxiety into words.

"What luck?" was all he permitted himself to say, when they had shaken hands. (Montstuart said he was so accustomed to that meaningless ceremony that once, waking on a stormy night, unaware of his surroundings, he had tried to shake hands with the bed-post.)

"I've a good deal to tell you that seems to point to Michelet being our man," replied Latymer, generously giving him the cream of his discoveries in his first sentence, "I'm framing up a skeleton of a case, but there are a great many gaps to fill in yet. First of all, I have to check up dates and times. I must find out where the fellow was staying. I've got a telephone number that, even if it doesn't belong to his hotel, ought to put me on the right track. I suppose there have been no developments this end?"

"One very unfortunate development," said the lawyer dryly. "Mrs. Brodie's husband has turned up."

Latymer whistled softly. "What the deuce does he want?"

"According to her story, to ruin her. He sounds that type that would never forgive infidelity, nothing that would detract from his own personal vanity. He doesn't really mind so much that she spent the night with this other man, but he looks on her as a thief because she gave Salomon what he chooses to think he's bought and paid for. Anyway, he intends making all the trouble he can, and I'm afraid that's rather a lot. I've had some bad cases in my time— there was young Livingstone who was supposed to have shot his partner, and that solicitor's wife at E—— who stood her trial for eight days, accused of poisoning her husband's lady-friend, but I don't know that I've ever been up against anything tougher than this."

Latymer was amused and informed by the change in the man. At the time of his own departure, Montstuart's attitude had been aloof, if not definitely hostile; but now he was warmly championing a woman whom in colder blood he despised. It wasn't, as Latymer saw, a triumph of personalities. Montstuart was in love, not with the lady, but with the case itself, with its intricacies, its problems, with its hard points, its opportunities, its novelty and its mystery. Mrs. Brodie was no longer an individual to him, but a symbol of that work that was his love, his life, the mainspring of his being, and, like the natural actor falling into the correct pose as a familiar line falls on his ear, so now, presented with a situation that enthralled him, calling forth all his professional ability, he ceased at once to be a person of definite prejudices and outlook, becoming merely the legal mind, an abstraction automatically summoning all the strength of his material to present as guarded a front as possible.

"What precisely does he propose to do, by way of ruining her?" Latymer asked.

"It seems he's been suspicious for a long time—my experience of his type is that it always is . . ."

"Apparently this time with some reason," cut in Latymer dryly.

Montstuart assumed the impassive air his clients had come to know. "We're not judge in this case, thank heaven. We're unofficially briefed for the defence. The point is that this fellow didn't get any farther than the coast. Then he left the train and came on down here to do some dirty spying work on his own account. He put up at a local hotel, and proceeded to trail his own wife. He knows exactly what she did that afternoon and evening, and he saw Salomon go in with her after dinner."

"And saw him emerge again next morning?"

"I don't doubt it, but that's not the story he's going to tell the court. He's going to swear that he saw Salomon leave the flat again within a few minutes, that is, about ten o'clock. Oh, he's damned subtle. He's going to have his cake and eat it. He isn't going to let his wife proclaim to the whole world that she's got a lover, that she's been cuckolding him for four years. No, he's her husband and he can swear that her companion left her at ten, and that during the night no one else went near the flat. He's prepared to wear a white sheet for a very brief time and confess to unreasoning jealousy that, happily, was quite unfounded."

"He doesn't go so far as to say that he knows Salomon did away with Marks?"

"Oh, no. Marks is nothing to him. He's only concerned to defend his wife's honour. There may have been rumours for all I know."

214

"Presumably he knows the truth of the relationship between them?"

"Of course he does. Equally, of course, he saw Salomon slip out in the early hours of the morning, six or seven, or whatever time it was. The fellow's one of these sallow restrained devils, the best possible material for psycho-analysts. Now the inhibitions he's suffered for years have flowered into the kind of cruelty you find in elderly people of both sexes, a most dreadful lust for power. Of course, it does come out in other ways, but if you'd heard, as I often have, quite old men on the bench displaying the most frightful demands for vengeance against young things for comparative trivial offences—I warn you, it alarms you for the lengths to which distorted humanity will go. Anyway, here is Brodie's one perfect chance. He's the sole witness we could have produced to show where Salomon was during the important hours, and he'll go into the box and blandly swear that fellow's life away."

"Has he acknowledged in so many words that he saw Salomon leave the flat in the morning?"

"Oh, he hasn't spared his wife anything. He's put all his cards on the table. He told her that he watched Salomon go back to his hotel, and tried to plan some way of getting even with him that wouldn't involve him (Brodie) in a scandal. And then came the story of Marks' death, and suspicion falling on Salomon, and he was quick enough to see his opportunity. Short of murdering the fellow, I doubt if we can do anything to shake him. He's not the kind you can buy off, even if that kind of thing were safe or possible."

"You said the only witness. There's the maid."

"Haven't you seen the glaring weakness of her in the box? Mrs. Brodie rang and asked for shaving-water, and the girl brought it. She didn't actually see Salomon at all. She's bound to be asked that, and she'll agree that it was Mrs. Brodie who did all the talking. There's no proof whatsoever that Salomon was there at that time."

"And Brodie has realised that?"

"I should say Mrs. Brodie let it out. It was a frightful shock to her. Or, of course, he may have questioned the maid at once. And there is the fact that so soon as he reached the hotel Salomon rang for shaving-water."

"That was to throw dust in the eyes of the chambermaid at the Cordon Bleu. He didn't want a scandal any more than Mrs. Brodie did."

"I'm afraid that won't be a very good card to play in court, if French justice is anything like English. And I don't see that we can shake Brodie either."

"If you wanted convincing you've got your proof," suggested Latymer dryly.

Montstuart looked doubtful. "Have I? I've only Mrs. Brodie's word that Brodie said he was going to lie in order to be revenged. He, of course, in court, will deny any such suggestion. Now what's our next move?"

"I'd better go on trying to implicate Michelet. And when we've done that we've got to find his accomplice. We don't want the intelligent police force to suggest that Michelet is simply Salomon's nameless accomplice. After all, Michelet's not in a very enviable position at the moment. I'm going to find out where he was staying and see if I can learn anything that way. He may have had this other fellow coming to see him at the hotel, or there may be trivial details noticed by a waiter or a fellow-guest that will put us on the track of evidence. We can't afford at this ticklish stage to disregard the faintest hope."

He went out and rang up the number he had scrawled in his note-book. The answering voice said at once, " Hotel Bordelaise," and Latymer returned, " Wrong number. I am sorry," and clicked off.

" So that's where he was staying. I'll go down and get dates and times," he told Montstuart. " Meanwhile, here's a note of my Paris discoveries, and if you can find anything else that helps us there, we may be able to shuffle Salomon yet one more step away from the guillotine."

The Hotel Bordelaise was a small cheerful second-class hotel, with flowers in pots on a yellow balcony, and a thin agile waiter standing in the doorway, his hands behind his back, his eyes roving inquisitively up and down the hot road. As Latymer approached he melted deferentially into his background, and the visitor found the entrance hall empty except for the reception clerk. He advanced to the desk and asked immediately for M. Michelet. The clerk looked puzzled.

" He is not staying here, monsieur."

" Oh, but I have a letter from him." He pulled out a thin sheet of paper on which were scribbled a few lines carefully copied from the handwriting on the ground-map he had found in Michelet's room. " Written from this address." He exposed it for the clerk's benefit.

" But that was written on the 31st October, monsieur. He is not here now."

" Oh!" Latymer looked blank. " When did he go back then?"

" I think the next day." The man turned over the leaves of a large shiny note-book. " No, monsieur, on that same day itself. He was here the two nights. He came in the afternoon of the 29th, and departed on the 31st."

"Oh. How very disappointing. Do you know if he went straight back to Paris?"

"He told the porter to send his bag to the station as he would be catching the 10.12 train that night. He was due to leave his room at 6.30."

"And he did actually go then?"

"He went much earlier. We did not see him after midday."

"So that he went in a morning suit," reflected Latymer. "But there's no evidence, is there, that both or either of the men Mrs. Fellowes saw were in evening dress? We can square that." And aloud he continued, "You can tell me perhaps if another gentleman, a friend of his, was staying at the hotel at the same time."

"And his name?"

"Rollin, M. Giuseppe RolliVn."

The clerk looked through the pages of his record. "No, monsieur. I do not think I have ever heard the name. No such gentleman has stayed here."

"But he came to see M. Michelet while he was here perhaps? A tallish thinnish man, rather sallow."

But the clerk said no, he could recall no such visitor. He could not remember if Michelet had had any letters or telephone calls. Latymer came away perplexed and frowning. He went to the station now, and explained that he was trying to trace the movements of a relative of his who was missing from his home and who might be suffering from loss of memory. He produced a photograph, a snapshot he had found in Michelet's rooms with a note—"A. M. —Juan-les-Pins, September '33" on the back, and showed it to the station-master. "This is he, and the matter is very urgent. We traced him to an hotel here, that he left on the 31st October, in the afternoon, saying that he would be taking the express to

Paris at 10.12. And from that time onward we've lost him."

The station-master suddenly looked alert. " He's a youngish man," he said, " brown-skinned, a little . . ." he snapped his fingers, " a little *exalté* perhaps."

" He might be," said Latymer grimly. " You do recall him?"

" There was a gentleman who came running into my office—my office—on the night of the 31st. I remember it quite well. There was so much noise and scuffling. I think he had been taking a little too much to drink. He said that he had booked a ticket, reserved a sleeper, I think, on the 10.12 and that his luggage was in the cloak-room, and now it was 10.34 and the train was gone and his luggage was still in the parcels office. And what did I propose to do? I told him he must wait till the morning or travel by slow trains with changes. He seemed greatly distressed."

" Did he say he had some important appointment in Paris that he should be so troubled? He could have his money refunded, couldn't he?"

" He did not say, monsieur. Only again and again he repeated, ' I was mad. I must not be found in Monte Carlo to-night.' "

" And you thought . . . ?"

The station-master shrugged tolerant shoulders. " A woman—or a husband, perhaps. Who knows?"

" Or the police?" wondered Latymer.

" You mean, some gambling trouble? No, monsieur, I had not thought of that."

" And what did he do?"

" He asked if it were possible to stop the express anywhere. He said he had money . . ."

" He needed it very badly."

"He was so upset, monsieur, so afraid. I have not often seen a man afraid like that. And he looked over his shoulder again and again at someone who was not there."

"You didn't gather what the trouble was? This is all very disquieting to his relatives."

"He was afraid of being followed, I think. And he looked at his watch several times."

"And it was now about half-past ten?"

"It was later than that, monsieur."

"Did he say where he'd been?"

"He said, I have been at the Casino. I did not notice the time. I was fortunate. Certainly, monsieur, he had money in his pockets."

"Did he stay here till the next train went off?"

"No, monsieur. He called for a taxicab, collected his luggage, and drove off."

"Did you notice the driver of the cab? Or perhaps some man would remember so excitable a passenger. Was there much luggage?"

"Only a suit-case, monsieur."

"Of course," thought Latymer, "he wasn't here for more than a night. And the driver?" he urged aloud.

"I remember him, monsieur. He is a new man, lately from Paris. He has his own cab, a new smart affair, and he is anxious to make contacts. A superb driver, monsieur. Several people have remarked on his skill."

"A man from Paris, eh? And how long has he been down here?"

"I should say a month, monsieur. Not more. But Paris, he says, is too full of the commercials; there is more money to be made here. Ladies are more kind."

"An ambitious fellow," commented Latymer

smoothly. "I wonder where he deposited this unhappy gentleman."

The station-master summoned an assistant and rapped out an instruction. A minute or two later a neatly-dressed alert man in the early thirties came in.

"I can be of assistance to monsieur?"

"I believe you may have carried an unfortunate relative of mine on the night of 31st October. The station-master here remembers him as being very excitable and distressed at having lost his train. He had a suit-case with him, and we think entered the cab. Since then he has disappeared."

The driver looked anxious. "I remember him, monsieur. I remember him quite well. I knew there was something strange, but it is no concern of mine what people do so long as they pay my fare and do not damage my cab."

"I hear it's a very handsome one."

The man smiled. "It is my capital, monsieur."

"I hope it doesn't pass its dividends, as so much of ours does just now."

"It suffices," said the driver vaguely. "About this gentleman, monsieur. . . ."

"Yes. Now where did you drive him to?"

The man was looking rather wretched. "Pardon, monsieur? You are from the police?"

"No, no," Latymer reassured him. "But this passenger is a relative of mine, and he is a little—you realise." He tapped his forehead significantly. "So I am afraid he may have got into some trouble, or have forgotten who he is. That has happened before, you understand."

The man's face twisted into yet more perturbed lines. "I don't know how to answer you, monsieur," he said frankly. "You see, a bargain's a bargain."

"And he bargained with you?" Latymer's voice was soft and persuasive.

"Mind you, I didn't think at the time it was anything but a lark. I hadn't heard about all this Marks trouble then."

"Marks!" The word shot from between Latymer's thin lips. And "Marks," he repeated more gently. "Will you tell me what you mean?"

"I didn't think much about it at first. You know how it is, you're busy and I had my own plans. Then suddenly it flashed across my mind—a red-bearded man. Wanted by the police. That's why I asked you that question just now."

Latymer and the station-master spoke together. "But you've got it wrong, this man you took up hadn't got a red beard," said the latter. And, "A red beard. Go on," cried the former.

"Ah, no, he hadn't got a red beard, not when he got into the taxi. But when he got out he was quite different. I didn't think then it was anything but a game, as I say. There's a lot of money spent on that sort of joke hereabouts, so when a man with a little black moustache and dark hair got into the taxi and said, Z—— Station, and twenty minutes later a man with red hair and beard and wearing different clothes got out, I went on thinking he was going to one of these parties most like. Especially when he said, Now if any one hails you and asks if you've seen me, you haven't. I'm going to win."

"And did any one hail you?"

"They didn't have the chance, monsieur. The gentleman gave me a handsome tip and I had been up since very early, and, since his destination was near my garage, I put the car up and decided to have an early night for once."

"How wise!" approved Latymer gravely. "And

where did you drop my unhappy friend? Ah, I recall. To Nice. To a particular house?"

"To the station, monsieur."

"And you?"

"I returned at once to leave my car at the garage. This would be about eleven-thirty. It is Moineau's Garage, where I have kept my cab ever since I came to this place."

"I see. Now, you didn't observe what your passenger did on leaving the cab?"

"He went into the station."

"You didn't happen to look back and see if he came out again?"

"I did not think, monsieur. I was so sure it would be some game. And I did not wish to meet any of the others who might ask me questions. So I put up the cab and I went to bed early."

Latymer laughed, a queer half-stifled sound, as though laughter were an effort for him. "I thought you were going to say you decided to give yourself a treat."

Flambeau's face remained grave. "No, monsieur. For that I can wait. But I am ambitious, and I have my plans. One day I shall own not just a single taxi that I shall drive myself, but a fleet of taxis, and that is not done by spending one's pourboires." He smiled suddenly, flashing excellent teeth.

"You're right, I'm sure," Latymer agreed. "And I'm grateful to you for what you have been able to tell me. It gets me on to a further point, though whether that's going to prove a blind alley or not I can't say yet."

The man hesitated, twisting his cap, showing his first signs of embarrassment. "Monsieur, I would not like you to believe that I am accusing this gentleman of—of anything, not even of being the man that went into the inn and, perhaps, drank a little too much. I thought once that he might be a little—a little unlike other people." He put the words in the form of a question.

"That's just it. He isn't quite normal. That's why we're so anxious about him. No, I don't for an instant in my own mind connect him with Marks' disappearance; I don't think the police support the theory that the man who made so much publicity for himself at the outset has anything to do with the crime. It's a form this kind of madness takes. It's what you might call a money mania. He'll be sensible for days, weeks perhaps, and then he'll hear of some particularly outrageous feat of a millionaire and he'll begin to seethe. It'll go on for some days and then it'll die down. It's like a volcano; it may be quiet for years, centuries even, and then there's a terrific explosion."

"I understand, monsieur. I have a brother who was shell-shocked in the war. There are occasions, impossible to foresee, when he is like—like an animal. He cannot reason or understand. And then for weeks he is like everybody else. But this gentleman seemed all right, only that he was very excited, and that I accounted for by saying, There is some joke on."

Latymer thanked him, and took out his note-case. "You'll give me your address in case I want to get in touch with you again. Of course this wild cousin of mine may turn up safe and sound at any minute. Good-day, and thanks very much."

He had learned a good deal, he decided, but now came a complete check. Every inquiry rebounded on itself; no one remembered seeing a red-bearded man, not in the station or the trains, not on the platform. No policeman in the neighbourhood recalled him; Latymer tried the nearest shops, a tobacconist, a baker, a drinking-shop, a paper-shop, but he learned nothing. The red-bearded rascal had vanished as though, when the taxi deposited him, the earth opened and swallowed him up.

CHAPTER XVII

1

DISCUSSING the matter some hours later with Montstuart, Latymer said, " I'm trying to put myself in Michelet's shoes. To begin with, what was his motive for changing his appearance in the taxi? I think to avoid being noticed. He isn't a very striking man, but it's normal human conceit to imagine that one has memorable features, habits, tricks of standing and walking, and the last is true. There are familiar gestures by which men more easily betray themselves than by their faces. I remember going into a film one night in London, and there was a picture being shown as I entered. All I could see was the back of a man disappearing down a corridor. But I didn't need to look at my programme to know who that was. There was a gracefulness of movement from the hips, a kind of ease that marked out the greatest actor of our time. When he turned, he was so disguised I'd never have guessed his identity. The way I reconstruct Michelet's action is this. He told the truth to the station-master; his watch was slow or had stopped. He honestly thought he was going to catch that train. It went at 10.25. A man with a car could have helped in the Marks murder and got away just in time, if the luck had been with him."

Montstuart shook his head. " You're forgetting one

very important point. There were two men on the
lorry."

"That's true. But there's no reason why we
shouldn't believe Michelet's story about the time. If
he'd known it was after half-past ten and the train
had gone, I doubt if he'd have rushed down to the
station and certainly he wouldn't have gone in his
own identity. Then, when he found it was hopeless,
he took steps immediately to prevent acquaintances,
etc., saying to one another, Michelet was hanging
about the place till after midnight. No one, of
course, would recognise him in his red beard. And
we know that was his, because we've traced it. Now,
let's see how quickly he could have got back to Paris
if he'd put his mind on it. Suppose he got a train
from Nice to Marseilles. Or he might get a car. Let's
look up a railway guide." He procured one and sat
keenly over it, making calculations. "No, that's all
right. There was a train at 12.30 and he could pick
up the 2 a.m. from Marseilles that reaches Paris about
lunch-time. Probably he looked up these trains to be
sure his story hung together. A neat-minded man,"
he added approvingly. "But why not spend the night
at Nice—if he's innocent—or at Marseilles?
Obviously, because he wants to give the impression
that he wasn't in the neighbourhood when the murder
took place. But it's too late to prove that, so why
make that mad cross-country rush? The answer is, of
course, that he had other things he'd got to do. Now,"
he pulled out a map and spread it on the table, " here's
the place where the body was found. There's a local
train from Nice that would have got him there about
2 a.m. And from there he could catch an early morning connection to Paris (while his accomplice drove
the lorry to H—— where he was going to sell it),

arriving about 1.30. Our problem is to show that he was on that train."

"You're assuming that your version must be right," suggested Monstuart dryly.

Latymer looked amazed. "The defence has to base its case largely on assumptions," he retorted. "Besides, there's the map, there's the telegram. You know, sir, the time's coming when our friend will have to be asked to explain his movements."

"It hasn't come yet," said Montstuart quietly. "In my experience it's no manner of use trying to rush things. I wonder if your taxi-friend could throw any more light on a difficult situation."

Latymer moved sharply. "So that went through your mind, too. Interesting!"

Montstuart stared. "I don't know what you mean. Nothing's gone through my mind beyond the possibility that we might do worse than talk to this man again. He seems an unusual type, keen, well-spoken."

"Exactly. And very helpful in giving you just enough information to win your confidence, but not enough to get us anywhere. Has it occurred to you that perhaps he's the other man we're after?"

It was typical of his companion that, instead of instantly pooh-poohing such a notion or demanding irrefutable proof, he said, as soon as the amazed silence ended, "It's a theory. Let's see how it would work. What, to start with, do we know of the man? That he's a Parisian, that he hasn't been down here long and knows no one, that he did carry a man we have every cause to suspect, and dispose of him in rather mysterious circumstances, that thereafter, instead of returning to the stand, he goes calmly to bed. . . ."

"That he's an unusually good driver," Latymer took up the tale, "and that we are looking for a man

227

of that description; that already he's begun to drop hints about going back to Paris; that of his own accord he's suggested a link between his anonymous passenger and Marks' murderer. . . . Of course, if there's anything in these suspicions, this story of the red beard donned in the taxi may be all my eye and Betty Martin."

"If you could prove that," said Montstuart keenly, "you'd have them on toast. Because if he wasn't really wearing the beard then, how did Flambeau know about it at all? He couldn't, unless he were Michelet's confederate."

Latymer said, without much enthusiasm, "It means starting a fresh trail, I suppose."

"And you're tired of them?"

"I get a little rattled in case they discover they're being trailed. The fat would all be in the fire then."

"If you were to approach him openly, think up one or two more questions you might reasonably ask, surely he wouldn't be suspicious. You'd be far more likely to learn what we want to know than if you start sleuthing straight away. It's no use my offering to come in on this. Once he found a stranger asking mysterious questions all our chances would be ruined." He seemed to assume that he had said enough on that point. "One other thing occurs to me in connection with this affair. Assuming, as we must, that Salomon and Mrs. Brodie are telling the truth, and that he never so much as saw the lorry in which Marks' body was taken away, there must be some other man in France who, on the morning of the 1st November, discovered himself minus a pearl in his dress studs. Of course, if he keeps his head he won't advertise that. But suppose he went to a jeweller straight away, and suppose we could find that jeweller? It might be worth trying. Our case isn't so strong that we can afford to disregard any detail. We might circularise the jewellers. . . ."

"Of Paris? We might. It sounds a little improbable to me, because surely a man would come forward when he heard about the missing pearl."

"Not if he knew his customer. Particularly in Paris. It wouldn't occur to him that the man would be mixed up in a murder. It's this glorious habit of assumption that makes crime far easier in our country at all events than it might be. I've been told—I only quote the opinion, I won't swear to it—that in France a man's guilty till he's been proved innocent, whereas with us, of course, the process is the reverse. Our criminal gets all the benefits of the doubt. And, you know, it isn't in human nature to suspect the man you've neighboured for years to be a murderer."

"But aren't you thrilled when you find he is?" murmured Latymer cynically.

"That doesn't alter my argument," retorted his companion in good-humoured tones. "Besides, the jeweller was traced very quickly here, and a good deal was kept out of the papers. News didn't trickle in much, and the story of the replaced pearl was published almost simultaneously with the story of the discovered pearl in the lorry. There really was no time for speculation."

"Oh, I agree with you, it's worth trying," said Latymer. "All's grist to our mill. I must say," he added in distressed tones, "I wish I knew a little more what was in Brodie's mind. That fellow holds us at the moment in the hollow of his hand. You saw him while I was away, didn't you? Is he the kind to be shaken in the witness-box?"

"Ever seen a rabbit try to shake off a stoat?" demanded Montstuart. "It's a horrible sight, and the

wretched beast's absolutely helpless. So will the law
be when it tries to stump our Mr. Brodie."

"We certainly are up against it. Salomon, granted
he's innocent, could hardly have woven a worse net
for himself. It only shows that, if you're going to
spend the night with another man's wife, you're
better advised to shout it from the house-tops."

"Not that anybody takes much notice these days.
Married couples change partners so often you have
to be constantly on the watch to preserve yourself
against a gaffe. It's unfortunate that Salomon did
lose his pearl that night. I hadn't thought of it for
the defence earlier, but it would have been a godsend
to us if he'd chanced to remark to a friend that he'd
lost the pearl before Marks was murdered."

"I'm afraid that's no good. He isn't that type of
chap. Extraordinarily meticulous about that kind of
thing. But these methodical fellows are the ones that
end in trouble. He's in no end of a mess at his end,
too, you know."

"I heard a rumour of that. What was it, actually?
Or is it confidential?"

"It's safe enough here. We can't be overheard.
He's in trouble for forged bonds or something precious like it."

Montstuart whistled softly in dismay. "If that
comes out we shall have a job defending our man."

"It's bound to come out. It's one of the planks in
the police case."

2

Latymer went back to Paris yet again, tireless,
patient, implacable. Montstuart, watching him de-
part, thought suddenly, "If I were on trial for my
life, that's the kind of chap I'd like to have working

for me. You'd never wear him down. If he were trying to save his own life he couldn't be more devoted."

Latymer sent out his advertisement, took a temporary apartment, and waited. On the evening of the second day there came to see him a small flustered man carrying a letter.

"With reference to your advertisement," he began, "I doubt if this is relevant at all. Probably I'm being ultra-careful, but I think it best to be candid. There's nothing to be lost. . . ."

Latymer smiled wisely. "A charming belief," he murmured, but his visitor was too agitated to hear the words.

"Of course, I know this unfortunate gentleman was found dead some time ago, the 1st November was the date, I believe. . . ." He paused, staring at Latymer with protuberant green eyes, twitching the letter between his fingers.

"He was killed on the 31st October, so far as we know, and the body was found a few days later."

"Yes, well, that's quite a long time ago, and of course this other man has been arrested, and I daresay the police are quite right, though naturally his friends and his lawyer don't agree."

"You've got some information that might be of use to us?" questioned Latymer patiently.

"I did warn you—you'll remember I warned you at the outset—that most likely it would prove irrelevant. But as I say, there's nothing to be gained by keeping silence."

"Is that the letter?" asked Latymer, despairing of bringing the man to the point.

"Ah, yes, this letter. Now you realise, do you not . . . ?"

"That this is probably all beside the point and

nothing to do with the Marks case at all. Yes, I've taken that in. Perhaps I could see it."

The man seemed rather reluctant to yield up the sheet. "We only had this yesterday morning," he told Latymer warningly. "It's a letter from a gentleman called Michelet, enclosing a stud, and saying that he has just lost the pearl and asking if we can replace it."

"You don't know him?"

"No, monsieur. There is just this letter and the stud." He gave up the letter at last, and Latymer immediately recognised the writing as identical with that on the ground-plan he had found in Michelet's room. It ran:

"MESSIEURS,

"I shall be glad to know whether you can replace a pearl in the enclosed stud. I have had the misfortune to lose mine. As I shall be wanting the studs for immediate wear, would you be good enough to send it back by hand as soon as it is done?

"ANDRE MICHELET."

"And the date is that of the very day I was inquiring for him," reflected Latymer, leaning back, the letter still in his hand. "He couldn't afford to be found with an empty stud; probably numbers of people knew he wore studs of this nature. Questions might be asked, and it would be awkward if he had to say that he'd given them away since Marks' death." He told his agitated companion that he must have the letter for the time being, and promised him that he should not suffer any inconvenience, whatever the consequences. Then, his work in Paris done, he went back to Monte Carlo, where Montstuart awaited him eagerly. As soon as he had heard the story he made Latymer's own comment.

"The same night as you made inquiries! He must have thought up till that time that he was safe. Then he heard that a stranger had been asking about his movements on the night of the 31st, and, though that wouldn't have affected an innocent man, it was enough to rattle a guilty one, and rattle him badly, too. I suppose he thought it would be wiser to write, as then no one would see him. He wouldn't know about your having found the man. Or would he? Even so he wouldn't, probably, remember that you knew his writing because of the notes. It simply wouldn't occur to him. And I dare say he had forgotten he ever had the thing, or else he'd think he'd destroyed it, and everything was jane, as that yellow-haired young woman, Miss Blaise, would say."

"He's in a pretty desperate position now," Latymer agreed. "I'm going to see what I can find out about the chauffeur."

"H'm. That's another delicate matter. He'll wonder what on earth you're up to."

"He won't know who I am," replied Latymer serenely. "It oughtn't to be too difficult."

"And then there's the question of the weapon, that seems to have been very casually shelved by everyone. I suppose the police made the usual inquiries; I also suppose it's next door to impossible to trace a knife of that description. But a man in Flambeau's position would be far more likely to use such a weapon than a man in Salomon's. Unless, of course, it was a subterfuge on the part of the criminals to give the impression that it was an apâche crime."

"As it may yet turn out to be," supplemented Latymer a little gloomily.

"I believe Dupuy tried to get the knife identified, and was assured it was absolutely impossible. Of course, he hasn't been able to bring the knife home to Salomon, that's one thing, though I dare say that's not for want of trying."

"It's equally probable we shan't be able to bring it home to Flambeau, even if he's involved," was Latymer's blunt reply.

At the close of the next day he came back, pale and dusty, and asked in a moment of absent-mindedness for China tea. Then, remembering that he was in a Riviera hotel, and that the tea hour was past, he changed his mind and said hastily, " A whisky-and-soda."

" This is a pretty good busman's holiday for you," Montstuart remarked, as his companion leaned back and waited for his drink. " But then holidays generally are, I find. I have a brother who's a bishop out East, and when he comes back on furlough he finds that the London secretary has booked him up to attend meetings and preach and deliver lectures for five months out of six. He says the diocese on the whole is less wearisome, because at least he isn't asked silly questions there, and isn't expected to sing for his supper, which he found devolved on him at home. Personally, I'm enjoying the whole affair. They say there's a criminal tendency in all of us, and I'm inclined to believe it. Look at the women who cheat the 'bus companies of coppers, and as likely as not give them to a pavement artist when they alight. It isn't just the money saved that appeals to them; it's this criminal instinct we all share. Like doing the Inland Revenue—oh, there are dozens of ways. And why this passion for detective stories? And the people who write 'em! They're lucky, of course, as I'm lucky and you're lucky, because we can sweat it out of our systems by proxy so to speak. And, as I say, I'm in my element now."

"Only wish you could take over the defence, I suppose?" murmured Latymer. "Well, why not?"

"Oh, that's Salomon's affair."

"Salomon will do what we tell him. He's quarrelled with his own lawyer, you know. Got the idea that the fellow believes him guilty and I dare say it's true."

"That he's guilty?" Montstuart sounded startled.

"No, no. That the lawyer believes he is. Anyway, Salomon's put himself completely in our hands. I was going to suggest, if you would, that perhaps you'd act for him."

The Scots barrister looked doubtful. "He's a Frenchman, being tried in his own country. French law and ours isn't identical, and they stress points that are immaterial, comparatively speaking, to us. I'm no advocate of false modesty, but I feel he'd be wiser to stick to one of his own countrymen. Besides, I don't really know the case sufficiently well. What's his line of defence going to be?"

"We ought to produce the actual criminal. That's what I'm working for. We haven't as yet got a strong enough case against Michelet. But I shall probably know more in two to three days' time when I've been on Flambeau's trail for a bit. I admit it's leaping in the dark, but these leaps are sometimes lucky. I wonder what he was doing on the night and early morning in question. That's the next thing I've got to know."

"You're inclined to be optimistic, aren't you?" murmured Montstuart. "When you know that, how much further on will you be?"

"I shall know how much of his yarn is true; why his happened to be the sole cab hanging about the station when Michelet arrived, and why, if he's so ambitious, he tamely disappeared to his garage at an hour when the crowds are thickest. It doesn't hang together to my mind."

"You've practically made up your mind he's the accomplice we're looking for?"

"Nothing of the sort. I've nothing to go on. But I can't dismiss the fellow from the case till I'm sure he's merely incidental to it."

3

Wearing a small moustache and exchanging his customary hard black hat for a soft shapeless one of grey felt, Latymer called the same evening at the garage and asked for Flambeau. The garage proprietor laughed. "You won't find him here yet, monsieur. It's pretty late of an evening before he puts up his cab."

"Not always, surely. A man must rest."

"Not he. He's got something in him that won't let him rest. He's going to be a big man one of these days. Big men can't afford to enjoy themselves."

"So if one were to come at nine or even ten o'clock . . ."

"That's when trade's briskest. You wouldn't get him then."

"The other night," said Latymer, "two or three weeks ago, that night he came in early."

"Did he?" The other looked dubious. "There must have been something up. It isn't like him."

"I suppose you're not always here," suggested Latymer.

"Maybe I'm not, but someone else is always about. Why, Flambeau is the joke of the place. The other men laugh at him, ask how he gets on without any sleep. That man isn't sane, monsieur. He thinks of nothing but his work and getting on. One of these days he'll do something terrible, I shouldn't wonder."

"Something terrible?" Latymer's voice was speculative. "In order to get on, do you mean?"

His companion nodded. "One of these days he'll be so beside himself with wanting to be where he intends to get to, that he'll lose his senses and when he gets his chance, he'll snatch. You see, monsieur, I know. I have seen it happen before."

"You—don't like him?" asked Latymer, frowning in some perplexity.

"I am afraid of him," said the older man simply. "He is not a human being, he is a machine, and machines are ruthless. They drive on no matter what or whom is in their way."

Latymer continued the conversation desultorily. Then, with the Frenchman's interest thoroughly aroused, he said, "I'll bet with you if you like. I'll bet you that Flambeau isn't really so industrious as you think. There's been one evening anyhow, one week-night evening, when he's put up his cab by—say—midnight."

"I think you will lose, monsieur. Nevertheless . . . you can prove what you say?"

"No, I can't, but I dare say some of the other drivers might remember, if he's the subject of gossip that you say."

"I would ask them, monsieur, but, as I say, I think you will lose."

The next day Latymer returned to the garage and the proprietor met him, smiling generously and crying, "You have won, monsieur. You were right. There was one evening when Flambeau's car was back before midnight, a little after midnight it was first noticed."

"Do you remember the night?"

237

" It was the night of the 31st October, All Hallows. That is remembered because there are many English here who keep that night as a—what shall I say?"— he spread his hands—" as a gala. It is a night when there is money being spent, a bad night for an ambitious man to be home early. Unless, of course, he also has his reasons."

" Or realises that there will be so many cars on the road that he won't be missed," parried Latymer casually, but the other looked derisive. " That's no reason for a man like him. No, no. He had his own party that night perhaps."

A fresh thought struck Latymer. " If all your other men were out, how did they know Flambeau wasn't?"

" One of them brought his cab in just after twelve o'clock, and he says that Flambeau's cab was already in. He taunted him with laziness next day and Flambeau said he had made good money and was satisfied. He didn't wish the windows of his vehicle broken. Sometimes there is trouble after these parties."

" How wisdom is justified of her children," speculated Latymer aloud. " I dare say he was up very early next morning, though."

" Oh, no doubt." Latymer tried to get some proof as to the time that Flambeau had taken his cab out of the garage but he could learn nothing. Nevertheless, he was not ill-satisfied with the evening's work. Flambeau had left the taxi at twelve o'clock. It could be argued from that that he was at the Fantastique at 10 to 10.15, helped to conceal Marks' body under the sacks, took his place on the front of the lorry where he was seen by young Paul, and then picked up his taxi, that he had stalled in some convenient place, and driven home to the garage.

" He has established the fact of his having returned

earlier than usual. That would create the impression in a jury's mind that he wished to provide himself with an alibi. Alibis are suspect just now; they're like oysters in R-less months. Innocent men aren't supposed to need them. Now, what was he doing in the early morning? My line of defence is going to be—unless I stumble on some insuperable difficulty—that he put up his cab, rejoined the lorry, drove with it to the shed where he helped in the repainting, let the lorry go on in charge of Michelet, who abandoned it at H——, and himself came down and collected his taxi very early in the morning. I dare say there was someone on duty but the sight of Flambeau appearing at six or so wouldn't surprise him. It's happened too often. I wonder if one could get any information from the house where he lodges."

It was difficult to make such an inquiry and all his tact and energy got him nowhere. "I'd better talk to the man himself and see if he gives anything away," Latymer resolved. Faced for the second time with the lynx-eyed Frenchman, Latymer suavely explained that he was a detective trying to trace a thief who had reached Monte Carlo on the night of the 31st October and was believed to have taken a taxi early the next morning and driven to the station from some insignificant hotel. "We're interrogating every driver in the neighbourhood of the hotel," he added, "in the hope that someone will remember the man. Of course, it's some time ago now and so many things happen and memories are short, but you might recollect the man if you had driven him. He had a great scar down the right side of his face."

Flambeau shook his head. "I recall no one like that," he declared. "In any case on that morning I drove a lady a considerable distance to an hotel at Cannes."

"Ah, but I mean really early. Some time between five and seven, we believe."

"It was about six when I picked up the lady, and it was after seven o'clock when she dismissed me. And eight o'clock when I returned."

"It's an odd hour for a lady to be abroad."

"It was a strange story altogether, monsieur. Listen! I had, as I said, a quiet evening the night before. I felt very rested and eager to be at work. You know how it is in the morning, one wishes to start at once. There is a whole day and much to be done." The man's blazing vitality fired Latymer, who felt himself shivering from contact with so fierce an ardour. But he felt, with the garage proprietor, that here was an energy barely normal. Like flame it leaped in the still air between them, till Latymer half-threw up a hand to shield his eyes from the glare and heat. "For some reason—I don't know why—I didn't go by my usual road. For one thing I was a little earlier than usual, and there would be no train coming for nearly an hour. So I thought I would go the long way round on the chance of picking up a passenger coming back from a dance, perhaps. And in the Rue Rivoli I was hailed by a lady who wanted to be driven to Cannes."

Latymer's brows drew quickly together. "That's a long distance," he observed.

"Yes, monsieur. As I said, I was more than an hour taking the lady there."

"Did it strike you as strange that a lady going such a distance should trust to luck to pick up a cab? The houses in the Rue Rivoli are large and expensive. Most of the tenants have cars of their own."

"There was much that was strange about this, monsieur. The lady was so frightened. She carried a little case. As I drove her I could hear her moving about in the cab; she could not rest. Several times she spoke to me, though there was nothing she needed to say. And at such an hour, monsieur, without so much as a servant to carry her bag—but it was no affair of mine."

"Of course not. And yet—you're not precisely Peter Bell, are you?" He said the last words almost to himself, and Flambeau paid no heed to them. "You saw the lady safe to her destination and then drove back, of course," he added carelessly.

"Yes, monsieur, and I was glad when she arrived. I was afraid of some collapse, and seven o'clock of a morning is no place for an hysterical woman in a taxi. Besides, I knew nothing of her . . ."

"But speculated a lot? Well, that seems to put you out of court so far as our thief's concerned. I wonder what did happen to the lady," he added reflectively.

Flambeau shrugged. "She went to a lover perhaps, flying out of the big house with the bright blue door, she went in fear and in no joy. Women, monsieur," he added unexpectedly, "do not even enjoy their sins."

Latymer capped that. "They believe the joy constitutes the sin, that's why," he said. "So long as they can sin miserably they feel they're justified. Well . . ." he passed his man a note, a fairly large note. It was going to be worth it. Then, turning away, he told himself, ' Now for the Rue Rivoli and make sure there is a house with a bright blue door."

CHAPTER XVIII

1

THE house was there, about half-way down the road,
an imposing building, through whose open window
Latymer caught sight of lovely curves and mouldings,
of tall larkspur in a great blue glass that caught every
shimmer of the mid-morning light, of pictures in
clear glancing reds and silvers on a pastel wall, of a
pair of blue lustre dolphins so vital that the air might
have been their transparent, immaculate ocean. He
paused a moment, thinking of the wealth from which
that shrinking, terrified woman had flown, and wondered if it were true she had fled to a lover, or if
she had gone in fear, lest some dreadful fate engulf
her did she remain. His curiosity whetted by the
story Flambeau had told him, his own zest adding
fuel to the flame, he mounted the flight of marble
steps and rang the bell. He had ascertained that the
owner of the house was a M. Dubois, and it was for
him that he asked. He was put to wait in a small,
square room with a ceiling and wall moulding of such
perfect proportions that he failed to notice how long
he was left alone, until an automatic glance at his
watch warned him that he had been here almost half
an hour. He stood up and walked over to the window. The room was some steps above the level of
the road, and he had a pleasing sense of being remote
from the world without being actually separate from
its activities and achievements. This delightful sense
of superiority engaged his attention until the door
behind him was flung open and Dubois came in. He
was squarely-built, dark, aggressive man with a certain dignity that was unexpected and unassailable.

"If she went from him she had good reason," thought Latymer. "He'd never forgive. God help any human being that got into his power."

Dubois, stooping slightly from powerful shoulders, with an instinctive habit of thrusting forward a handsome fierce face, said in abrupt tones, "And what can I do for you, monsieur?"

Latymer presented a card. "Mr. Paul Harrison," Dubois read aloud and an address in London. "I don't understand," he said harshly.

Latymer, who had been looking away from him, turned without warning and surprised upon the face of his companion a most dreadful look that involuntarily silenced him. It was not only a look of rage and fury, it held desperate suffering and humiliation, it held fear and bitterness, it was a look that no man should ever see on the face of another.

"I will explain," said Latymer hastily. "I am an English private detective, working on a jewel thief case, one of these gang affairs, you understand? I am trying to trace the movements of a man masquerading as a taxi-driver, now in this place. And you will realise that I have to confirm the story he has given as to his movements on a certain day."

Dubois made an impatient movement. "And what has this to do with me? For one thing, I don't take taxis, and, even if I did, do you suppose I should remember individual drivers?"

"Not that exactly. These circumstances are sufficiently peculiar for them to be remembered. My driver's story is that on that morning, the 1st November, at about six a.m., he picked up a lady in front of this house, a lady who had just emerged on to the pavement carrying a small case. He took her a considerable distance. He gives the story in a good deal of detail. He says he would know the lady again, describes her rather closely. . . ."

Dubois' hands were slowly clenching and unclenching; his voice was stiff and brittle as he asked, " And you wish me to tell you—what?"

" If the story's true. If a lady did leave your house at that hour of the morning carrying a case."

Dubois looked as though he were going to burst a blood-vessel. His face was suffused with blood; the muscles round his mouth worked powerfully and agonisedly. He opened his lips and seemed about to speak; then he closed them again. Latymer remained silent and perfectly still. At last, thrusting his hands into his pockets with a force that strained at the close-fitting black stuff, Dubois threw back his head and cried, " No. I won't. I won't have my affairs dragged into some infamous private scandal on which you're employed."

" I'm sorry," said Latymer in his colourless tone. " I'm most reluctant to lengthen this interview for an instant. It's very painful for you and most embarrassing, believe me, for me. But surely you realise what'll happen, what must happen, if you go on refusing to answer me. We shall be forced to bring this man into court, where he'll explain his movements. He'll repeat the story I've just told you. That will be a public scandal right enough. You or the lady, probably the latter, would have to appear in the box. Every paper would be on to it."

Dubois uttered a sharp groan; his genuine agony at this scene was so strongly marked that Latymer walked over to the window of the apartment and stood staring down into the street. From behind him sounded the Frenchman's voice: " You are right. I must acknowledge it. It was my wife."

" And—she's here?"

" She's here, of course she's here. Good God, do you want to see her too?"

" I wondered if she could recognise the driver from a photograph. We daren't leave the smallest earth unstopped."

Dubois, with the gesture of a man to whom now little is of significance, strode across the room and pulled a long gold tassel. Somewhere the faint tinkling of a bell was heard and Latymer was left to stand by the window brooding over the square and becoming mystically reflective, a phase that seldom attacked him. For instance, he thought, how magnificent is that gilded rope, and how small, how feeble, the response. But adequate, his topsy-turvy thoughts assured him, for here comes a servant. And a moment later a man entered to be charged with a message for Madame. When Dubois' wife came in, Latymer, not easily astonished by beauty, was shocked into involuntary silence. Shocked, though not repelled; but a sensation like an electric current ran through his body, and this although he was far from being a sentimental man or one easily moved by such causes. Her face had a locked expression that set the least imaginative to speculating what must lie behind her frozen silence. Warmth and eagerness and delight must have animated her once; now she reminded Latymer of a carving he had seen in Vienna entitled The Living Death. She approached the table by which her husband stood, and waited, glancing from one man to the other with a look utterly devoid of curiosity or liveliness. Something had happened to her, something so intolerable it had quenched her spirit, like a shade put over a candle. Nothing mattered to her any more, not her husband, not this tiresome stranger with his inquiries about taxi-drivers, not even his colourless references to that wild morning when, with the sensations of a bird escaping from a nest whence he never dared hope he might be free, she had stood on a grey pavement, looking desperately up and down and espying at length a taxi materialising like a miracle out of the empty street. She was like a woman slain upon her feet, moving by mechanical volition. She took the photographs Latymer gave her, glancing at them quickly because they were so unimportant to her, yet with a certain degree of scrutiny because other men's lives might still have value. She picked out the picture of Flambeau after a moment or two. " That is the most like him," she said, " but I couldn't swear to any of these pictures. I didn't notice him particularly."

Latymer thanked her and said that identification was sufficient to reassure him; then he took up his gloves and stick and went quietly out.

" That might be checkmate," he reflected, turning out of the charming square into the busy high-road, " but need it be anything more than a well-thought-out alibi? Flambeau meant to have someone who would remember him to come forward if neces-sary—can't we work up that line of defence? And though it would be a tight fit, still it is possible to show that he came dashing back from repainting the lorry and collected his taxi. Let's see how that theory would work."

It could be made to work, he decided several minutes later, but so far it was a theory only. He had no facts whatsoever to connect Flambeau with the murder beyond the mildest of coincidences, an over-whelming ambition and the fact that the man couldn't supply an alibi for the hours eleven to, say, half-past five. But then he was an unmarried man, notoriously quiet and secretive in his personal life, lodging at a house where every other member had been out at some gala or other on the night in question. How could anyone say whether he really was in his bed, as he himself asserted, during the fatal period?

"I wonder if I could possibly get at his room on some pretext or other. Suppose I could find something there that would link him up with the crime? What reason can I give for wanting to see the place? And how to do it without rousing suspicions and making trouble?"

He decided to wait a day until some probable excuse occurred to him; he knew by this time that the position was about as serious as it could be. Montstuart was suggesting that they were raising mountains out of molehills. "Put that fellow, Brodie, in the box," he urged. "He'll be under cross-examination. . . ."

Latymer interrupted him. "You suggest we call him for the defence. But he wouldn't agree to that. You can't subpœna men to speak for a prisoner, if you're not the Crown."

"We could get that man into the box. We need only go to Dupuy with the story. Dupuy's an honest man and Brodie isn't. And from the time of the psalmist, and no doubt long before that, it's been a truism that the unrighteous flourish like green bay trees. I dare say that's fair enough according to the theological and philosophical authorities. The righteous have so much coming to them they can afford to be a little downtrodden here. But imagine Dupuy approaching Brodie with this story: You were watching your wife's flat, Mr. Brodie, on that evening, and you saw the prisoner enter at about ten o'clock. And a little later, according to you, he left the flat? Suppose Brodie agrees, how's he going to answer the next two questions? Why didn't he follow Salomon and raise hell on the spot? Or, alternatively, why didn't he go in and beat up his wife? Will any jury believe that he tamely spent the night in the street? And in the morning he said nothing to his wife or to Salomon? The thing's abnormal. Why did he want evidence if he wasn't going to act? He hadn't approached a lawyer, and at that stage he knew nothing of Salomon's connection with the Marks affair."

" He's the patient type, the terrible, pitiless, unforgiving type. He wouldn't act in hot blood. He hasn't any. He's like ice. And he could afford to wait, though he couldn't have expected fate to play into his hands as completely as she has. When he heard that Salomon was suspect he saw his chance. Oh, he won't come forward if he can help it; he doesn't want to admit that he's been cuckolded by a French tradesman. That's how he'd regard it. But if necessary, if there's any likelihood of Salomon getting off, then he'll come forward with his story. . . ."

" And be asked why the devil he's been quiet for so long."

" The answer to that will be obvious. He didn't wish his wife involved. No one will carp at him for that."

" And when our side cross-examine him, you think we shan't get the truth out of him, then? Trip him up somehow."

" It's a great risk. I'd like something more certain, more satisfactory."

" You don't call this satisfactory? To get your client off?"

" I aim at doing more than that. I want the real murderer. Besides, there's Mrs. Brodie. If we get Salomon off on her husband's evidence, it'll mean a horrible ordeal for her. Why didn't she come forward? Why let the wretched man be tortured all this time while we're laboriously scraping together evidence in his favour? Illimitable selfishness, a woman without morality or sympathy. That's how it and she would be described."

Montstuart, whose habit of regarding the protagonists in these affairs as puppets, subservient to the circumstances, protected him from personal emotional strain, believed he had, of a sudden, the key to the situation. So that was the answer to Latymer's tireless activities. Now, in his middle years, he was being swept away by sensations entirely unacademic, and Montstuart thought it was a pity.

"Now," he told himself, "he'll be utterly prejudiced. He'll find a way of turning the smallest detail into a weapon."

But Latymer, apparently unaware of his companion's trend of thought, had continued with a scarcely perceptible break:

"And even then I'm not sure the evidence wouldn't be suspect. It's funny, someone would observe, that no inkling of this story has leaked out before. What about the maid? Why didn't she talk? Loyalty? Oh, well, that might be the truth. But look at it how you will, it's infernally odd. Rather like a put-up job, isn't it? You must have heard that kind of thing, sir, often enough."

"And Brodie's reason?"

"Cash, of course. He's being heavily paid. . . ."

"By Salomon, who's more or less bankrupt?"

"More likely by the defence, who haven't another horse to send to the post."

Montstuart stared. "My dear chap—oh! this is fantastic. I'm aware that the law is a very peculiar and often a very incomprehensible institution. I'd be the last person to suggest, with my thirty-odd years of experience, that there is such a thing as justice. We can only tilt the scales as best we know, but we're little more than children, blindfolded, making wild guesses. Now let's examine this amazing suggestion of yours that, when we produce a witness who can provide an alibi for our client, all the community's going to leap up and say we bought him. Your cynicism horrifies me. Believe me, the community isn't so immoral as that."

"I'm not suggesting the idea would spring up in their minds without assistance," replied Latymer dryly. "But Brodie has coolly assured me that the impression left on the minds of the jury will be that he, a man in poor financial circumstances, was induced, by the sacrifice of his wife's honour, to earn a large sum. . . ."

"You're serious?" said Montstuart, after a long pause.

"Absolutely. You can talk to Brodie yourself, if you like. Your words would probably carry more weight than mine. You're a lawyer; you may be able to alarm him into decent conduct."

Montstuart pondered. "That's the very last thing we want to happen. Our case would be ruined from the outset."

"Precisely. That's why I'm so dead keen to discover who Michelet's accomplice is. We've got to go carefully here. We can't afford a single false step. I doubt if we've got enough on Michelet to justify even detention. And then Dupuy has taken his man. He can't move at present. I want to get my case complete before I drag the police into it. It would be easy to blow it to smithereens as it stands at the moment. And if Flambeau has an idea that the police are on the trail he'll cover his tracks at once."

"Supposing he has tracks to cover. If you don't mind my saying so, it appears to me you're taking a great deal for granted where that man's concerned."

"I'm taking everything for granted," Latymer acknowledged. "But if I don't start with some hypothesis we shall never get anywhere. However, I'm quite prepared to drop Flambeau out of the case as soon as I can find someone to put in his place. Anyway, I don't think Michelet can escape scot-free. That letter about the stud will be pretty difficult to explain away."

"And Dupuy would be more likely now to get at the facts," suggested Montstuart, who believed in authority doing its share, and also in the acumen of experts.

Latymer still looked doubtful. "You're thinking this is all professional pique," he exclaimed after a minute, "and that's partly true. I've discovered Michelet and pinned him down, and I don't want Dupuy to get the credit. This job isn't just my hobby, it's partly my living too. It would be a good bag for me to have tracked down the murderer of Marks in the teeth of the French police. And then I've the sense that an artist has when he finishes a canvas or a book, something done economically and well. You know that feeling, of course. To deliver up a thing all ragged ends distresses me."

"I'm afraid I was thinking more of Salomon's point of view," said Montstuart dryly. "The sooner he's out of his present predicament the better from his way of looking at things."

"Give me twenty-four hours," urged Latymer. "I want to get inside this fellow Flambeau's room. It may all amount to nothing, but—oh, I'm not superstitious. I haven't what the Americans call a hunch that I shall find the missing pieces there, but it's part of a theory I haven't yet rejected. And I should hate to have to reject it until I was satisfied that it's no good."

Montstuart shrugged. "All right. Have your twenty-four hours. You don't need me to tell you that what you're planning is an extraordinarily risky thing for which you take the chance of being run in for theft or, alternatively, if you plead justification in view of your opinions, libel in the first degree."

"I didn't need you to tell me," Latymer agreed, smiling, "but you've given me my chance just the same."

2

Fortune favoured Latymer. That night, as he passed the house where Flambeau lodged, he saw a card in the window, saying that a furnished room was vacant. There's an excuse for getting inside the house, he thought. That's my first step. Now I've got to devise a plan by which I can have Flambeau's room to myself for ten minutes. And before he went to bed the plan was devised.

The next morning at half-past nine he called at the house and asked to see the empty room. The landlady, an entirely typical woman, plump, shrewd, voluble as to the room's merits, took him up two flights of stairs carpeted in drab into a room of fair dimensions overlooking a small yard. Latymer regarded it appraisingly. "I hope it's quiet," he said. "Who works in that yard?"

"It's a garage, monsieur. But you will not notice the noise."

"It's open all night, I suppose?"

"Yes, but there are not so many cars coming in late."

"They start going out early, though, don't they? What sort of cars are they? Taxis, tradesmen's carts?"

"All kinds," the woman told him vaguely. "It

doesn't matter, does it?" And then she asked him what he did himself.

Latymer said he was a clerk, and added, " What about the man whose room is opposite mine? What does he do?"

" He drives a taxi. He's quiet enough. Why, you never know if he's in the house or out of it. And mostly it's out."

" Works late?"

" That's right. Going to be a rich man one of these days. And I shouldn't be surprised if he was, what's more."

" There's a lot of luck about it," murmured Latymer, and the woman said sharply, " He's not going to leave anything to luck, Flambeau isn't." And then the front door bell rang.

She turned. " That's my bell. I haven't a girl to answer it."

" That's all right," Latymer assured her. " I'll wait up here. I haven't quite made up my mind about the room."

As he heard her list slippers moving along the linoleum in the hall, he crossed the passage and opened the door of the front room. He had ten minutes, he knew. The woman might be ill at ease, but she wouldn't get away under ten minutes. Latymer had chosen his ally well.

Flambeau's room was very like the one he had already seen, small, square, with the windows carefully shut. There was a small press in one corner, in which hung two neatly-kept suits; there was a hard, narrow bed, two plain chairs, a rag carpet, a square table with a red cloth on it, some old-fashioned pictures and photographs on the walls and mantelpiece, and a shabby despatch box full of papers, accounts, notes and letters. Latymer looked through the latter rapidly. They dealt chiefly with offers of employment, some correspondence dealing with a possible partnership that had apparently come to nothing. Latymer put them all back carefully and relocked the box. It was an easy lock, too easy for so shrewd a man as Flambeau, one would have thought.

Downstairs the man had exhausted all his persuasiveness. There was the sound of steps on the stairs, and in an instant Latymer was through the door and was standing thoughtfully beside the window in the back room when the landlady returned.

"I'm sorry to keep you so long," she said. "One of those men asking any number of questions that get you nowhere. Now what about the room?"

Latymer said, "Well, I shouldn't want it for three or four days, and I had another address to look at, but if you can assure me that this garage man won't disturb me I'll take it. Anyhow, I'll reserve it for a week," and he drew out some money. It was improbable, he thought, that he would want to return here, but it was as well to have the entrée lest occasion arise.

Montstuart was waiting for him when he returned. "You've got something?" he demanded shrewdly.

Latymer looked a little crestfallen. "Was I so obvious? Yes, I've got something," and he put into Montstuart's hand a slip of white paper of cheap quality, with a printed heading and a blue carbon legend scrawled along a dotted line.

"This is a bill," said Montstuart. "A bill for 200 frs."

"Exactly. Have you noticed whom it's from?"

"Mouillet—oh, the big carnival people, fancy dresses and so forth. Well, I dare say fancy dress sounds incongruous in a taxi-man, though that's simply the association of unfamiliar ideas—there's no reason why he shouldn't spend his evenings decked out as a Viking, I suppose—but what in thunder has this got to do with Marks?"

Latymer retrieved the paper. "October 31st is the date," he pointed out gently. "And the bill is for a box of carnival hats and caps. Two hundred francs is a lot for a taxi-driver who's out to save money and on his own showing spent the evening of the 31st in bed."

"That's true enough. But what on earth are you driving at?"

"Oh, there was obviously a second box." Latymer seemed surprised at his companion's obtuseness. "Dupuy realised that from the outset. Only we couldn't discover who had bought it. *Why* it was bought has been clear from the beginning."

3

Latymer was now ready to hand over the position to Dupuy. He recognised that he had reached his own limits; he had neither the authority nor the desire to examine his suspects himself, and he agreed that the combine was far too subtle and too well prepared to admit of the slightest risk being justified.

"We might talk to him unofficially," Montstuart suggested. "He may have realised that you were dissatisfied with his conclusions; he's a sharp chap. And, since you were in the affair from the outset, it won't seem odd your going over the ground with him."

Dupuy, ardent, imperturbable, eager as ever, came at once to the hotel and listened to their story. At the end of it he passed a hand over his forehead. "This is very amazing," he said. "I must thank you, messieurs, for taking me into your confidence. You will let me keep the letter and the plan from Michelet's room, and the bill found in the room of the chauffeur?"

"What's the next step, if it isn't presumptuous to inquire?" Montstuart wanted to know.

"I must satisfy myself on the purely technical points. That this letter is in Michelet's writing, for instance, that the story M. Latymer has told me is not fiction," he beamed at them benignly. "You will realise that the police can take no story at its face value. The story of detection is proof and proof and proof again."

"That's fair enough," Latymer agreed. "You won't keep us in the dark longer than you can help?"

Dupuy bowed. "It is to you that I shall come first of all, monsieur," he replied. "Rest assured of that."

For thirty-six hours they saw nothing of the keen little man, though rumours of his scurryings in the neighbourhood reached them. Flambeau continued to drive his taxi tranquilly, and Michelet apparently was carrying on in Paris. Salomon languished in gaol, and Montstuart was frankly impatient at the delay. Latymer had reverted to his original pose, that of a non-committal passivity. On the second day Dupuy appeared, shot like a blazing meteor into their midst and fled again. He left one pregnant sentence behind him.

"Always I have wondered about that well," he said, "why it should be partly freed, and now at last I think I know."

"Which is more than I do," confessed Latymer frankly. "Oh, I hadn't forgotten the well, of course, but I hadn't been able to fit it in anywhere, and that left me vaguely troubled. I don't believe any detail so definite as that is without significance. And I couldn't see what that was. I'll be excited to know what Dupuy makes of it."

All those remaining in the hotel—by no means a large number, since many had returned to their own country, since the long painstaking inquiry began— were astonished and excited when next morning Dupuy marched up accompanied by two men, a box of candles and a great quantity of rope.

"What on earth's he going to do?" Miss Hoult breathed into Montstuart's ear.

"Something to do with the well, I imagine," returned Montstuart, removing his ear to a safer neighbourhood.

"The well?"

Montstuart remembered that she had not been present at Dupuy's cryptic announcement two days before.

"I can think of nothing else that would explain the candles. To test the foulness of the air," he explained. "But, of course, I may be absolutely wrong. I'm not in the French police."

It turned out, however, that on this occasion he was absolutely right. The inmates of the hotel grouped themselves in the grounds and waited to hear results.

"What do you expect to find, M. Dupuy?" asked Miss Hoult. "Not another body?"

"Oh, no, nothing like that," said Dupuy tranquilly.

"Then—oh, not the famous diamond?"

"Nor the diamond."

A chilling little man, she thought him, remembering the charges of warm blood and passion commonly made against his race. She didn't, of course, expect him to give his confidence wholesale, but surely she, an expert, an unofficial detective, you might almost say, stood in a different relationship. But the police always resented lay opinions. She adopted an attitude of cool reserve, but her eyes, like burying-beetles round a corpse, scuttered desperately to and fro, lest she lose a single detail. She was acting on the suburban assumption that if you do not want to know about things you are generally told.

Dupuy's men let down a candle into the well, and when they drew it up again its flame was not extinguished. So one of the men bundled over the side, and there was a period of suspense before he was seen again.

"How deep is the water?" Miss Hoult hissed in Potain's ear.

"Oh, nothing at all, madame," Potain assured her. "It is just the atmosphere. One must be careful."

"Yes, indeed," agreed the lady novelist, laughing heartily. "You don't want another death on the premises."

The search lasted some time. At first nothing was brought up but stones, weeds and ancient pieces of metal. But at last something appeared that centred the attention of the whole group, something large, irregularly cut, with glints of burning crystal showing through the slime with which the object was coated. Dupuy took it up and rubbed away the mud and weed, and instantly the thing glowed with a brilliant light.

"The diamond!" cried Miss Hoult.

Dupuy looked up, his thin mouth twisted in an ironical smile.

"No, not the diamond," he told her, "but all the diamond that Julian Marks ever brought to this hotel."

CHAPTER XIX

1

" I was not happy about the well from the beginning,"
confessed Dupuy to an intent audience of Montstuart
and Mr. Increase Latymer later the same day. (Miss
Hoult, incensed and outraged, had been excluded
from the conference.) "I know that numbers of red
herrings obscure the paths of the police when a crime
has been committed, but this, I thought, was different.
The stems had been cut before the police intervened;
there could be no mischief or design there. And that
kind of thing is only done for a purpose. I tested the
lid of the well, and it rose easily; you saw it this
morning, I dare say. So, I argued, it would not be
difficult to raise it two weeks ago. It fits loosely to its
frame. Now, messieurs, there is only one reason why
a man wishes to open a well in such circumstances,
and that is to conceal something. I might have sought
the weapon there but that it was found in M. Marks'
back; and indeed, the truth did not strike me until M.
Latymer brought me the plan he had found in
Michelet's room."

" You mean, Michelet opened the well?" Montstuart
sounded puzzled.

" No, monsieur. I think Michelet was never inside
the grounds."

" Never? Then how on earth did he make the
plan?"

" I think he did not make the plan, monsieur.
Otherwise he would have destroyed it, realising what
a danger it must be. That, indeed, was how I learned
the truth. For, said I, Michelet is no fool. I looked
up his record. He is a bit of a rogue, perhaps, a man

who lives by his wits, but hitherto no criminal, certainly no murderer. Nor, as I say, is he an imbecile. So, if he had killed M. Marks, he would at once destroy that plan that might bring him to the gallows. It was dangerous to make it in the first place; but afterwards, when the whole world knew of the crime, then he must be a madman not to destroy it. And he does not. It lies among his papers, and he does nothing, nothing at all. It is there for any curious or light-fingered person to find. And I begin to tell myself, It is you, *mon cher*, who are the fool. He has a reason for keeping this chart. It is for you to learn what that reason may be. I say to myself, many times I say it, Here is a man, murdered; and here is another man who naturally wishes to dissociate himself from the crime. Why, then, does he keep the one piece of evidence that links him to it? There is one answer and one only to that, for when their lives are forfeit men do not forget to destroy such glaring evidence. There is some significance, I discover, that I have missed. Michelet is keeping this map because it is precious to him as security. But it is difficult, for a long time it is impossible, for me to see what that security is. Particularly as the map is marked in great detail in the precise places where this crime was committed. Well, for the moment I thought I must abandon the chart; I must wait for inspiration. And then, as a formality, as a matter of routine, I compared the handwriting on it with that of Michelet himself. And I tell you, it is not his writing." He paused dramatically. Latymer stood up, half-dazed.

"And I—I never thought of a simple test like that. I was elaborate—I . . ." he broke off, staring incredulously at the detective.

"No, monsieur," Dupuy agreed. "I have realised that. And I blame myself most severely that the explanation did not occur to me until I had the proof under my hand."

"You're quite sure you're not pulling our legs? making a mountain out of a molehill?" suggested Montstuart, who had not moved. "Did it have to be in Michelet's writing? Mightn't it be that of his accomplice?"

"It was indeed, monsieur."

"Flambeau?"

"Flam——? Ah, yes, the chauffeur. No, no. The writing was that of M. Marks himself."

He had no cause to complain of the inattention or indifference of his audience. They remained spellbound. Latymer's face was informed by something stronger than chagrin, something Montstuart translated as anger, though whether at his own lack of enterprise or at Dupuy's superior genius was not altogether certain.

The lawyer spoke first. "You must give us a moment, M. Dupuy. We're literally dumb. We have to adapt this astounding statement to the facts already in our possession. Are you trying to tell us that Marks himself cut the stems and opened the well?"

"That is so, monsieur. You recall the scissors found in M. Marks' pocket? And that they were discoloured? The sap from those stems would discolour a steel blade in precisely that way."

"But his purpose?"

"That surely is clear. To conceal the faked diamond."

"And give the impression that he'd been robbed? What a scoundrel! But, if I may ask, have you any proof to back up that startling theory?"

"I think we have a great deal of proof, monsieur. Consider M. Marks' behaviour, how strange it was, how indiscreet. He made no secret of the fact that he was carrying the stone; he took no precautions; he did not even get about his business with despatch. He lingered in Paris, he lingered at this hotel; he spent a whole day before he telephoned to M. Salomon; he arranged for the motor to take him to the Cordon Bleu in as public a manner as possible. He announced that he had a very heavy chain to secure the diamond; yet when the body was found the chain was nothing remarkable. If it had been too strong, you see, it might be difficult to show how a thief severed it. He behaved then in an amazing manner that must have attracted universal suspicion. That, too, explains his elaborate fears at the Hotel Cosmopolitan. I think there were never any threatening letters except, perhaps, those he wrote to himself. And he agreed to play that very foolish game that ended with his death. He knew his peril there, knew he might be attacked, that Monte Carlo was full of men who wanted the stone, and that there might be many who would proceed to take it. Yet he behaved with no more caution than an idiot child. All this seemed to me strange. And there were the collar and tie disarranged, and I remember how M. Marvell said that perhaps it had been nervousness and not dandyism, as he at first supposed, that made him finger his collar and tie as he went across the lawn. Suppose, monsieur, that instead of settling his collar, he were unfastening it? Suppose it is essential for his plan that it should appear he has been attacked?"

"And there is no real assailant?"

"Only M. Marks' clever wits. He will be found with marks on his throat, with his clothing disarranged; he will tell his story. He was attacked by a man who came over the wall, who wrenched the diamond away and fled. The police, messieurs, will not busy themselves looking for the stone inside the grounds. There is no thief, so how can he be apprehended? And when the chase has proved fruitless, who will return to notice the cut stems, already growing together again? Or who know when the knife was used?"

"And Michelet—Michelet was an accomplice?"

"In the theft, monsieur. Not in the murder."

Latymer sat up. "This is the most ingenious solution I've ever encountered," he acknowledged handsomely. "All the same, aren't there a few gaps? I'm a bit in the dark about Michelet still. What precisely was he to do when he'd finished making fake inquiries and rousing suspicion against himself?"

"Nothing more, monsieur, but procure his own safety from arrest by catching the 10.25 train and providing himself with a perfect alibi. I think he had a bad shock when he found he had missed the train. For now, when Marks reported the theft, how was he to clear himself? He had taken no pains to cover his tracks; it might not be hard for the police to show that it was he who came once at least to the hotel, breathing threats against millionaires in general and M. Marks in particular. And now, if he is asked about his movements, what can he say?"

"He could tell the truth, presumably."

"And hope that M. Marks would back him up? But that was criminal fraud, monsieur. Would a man confess that, a man of Marks' ambition and history? Oh, he was in a tight corner, as you say, was Marks, so tight that he was almost crushed to death. Those stories of his bankruptcy being close at hand were not so very false after all. Even the diamond, it seems, could not save him."

"There really was a diamond?" said Latymer sceptically.

"Oh, yes. It was seen by experts, though it never left England in Marks' possession. The last persons to see it, except the man who took it away from the hotel at Dover, were the proprietor and the chambermaid, the mysterious, vanishing chambermaid. And there you have the explanation of M. Marks' delay at the Sumptuous. He could not leave until his colleague had come for the diamond; and he did not come for two days. Then M. Marks crossed to Paris with the diamond you saw me take from the well. He was safe enough, he thought. A man seeing it by chance, with no opportunity to examine it at close quarters, would have said, Oh, the wonderful jewel! And perhaps, Oh, the mad, the crazy owner of it! To Paris, then, goes M. Marks, and to Paris goes the lady who is part of the plot. Why he stays that extra night I do not know, but there are strange stories told of him in that city, stories I need not detail now. You will find them told later with a greater picturesqueness by the press. But I do not think the lady was any part of his plan."

"Just Act of God," suggested Montstuart flippantly.

"Oh, no. She was no part of his plan, but he was part of hers. She had followed him from Dover, to learn his movements, that she might send the details to her accomplices here."

"She seems to have had plenty of money."

The little Frenchman leaned forward to say impressively, "Believe me, monsieur, if you wish to be a criminal, you must first be a rich man, if you are to be successful. Remember, the criminal on a grand scale has to support himself in two rôles, and both are expensive. Oh, it cost money, no doubt, but it was a speculation. And what a speculation! To spend the price of a ticket, an hotel bill, the purchase of a lorry, a half-load of straw, half a dozen sacks, the knife, perhaps—and for what a reward. And how terrible, when the deed was done, to find the stone already gone. To one with a sense of drama, messieurs, like myself, that must have been the supreme moment in all the events. To see those men staring at a man they had needlessly killed. . . ."

Latymer said dryly, "Your imagination does you credit, monsieur," and Dupuy replied at once, with the utmost good humour, "You are right. I am wasting your time. But these adventures of mine enthral me. One sees them as pictures. Well, then, next morning Michelet learns that the plan has failed, Marks is missing, possibly dead. And presently the body is found. Think then of his dilemma. Now he cannot even rely on Marks agreeing to his story. Once let him be identified as the man who made himself so conspicuous at the Fantastique, and he is undone. He missed his train, he was away all night, he has no alibi. And then he remembers. He has the map, the map with directions on it in Marks' own writing. Now if he tells his story he has some proof to show. No wonder he kept that map, but he should have kept it more securely."

Montstuart, not much impressed by these histrionics, was struggling with facts. "And the telegram that we thought came from the chambermaid— or the lovely lady, which you please? That came from Marks, too?"

"That came from Marks."

"Are you sure the woman's concerned, after all? That we're not being unduly romantic about her?"

"Oh, she was concerned, believe me; she was in the centre of the stage. If she did not send a telegram she could telephone to her confederates, and indeed she put through a call from Paris to Monte Carlo on the night of the 28th."

"And you're after her? Or have you found her?"

"I could tell you her name, I think."

"And that is?"

Both listeners were now strung up to the highest possible pitch of suspense.

"Mrs. Brodie," said Dupuy.

2

Latymer dropped limply back into his chair. "That woman!" he muttered. "My God, what a mind. To come forward and ask for our help—but why, M. Dupuy? What's Salomon to her?"

"Her confederate in the murder of M. Marks. That certainly. Her lover, perhaps." He shrugged. "I know nothing of that. And it is not in any case important."

"And was she the second person Mrs. Fellowes saw in the grounds that night?" Montstuart sounded sceptical.

"How should she be, monsieur? She was to be his alibi. He had spent the night with her, remember. But Salomon, that man of straw, overset all her careful plans. He asked for shaving water as soon as he returned to his hotel, and the only evidence she had of his presence in her flat on the morning of the 1st November was his demand for shaving water before he got up. Any good counsel could have pitched on that discrepancy. Besides, no one saw him leave early that morning."

"Except her husband," contradicted Latymer. "Your good counsel might have got the truth out of him."

Dupuy shook his head. "He would never have brought that story into court. He could not, monsieur."

"No? Who would prevent him?"

"I, monsieur. You have perhaps forgotten a small incident occurring that night. There was a lady in the Rue de la Rose, one block distant from Madame

Brodie's flat, who flung herself from an upstairs window, and lay on the pavement for two hours before she was discovered. You will remember," he looked at Montstuart, " there was some talk of police negligence. Why was the street not patrolled? But it is a small street and quiet, and the shadows were very deep. I think one might have passed down the street and seen nothing, after the moans had died away. But to be standing there, not fifty yards distant, and to tell a court full of people that you heard, saw, comprehended nothing, that is too much for even a wooden-headed jury to swallow. M. Brodie knew that; in these matters it is chance who holds the last card. He could make many plans, but he could not know that his alibi would be destroyed."

" Then where was he that night?"

" In the lorry with M. Salomon, of course. You do not perceive the subtlety of their scheming, monsieur. Each was to be alibi for the other. M. Salomon could not be guilty for he spent the night with Madame Brodie; and M. Brodie could not be guilty for he spent the night watching the flat. And now a silly, hysterical woman has brought both to the scaffold. Oh, yes, we have them both, never fear. There was nothing for them to do thereafter but fix the blame on another man. And they were almost successful. They were clever, you see, and cool; they told a great deal of the truth. If you should ever be tempted to adopt a criminal career, monsieur, remember that it pays to tell the truth. No one can disprove it; a lie cannot be witnessed, and witnesses are important. Moreover, when your stories have been found accurate, hereafter you will be believed as a matter of course. It was brilliant, it was almost genius on the part of Madame Brodie to divulge the plot of the chambermaid; for who would connect that woman with herself? She turned suspicion away by her candour. Yet one must allow for the unexpected in murder cases. Sometimes, as here, it is overwhelming."

But Montstuart had recalled another point, a point insoluble in the light of Dupuy's contention. He stood up in his eagerness, his face blazing with excitement. "But the letter, monsieur, the letter that Michelet sent to the jeweller's. I saw it. The writing was the same as that on the chart. How do you explain that? If the first wasn't Michelet's writing the second wasn't either. If the first was Marks' writing, how do you explain the second, with Marks in his grave?"

Dupuy cried contemptuously, "You are a criminal lawyer, monsieur, and you ask me that? Have you never heard of forgery? In so intricate a crime," he went on more temperately, turning his eyes away from the barrister, "it is always difficult to gather every loose end. One trifling slip unperceived may ultimately betray the criminal. Sometimes fate is against a man. When M. Brodie prepared his story he could not allow for the lady with suicidal tendencies. That was his misfortune. But I do not think, monsieur," he swung round suddenly to the tense and silent Latymer, "that a man of your experience should have committed the error of supposing that the writing on the chart was Michelet's writing, simply because the chart was found in his room. I do not mean to suggest that the difficulties at that stage were not very great, or that the plan was not intricate and original. It was fascinating, in many ways admirable, and it almost succeeded. That letter to the jeweller was, of course, to be the final nail in Michelet's coffin. It is not easy to regard a matter from more than one aspect at a time, and the public can be fairly easily decoyed. Draw their attention to one aspect and they will ignore the rest, as the party at the Fantastique allowed themselves to be decoyed to the ridge well away from the scene of the murder, by the mere dropping of a stone. Yes, M. Latymer, it was a well-conceived plan, but for that one fatal flaw. And it would have been so easy to avoid that mistake. One more instant of consideration. No, no, do not move, I beg you. I have you covered, and I should no more hesitate to shoot than you hesitated to give the signal to your confederates as you walked up from the well with M. Fellowes, whistling the Marseillaise—M. Brodie recognised no tune but the Marseillaise, did he?—that they might know the time had come, and that M. Marks would be alone in the garden."

Montstuart had had many shocks that afternoon, but this one seemed to paralyse him. His face exhibited no emotion whatsoever, neither incredulity nor anger nor scorn. It was blank and immobile; he heard Dupuy's words, but the meaning of the monstrous charge was blurred. He sat where he was, staring at the pair of them, Dupuy, taut as an electric wire, Latymer, white as paper, slouching back in his chair, not a muscle of the thin, fierce face moving. But, thought Montstuart, consciousness returning slowly, how he could hate, with what power he loathed his own bungling and his enemy's triumph. For Dupuy was not generous. Pity was a word to him, and nothing more. The air quivered with the passion of the condemned man, beside whose chair two gendarmes had already taken their stand.

At last the lawyer heard himself mutter, " But why —how did you guess? I believe you—one can't deny the letter, but still it seems to me incredible. . . ."

" The letter was the climax," acknowledged Dupuy, preening himself a little. " There were other details. In particular there was the necessity for discovering which member of the party was in the plot. Someone must give the signal that it is safe for the criminals to advance. I thought once it might be M. Fellowes. I am told that in England politicians have a great many interests; and certainly, just before M. Marks went to hide, M. Fellowes discovered he had lost his tiepin, and went to search for it, near the vegetable garden and near the well. Strange coincidence, I thought. But I could not make any of the facts fit in with such an explanation. You see, M. Latymer had gone with him also, and if there had been a signal, he, the trained detective, would have remembered it, particularly in the light of what followed. So, then, it might be M. Latymer, and I recalled that he had returned whistling the Marseillaise. And I thought, Is it not odd that an Englishman, not an Englishman resident here in Paris, but a man here for a brief holiday, who would scarcely know the tune, one might suppose, should be whistling it in the subconscious way in which men do whistle when they are much occupied or thinking deeply? I have been associated with M. Latymer a good deal since that day, and never since then have I heard him whistle any tune at all. Nor have I ever seen him manicure his nails in public. But on that night, when M. Marks was preparing to hide, he was on the back of the verandah cleaning his nails."

He spoke as though Latymer were no longer a sentient being, and to Montstuart this seemed the final humiliation, as though the poor wretch were already condemned and executed, a creature blind and deaf to consideration. Yet, despite his own rush of feeling for the man who had been his companion for many days, he could not prevent the questions that sprang to his lips.

" But what had he been doing?"

" You remember the stone that deceived you all, the

270

stone you supposed to be the body of M. Marks? That
was a heavy stone; it could not be prised up in the
few seconds' start that M. Latymer had of the rest of
you. No, he prised that up during the previous search,
at the time, I think, that M. Marks was raising the lid
of the well. For I believe the diamond was hidden
when he returned to the verandah. I think this is why
he was last ' home.' He had to have those few minutes
to himself, never guessing of the plot to destroy him.
There was red earth under the nails of M. Marks when
we found the body. But I do not think that earth
came from the ridge. I think he was never on the
ridge."

Montstuart's surprise outran his caution. " But he
was seen—seen by all of us."

" No, monsieur. You made one of the two cardinal
mistakes that detectives can make. That is, taking
facts for granted. You drew a premise, and it was
wrong. You saw a man, a rather short, spare man,
walk along the ridge wearing a certain kind of cap,
and immediately, because M. Marks was wearing a
similar cap, you declared that it was he whom you
saw. But, monsieur, there are such caps to be bought
by the hundred in any shop. A man who is preparing
to commit a crime has only to enter the shop and
buy a similar box of carnival favours, and then wait
and see which one his victim will wear. I knew from
the outset there had been a second box. For there
were two caps, the one M. Marvell found in the
spinney and the one M. Marks was wearing when he
was struck down. We found some silk threads in the
wheelbarrow, you remember."

" But could they not have been the same cap?"
Montstuart demanded.

" Monsieur, believe me, M. Marks was never in the
spinney. When the body was found, there was not in

his clothing one green spine such as made M. Latymer, M. Marvell, M. Degas, myself even, like little Sebastians of the new day. We were pricked even to blood; no man could go that way and be otherwise. That was something else the murderers forgot."

"And Latymer had that second pink cap hidden under his coat, I suppose, when he left the verandah? What did he do with his own?"

"He folded it and put it in his pocket. Did you notice when you were returned to the verandah that his was folded into neat creases?"

"I did. I remember that I absent-mindedly began to crease mine and happened to see his, and wondered if it were telepathy."

"And there was one more point," the inexorable voice went on; "even Potain did not know of M. Marks' arrival until the day he was to come, but already M. Latymer had told Miss Hoult about him. Miss Blaise gave them away. She said, ' They have talked of nothing else for forty-eight hours,' that is, twenty-four hours before Potain himself knew. You see, the lady had telephoned, and M. Latymer never dreamed that nobody would know."

Montstuart was frowning. "But what was his motive for dragging me into it?" he demanded. "It's true I was completely hoodwinked, but did they count on that in advance? And anyway, I wasn't in with the French police. I couldn't have hurt them."

Dupuy sent him a sly, faintly malicious glance. "No, monsieur, but you were a lawyer, you found it as difficult to keep away from such an affair as the sneak thief to abstain from picking and stealing. And M. Latymer knew that to have you on his side meant not only a valuable ally for him, but also that the enemy would forfeit your sympathy. He is clever enough to realise that. Indeed, I think his true motive was to keep you where you could do him least harm."

Montstuart looked crestfallen. " Humility's the bed-rock of the virtues," he observed. " I suppose I should be grateful to him for exposing to me yet another weak point. You know," calmly he changed the subject, " I wondered at first whether Potain mightn't be in it."

Dupuy vigorously negatived the suggestion.

" He was just blind fate playing into the criminals' hands. With his foolish English games. Not for one moment did I suspect him. His hotel is as dear, as honourable to him as my art to me or yours, monsieur, to you. He would not have the slur of a murder on its reputation for all the diamonds on the earth, not if he were consulted.

" And lastly there is this point, a psychological one this time. When a man makes himself conspicuous, I argued, he does so for one of two reasons. Because he wishes to be noticed, or because he wishes to be over-looked. Now, I did not think M. Latymer was the type that wishes to be noticed. He has a very proper pride in himself, and he would know that the approba-tion or indifference of the people collected at that time at the Fantastique—if you will pardon my candour, monsieur," again that swift mocking smile in Mont-stuart's direction, " was of very small consequence. So then, I think, he wishes not to be noticed. He wishes to be so obvious that if any mystery arises he will be absolutely overlooked. Am I right in my argument, M. Latymer?"

" You are not," said Latymer, who had recovered his habitual composure, though his voice was abnormally dry and his tongue grated against his teeth. " I take it you're referring to the boots I wear. I had the mis-fortune to lose a foot in the war, and since then there are periods when the ankle has to have special support.

This chances to be one of the periods. Too simple an explanation for the police, I'm afraid."

"That is another thing a man should remember. Not to take things for granted, and not to seek romantic explanations. I thank you for enlightening me.

"I do not think," he went on placidly, "that the notion went through any mind that Salomon would be arrested, and, so soon as that happened, one of the partners comes to the other and says, Now, what do we do? We must extricate our friend, or we shall ourselves be condemned. And M. Latymer agrees that a scapegoat must be found. Who shall it be? M. Marks helps them. He has provided a suspicious person who might perhaps be accused of the crime. M. Michelet helps them by missing his train. They believe that he has helped them once more by leaving that plan in his rooms, but here they are mistaken. That leads to their downfall. Yet how should they guess that the writing would be Marks'? How safe M. Latymer must have felt when he put that letter in the post! Everyone will argue that Michelet has just discovered he is suspect and is endeavouring to cover his tracks. Again, that was what M. Latymer counted upon. How many said, It is strange that this letter should be posted on the day that M. Latymer is in Paris and has just found what he thinks to be a specimen of Michelet's handwriting in his room? And now, let me give you advice," he swung round to Latymer as he spoke, then with a half-humorous shrug turned back again, " but why do I waste my words? It is too late for advice. You will have no second chance, monsieur. That is why to be a murderer is not profitable, because he is nearly always caught and he has no opportunity to perfect his art. A forger, a thief, he can go to prison where he will learn many things that may help him from his companions, but a murderer has no time. That is why murder is at the last less successful than any other crime. But I will tell *you*, monsieur," and back came his glance and his admonitory finger to Montstuart, "do not find too many good clues in your enemy's premises. The map —that was good fortune—but the bill for the carnival hats in the chauffeur's drawer—that was stretching probability. And it was perilous also. For unless Flambeau was implicated—and how easily it might have been proved that he was innocent—then there could be no shadow of doubt as to the truth. The bill found in his papers could have been put there only by one man, a man who knew of the murder, who was involved in the murder. Oh, if criminals would only be direct and simple, if they would take risks, draw their pictures with a bold sweep of colour and not be so much concerned with the tiny detail, how much more successful they would be! Figure to yourself— which are the crimes that have evaded detection? The bold crimes, crimes where a man has made no attempt to conceal the weapon and only the crudest to conceal the corpse. Women strangled in open fields, men and women struck down in shops and lodging-houses in broad daylight; and the weapons—knives and hammers and sticks. Not elusive poisons. That limits the field, and it helps us. There are not many people in any case who have much knowledge of poison. So it is only two or three that we need follow. But—your national poet, monsieur, says something of this and he is right: 'Be bloody, bold and resolute.' It is good advice, monsieur "

Latymer's voice came like a ghost from where he sat. His perfect composure was unflawed, yet Montstuart automatically shifted a little farther away. The man was helpless, was already to all intents and purposes condemned; yet his personality exercised so strange a spell that, in spite of Dupuy's indifference, he could not be wholly ignored.

"And in which degree did I fail, M. Dupuy?" he said.

"You were not bold enough. No, you were cautious," his voice gained in intensity, was strong and derisive, "you were so much afraid your plan would not succeed that you must manufacture a criminal of your own. Nature, M. Latymer, does not love a timid criminal."—Montstuart gasped at the implication, but the Frenchman swept on—" Fortune and Love, they say, love the bold heart."

"You are a little unreasonable," objected Latymer. "You have presented to you a corpse, a pseudo-amateur detective invented solely for your benefit, you have a stolen diamond, you have wild-goose chases across France, you have the whole attention of the French and British bourgeoisie fixed upon you, and you are dissatisfied. Your criminal does not reach your standards. You are exacting, monsieur." He leaned forward, clasping his hands and letting them swing loosely between his knees. "You will reap great credit from this case. What is it that three men should die, and perhaps a woman, too? There's an English proverb that one cannot make an omelette without breaking eggs." He dropped his head into his hands. Monstuart uttered a sharp exclamation. Dupuy leaped forward a moment too late.

"You needn't grudge him that way out," murmured Montstuart, "you've got every other card in your hand."

Dupuy fixed him with a wrathful eye. "You expected this?"

"You said yourself that he was a cautious man. One

would need to be utterly reckless to make no provision against failure, with you on his heels, M. Dupuy."

Dupuy seemed to hesitate for an instant between anger and resignation. Suddenly he exclaimed, putting his arm through Montstuart's and drawing him towards the door, " Perhaps you are right, monsieur. There was your English Nelson, whose philosophy I have often admired. It is wise for all of us sometimes to have a blind eye. And then," he reached the door and went out, drawing his companion with him, " there is always trouble when any foreign authority attempts to try an Englishman. And we have the men who struck the actual blow." They reached the bar of the hotel and Dupuy called for something to drink.

" He was right," he observed loquaciously, holding the little glassful of golden liquid in his hand and scrutinising it with care, " he has done me a great service. There is a position at headquarters that I covet; there is much competition, but I think this may turn the scales. It is a step upwards for me, and I am an ambitious man, monsieur." He fell into a brown study, forgetful of his companion. Suddenly he felt the need to be back in Paris, the hub of the world, where the great wheel of life revolved, that shining city full of passionate men and women, robbing and forging and uttering bad money, cheating insurance companies, murdering their neighbours, planning gigantic criminal coups, among whom he would thread his way, detecting their fine schemes, winning laurels, engaged in a perpetual battle of wits, achieving new triumphs, seeking fresh victories. He put down his glass; his companion, he saw with some surprise, had disappeared. Ah! well, he thought, the English were a strange race; he had seemed actually sorry for this Latymer. That was like them, sentimentalists that they were; when the fellow had tried to get Michelet hanged—though, of course, thought Dupuy vaingloriously, there was no danger to Michelet so long as he, Dupuy, was on the trail. Still, Montstuart took no joy from the situation that had throbbed for the Frenchman with dramatic intensity.

"But then," argued Dupuy, generously acquitting his neighbour of a lack of sportsmanship, "he will gain nothing from it. For me it is different." And again he began to see himself in that coveted position at the Sureté, detecting the causes of mysterious deaths, adding to that treatise on poisons that he would publish, with many examples of their use, when he was retired, scurrying like a rat through the Paris streets, watching the city with a thousand eyes, the invisible vengeance, the man no evil-doers should escape, and finally the head of the Sureté itself. He flung up his head and strode out of the hotel into the street.

"Life is very good," cried M. Dupuy, and with a lordly air he hailed a cab and was driven back to his hotel.

THE END

>>> If you've enjoyed this book and would like to discover more great vintage crime and thriller titles, as well as the most exciting crime and thriller authors writing today, visit: >>>

The Murder Room
Where Criminal Minds Meet

themurderroom.com

www.ingramcontent.com/pod-product-compliance
Ingram Content Group UK Ltd.
Pitfield, Milton Keynes, MK11 3LW, UK
UKHW022318280225
455674UK00004B/352

9 781471 910609